THE FRIENDLY PERSUASION

Books by Jessamyn West

THE FRIENDLY PERSUASION

A MIRROR FOR THE SKY

THE WITCH DIGGERS

CRESS DELAHANTY

LOVE, DEATH, AND THE LADIES' DRILL TEAM

TO SEE THE DREAM

LOVE IS NOT WHAT YOU THINK

SOUTH OF THE ANGELS

A MATTER OF TIME

LEAFY RIVERS

EXCEPT FOR ME AND THEE

CRIMSON RAMBLERS OF THE WORLD, FAREWELL

HIDE AND SEEK

THE SECRET LOOK

THE MASSACRE AT FALL CREEK

THE WOMAN SAID YES

THE LIFE I REALLY LIVED

DOUBLE DISCOVERY

THE STATE OF STONY LONESOME

THE COLLECTED STORIES OF JESSAMYN WEST

The Friendly Persuasion

By

JESSAMYN WEST

A Harvest Book
Harcourt Brace & Company
San Diego   New York   London

Requests for permission to make copies
of any part of the work should be mailed to:
Permissions Department, Harcourt Brace & Company,
6277 Sea Harbor Drive, Orlando, Florida 32887-6777.

Library of Congress Cataloging-in-Publication Data
West, Jessamyn.
The friendly persuasion/by Jessamyn West.
p. cm.
Previously published: New York: Harcourt, Brace & World, 1968.
ISBN 0-15-633606-5
I. Title.
PS3545.E8315F75   1991
813'.54—dc20   91-6468

Printed in the United States of America
G I K M O P N L J H

FOR
TWO REMEMBERING
E. R. W. — G. A. W.

Thanks are due to *Prairie Schooner, Collier's, Harper's Bazaar, The Atlantic Monthly, The Ladies' Home Journal, New Mexico Quarterly Review,* and *Harpers Magazine* for their kind permission to reprint stories in this book.

CONTENTS

THE FRIENDLY PERSUASION

MUSIC ON THE MUSCATATUCK

NEAR the banks of the Muscatatuck where once the woods had stretched, dark row on row, and where the fox grapes and wild mint still flourished, Jess Birdwell, an Irish Quaker, built his white clapboard house. Here he lacked for very little. On a peg by the front door hung a starling in a wooden cage and at the back door stood a spring-house, the cold spring water running between crocks of yellow-skinned milk. At the front gate a moss-rose said welcome and on a trellis over the parlor window a Prairie Queen nodded at the roses in the parlor carpet—blooms no nurseryman's catalogue had ever carried and gay company for the sober Quaker volumes: Fox's life, Penn's "Fruits of Solitude," Woolman's "Journal," which stood in the parlor secretary.

Jess had a good wife, a Quaker minister, Eliza Cope before she was wed, and a houseful of children. Eliza was a fine woman, pious and work-brickel and good-looking as female preachers are apt to be: a little, black-haired, glossy woman with a mind of her own.

He had a good business, too. He was a nurseryman with the best stock of berries and fruits west of Philadelphia; in the apple line: Rambo, Maiden Blush, Early Harvest, Northern Spy, a half dozen others; May Duke cherries; Stump the World, a white-fleshed peach; the Lucretia dewberry, a wonder for pies and cobblers. Pears, currant bushes, gooseberries, whatever the land could support or fancy demand in the way of fruits, Jess had them.

There were extras to be had, too, there on the banks of the

3

Muscatatuck: black bass; catfish that weren't choosy, that would come out of the water with their jaws clamped about a piece of cotton batting. Pawpaws smooth and sweet as nectar, persimmons with an October flavor, sarvice berries tart as spring.

In spring, meadow and roadside breathed flowers; in summer there was a shimmer of sunlight onto the great trees whose shadows still dappled the farmland: sycamore, oak, tulip, shagbark hickory. When fall came a haze lay across the cornfields, across the stands of goldenrod and farewell summer, until heaven and earth seemed bound together—and Jess, standing on a little rise at the back of the house, looking across the scope of land which fell away to the river, would have, in pure content, to wipe his eyes and blow his nose before he'd be in a fit state to descend to the house.

Yet, in spite of this content, Jess wasn't completely happy, and for no reason anyone could have hit upon at first guess. It certainly wasn't having Eliza ride every First Day morning to the Grove Meeting House, there to sit on the elevated minister's bench and speak when the spirit moved her. Jess knew Eliza had had a call to the ministry and was proud to hear her preach in her gentle way of loving-kindness and the brotherhood of man.

No, it wasn't Eliza's preaching nor any outward lack the eye could see that troubled Jess. It was music. Jess pined for music, though it would be hard to say how he'd come by any such longing. To the Quakers music was a popish dido, a sop to the senses, a hurdle waiting to trip man in his upward struggle. They kept it out of their Meeting Houses and out of their homes, too. Oh, there were a few women who'd hum a little while polishing their lamp chimneys, and a few men with an inclination to whistle while dropping corn, but as to real music, sung or played, Jess had no more chance to hear it than a woodchuck.

What chances there were, though, he took. He'd often manage to be around the Methodist Church when they had their midweek services and he felt a kind of glory in his soul that wasn't entirely religious when the enthusiastic Methodists hit into "Old

Hundred." And when on the Fourth of July, Amanda Prentis soared upwards on the high notes of "The Star-Spangled Banner" only Eliza's determined nudgings could bring Jess back to earth.

This seemed for some time about the best Jess would be able to do in the way of music without having Eliza and her whole congregation buzzing about his ears, the best he could do anyway until he took that trip to Philadelphia and met Waldo Quigley; though of course he had no way of knowing when he was planning the trip that it would turn out as it did.

Jess had been hearing for some time about a new early cherry and he'd made up his mind to go to Philadelphia, and if they were all he'd heard, order some for the Maple Grove Nursery. There wasn't, perhaps, any real need of his going as far as Philadelphia, but to a Quaker, Philadelphia was the place to go if nothing more than a pocket handkerchief was needed. So Eliza packed his valise for him, drove him to Vernon herself and saw him on the train.

The first word Eliza had from Jess was a letter mailed a couple of days after he left. He didn't mention Waldo Quigley in that letter, though as a matter of fact he was already hand in glove with him as Eliza discovered later. The letter was short: health good, scenery pleasant, that was about the whole of it with the exception of a postscript saying, "Thank thee, dear Eliza, for the little packet thee put in my nightshirt pocket."

The "little packet" contained peppermints, and it was through offering one of these to Waldo Quigley that Jess made his acquaintance. Jess was always sociable when he traveled. He used to say that sun, moon and stars were the same everywhere and only the people different and if you didn't get to know them you'd as well have stayed home and milked the cows.

After Waldo Quigley put the peppermint in his mouth he settled his big, portly, black-suited frame onto the seat opposite Jess.

"Well, sir," he said, "you a Hoosier?"

Jess said he was and the big man went on, "Got a president shaping up out your way. Got an up-and-comer there on your prairies, a man who can out-talk a trumpet and out-see a telescope. He's a little giant. Man to elevate somewhat and he'll set our country on its feet. He's the man we need."

Jess sniffed. He was a fiery Republican, as fiery at least as a Quaker's apt to be. "Friend," said he, "the man we need is no little giant, but a big one. Not a man busy rousing up the country-side, setting state against state, but a man with the interest of all at heart, little farmer as well as plantation owner, black as well as white."

Jess could see, "That's Stephen A. Douglas," work up Waldo Quigley's gullet as far as his back teeth but there he stopped the words, said, "Them's my sentiments precisely, Brother Birdwell, them's my very thoughts, only better said."

Jess wrinkled up his big nose. "I see thee's a man of harmony, friend."

"Brother," replied the big man, "you put your tongue to the right word. Harmony's what I preach and harmony's what I practice."

Jess listened to these words, took another look at the big man's black suit and decided that he was a preacher of some sort.

"Is thee, perhaps," he asked mildly, "a minister of the gospel? Though thy habit for a man of the cloth is perhaps a mite unorthodox."

Mr. Quigley cleared his throat, swallowing the last of his first peppermint. "I can't say as I've ever been ordained," he admitted, "but my work's been so much with them that has that I've fallen into a sedate manner of dressing. It strikes me as being a more seemly thing to do. Helps business, too," he added.

"Business?" asked Jess.

"You named it yourself, Mr. Birdwell. Harmony is my business. Do-re-mi. Also la-ti-do. Not forgetting fa-sol. Harmony. The music of the spheres. God's way of speaking to his children. The power that soothes the savage beast, the song that quiets newborn babes and eases the pangs of the dying man. In a word, music."

"In several words in fact," ruminated Jess. "Is thee then, Brother Quigley, a musician?" he asked.

"Musician? Yes. But I," said he frankly, "am that rather unusual combination, a musical businessman, or perhaps more truly a businesslike musician. There's plenty of men can keep a double entry set of books and there's a number more, though fewer, can tell a grace note from a glissando, but I," handing Jess a card, "can do both."

Jess took the card and read aloud, "Professor Waldo Quigley, Traveling Representative, Payson and Clarke. The World's Finest Organs. Also Sheet Music and Song Books."

Brother Quigley reached out, took the card from Jess and wrote "Personal Compliments" on it.

"I note from your speech you're a Quaker, and knowing the way that sect—not that it ain't the finest in the world," he said politely—"feels about music I wouldn't want you to think I was trying to work against your prejudices—convictions rather. So," he said, handing the card back to Jess, "I write 'Personal Compliments,' to show I'm free of any profit-making motives; that we meet man to man. Pays to be delicate-like where religion is concerned. Pays every time," he said, nodding to Jess.

Jess tried Payson and Clarke over once or twice on his tongue. "Payson and Clarke," he said. "So thee sells Payson and Clarke's. They've got one unless I disremember in the Methodist meeting house at Rush Branch."

"Sure they have," said Brother Quigley. "Sure they have." He took a little red book from an inner pocket and flipped a few pages. "Yes, sir. I sold them that organ three years ago April 19. One more strawberry festival and they'll have it paid for."

"Thee sells a good instrument then. I've heard that organ now and again in passing."

"Good? Mr. Birdwell, it's better than good. Three years ago after them Methodists at Rush Branch heard my concert and song recital, they said to me, 'Professor Quigley, we don't ever calculate to hear the voice of God any more plain while here on earth.'"

Jess said, "That's carrying it a little far, mebbe," but he was really burning to hear more about the Payson and Clarke.

"Well, of course," Brother Quigley reminded him, "you got to remember they's Methodists. Tending toward the shouting order. But this organ, Methodists aside, is pure gumbo, absolutely pure gumbo."

"Gumbo," Jess repeated.

"Rich. Satisfying. Deep. Gumbo, pure gumbo."

Jess knew a thing or two about organs though it would be hard to say how: perhaps from reading Chalmer's "Universal Encyclopedia," perhaps from an inspection of the Methodist organ. Perhaps in neither way. Knowledge of what you love somehow comes to you; you don't have to read nor analyze nor study. If you love a thing enough, knowledge of it seeps into you, with particulars more real than any chart can furnish. Maybe it was that way with Jess and organs.

So he asked, "How many reeds in a Payson and Clarke?"

"Forty-eight, Brother Birdwell, not counting the tuba mirabalis. But in the Payson and Clarke, number ain't what counts—it's the quality. Those reeds duplicate the human throat. They got timbre." And he landed on the French word the way a hen lands on the water, skeptical, but hoping for the best.

"How many stops?" Jess asked.

"Eight. And that vox humana! The throat of an angel. It cries, it sighs, it sings. You can hear the voice of your lost child in it. Did you ever lose a child, Brother Birdwell?"

"No," said Jess shortly.

"You can hear the voice of your old mother calling to you from the further shore."

"Ma lives in Germantown," said Jess.

If the conversation had followed in this direction, Jess would never have come home with a Payson and Clarke; but in every nerve Brother Quigley could feel a prospect retreating and he changed his tack.

"The Payson and Clarke comes in four different finishes," he said. "Oak, maple, walnut and mahogany. Got a cabinet that's purely elegant. Most organ's got two swinging brackets. This one's got four. Two for lamps, two for vases. Has a plate mirror over the console. There's not a square inch of unornamented wood in the whole cabinet. No, sir, there's not an inch of dingy, unembellished wood the length and breadth of the cabinet. But, Brother Birdwell, you're a musician yourself. You're not interested in cabinets. You're interested in tone. Tone's what the artist looks for. Tone's what Payson and Clarke's got."

He began to hum under his breath. Low at first, then louder, with occasional words. "Tum-te-tum—the riverside—tum-te-tum—upon its tide."

"That's a likely tune," Jess said.

"Can't do justice to it singing."

But he stopped humming, launched into the words. He had a fine baritone. Flatted a little, Jess thought, but not bad. When he exhaled heavily on a high note, Jess was sorry to find he'd had a nip or two, but before the piece was finished Jess was beating time with his forefinger on the red plush arm of the seat, completely forgetful of the spirits Brother Quigley had surely had.

"What's the piece called?" Jess asked.

" 'The Old Musician and His Harp.' It was written to be played on an organ. Mortifies me that you have to hear it first time sung, merely."

"Thee's a good voice," Jess said.

"Fair to middling. Fair to middling, only."

He sank a fat hand in one of his big black pockets and brought up a leather-covered flask. He wiped the mouth carefully on his coat-tail and held it toward Jess.

"Wet your whistle and we'll sing it through together."

Jess shook his head.

"Well, I didn't suppose you would, but it's a pity. Cleans your pipes. Extends your range. Gives you gumbo." He took a long swig himself.

"Try it with me, Brother Birdwell."

Jess said afterward he didn't have the slightest intention of making a show of himself in a B. & O. parlor car singing "The Old Musician and His Harp," or any other song, for that matter. But that tune was a hard thing to give the go-by; the mind said the words and the toe tapped the time; with the whole body already singing it, that way, opening the mouth to let the words out seemed a mighty small matter and before Jess knew it he was taking the high notes in his fine, clear tenor. Jess had the nose for a really first-class tenor—there never was a first-class tenor with a button nose, and Jess, with his, high-bridged, more Yankee than Quaker, had just the nose for it. Before he and Brother Quigley had finished a couple of verses half the parlor car was joining in the chorus.

> Bring my harp to me again,
> Let me hear its gentle strain;
> Let me hear its chords once more
> Ere I pass to yon bright shore.

When they finished Brother Quigley had another nip. "Got to cool the pipes," he said. "Now, Brother Birdwell, when you get to Philly, when you get them cherries located, you stop in at Payson and Clarke's and hear that the way it was meant to be heard. Hear it on the organ. No obligation whatever. Privilege to play for a fellow artist."

Jess hadn't a notion in the world of buying an organ when he went into Payson and Clarke's. He'd got the cherry stock he'd come after, had had a nice visit with his mother, and was ready to start homeward when he thought he'd as well hear "The Old Musician and His Harp," on a Payson and Clarke. Brother Quigley had been clever to him and it was no more than humanly decent to let the man show him what the organ could do. That was the way he had it figured out to himself before he went in, anyway.

When he'd walked out, the organ was his. He didn't know what he'd do with it; he didn't think Eliza would hear to keeping it; he thought he'd like as not slipped clean away from grace, but he had the papers for the organ in his pocket. He'd paid half cash, the rest to be in nursery stock. Clarke of Payson and Clarke was an orchardist.

As soon as Jess heard Waldo Quigley run his fingers over that organ's keys with a sound as liquid as the Muscatatuck after a thaw he'd known he was sunk. And when he'd found he could chord "The Old Musician" himself, when Waldo Quigley said, "Never knew a man with a better tremolo," when he pumped the air into the organ with his feet and drew it out with his fingers, sounding like an echo of eternity, he began casting up his bank balance in his mind. He was past figuring out the right and wrong of the matter; all he was interested in was getting it, having that organ where he could lay his hands across it, hear whenever he liked those caressing tones.

He managed to get home a few days before the organ arrived. He didn't say a word to Eliza about what he'd done. He figured it was a thing which would profit by being led up to gradually. He talked a good deal in those few days about music; how God must like it or He wouldn't have put songbirds in the world, and how the angels were always pictured with harp and zithern.

Eliza was not receptive. "Thee's neither bird nor angel, Jess Birdwell, and had the Lord wanted thee, either singing or plucking a harp, thee would be feathered now one way or another."

There'd been an early snow the day the organ arrived; a foot or two on the level, much more in the drifts. Jess himself brought the organ home from Vernon on the sled.

Eliza knew what it was the minute she laid eyes on the box, for all Jess' care in covering it over with an old rag carpet. Jess' talk about birds and angels had made her fearful of something of the kind, only she hadn't thought it'd be as bad as an organ; a flute, or maybe a French harp he could go down cellar and play had been the worst her imaginings had pictured for her. But she knew it was an organ before Jess had got the covering off the crate, and was out in the snow by the time Enoch had the horses out of the traces.

"What's this thee's bringing home, Jess Birdwell?"

Though she knew well enough. She just wanted to hear him put his tongue to it.

"It's a Payson and Clarke," Jess said, still trying to be gradual. But it was no use. "It's an organ," Eliza said. "Jess, Jess, what's thee thinking of? Bringing this thing here? Me, a recorded minister and the house full of growing children. What's the neighbors to think? What's the Grove Meeting to think?"

If she'd kept on in this sorrowful strain Jess would like as not have got shut of the organ, but Eliza didn't stop there.

"Jess Birdwell," she said, "if thee takes that organ in the house, I stay out. Thee can make thy choice. Thee can have thy wife or thee can have that instrument; but both, thee cannot have."

Jess had a heart as soft as pudding, and if Eliza'd said Please, if she'd let a tear slide out of her soft black eye, that organ would have been done for; but commands, threats, that was a different matter entirely.

Jess called to the hired man who'd taken the horses to the barn, "Come and give me a hand with this organ, Enoch."

A heart soft as pudding, till someone took it on himself to tell Jess which way to turn, then the pudding froze, and if you weren't careful you'd find yourself cut to the bone on an ice splinter. A mild man until pushed, but Jess solidified fast with pushing.

Eliza saw the granite coming, but she was of martyr stock herself and felt the time had come to suffer for the right. She sat flat down in the snow, or as flat as petticoats and skirts would let her. There in the snow she sat and said, "Jess Birdwell, here I stay until that organ is taken away."

Jess said, "We'll uncrate it where it stands, Enoch, then carry it up to the house. No use having the weight of the crate to move, too."

So they went to work on it, got it out of its case and the excelsior packing. Enoch kept his eye on Eliza sitting there in the snow. She made him feel uncomfortable, as if the least he could do would be to give her his coat to sit on.

"Well, let's not dally here, Enoch," Jess said, seeming not to even see Eliza. "Let's get it up to the house."

As they went up the path to the house, straining and puffing through the snow, Enoch said, "Ain't she liable to catch her death of cold there?"

"I figure," said Jess, "that when the snow melts through the last petticoat she'll move."

He was wrong about that. Eliza was wet to the skin before she came up to the house. She had sat there casting up the matter in her mind, but she knew that when Jess was set he was a problem for the Lord. And she had enough respect for both to leave them to each other. There was nothing ever to be gained, she thought, by dissension. Peace, she could at least have. Jess had just finished dusting the organ when Eliza came in, went to the stove and stood there steaming.

"Jess," she asked, "is thee set on having this organ? Remembering thy children and my ministry, is thee still set?"

"Yes, Eliza," Jess said, "I'm set."

"Well," she said, "that's settled;" and being on the whole a reasonable as well as a pious woman, she added, "It will have to go in the attic."

"I'd thought of that," Jess said, "and I'm willing."

So that's the way it was done. The organ was put in the attic and from there it could be heard downstairs, but not in any full-bodied way. It took the gumbo out of it—having it in the attic—and besides Jess was careful not to play it when anyone was in the house. He was careful, that is, until the day the Ministry and Oversight Committee called. He was careful that day, too; it was Mattie who wasn't careful, though unlucky's more the word for it.

Jess had noted right off that Mattie had a musical turn. She'd learned to pick out "The Old Musician" by herself, with one hand, and when Jess discovered this, he taught her the bass chords so that she could play for him to sing. That was a bitter pill for Eliza to swallow, and just what she'd feared: the children be coming infected with Jess' weakness for music. Still, she couldn't keep herself from listening when the deep organ notes with Jess sweet tenor flying above them came seeping down through the ceiling into the sitting-room below.

But in spite of Jess' being careful, in spite of Eliza's being twice as strict as usual, and speaking at the Hopewell Meeting House with increased gravity, the matter got noised about. Not that there was an organ at Birdwells': there wasn't anything definite known, anything you could put your finger on. It was just a feeling that Friend Birdwell wasn't standing as squarely in the light as he'd done at one time. Perhaps someone had heard a strain of organ music coming out of an attic window some spring evening, but more than likely it was just the guilty look Eliza had.

However that may be, the Ministry and Oversight Committee came one night to call. It was nearing seven; supper had been over for some time, the dishes were washed and the table was set for breakfast. Jess and Eliza were in the sitting-room resting after the heat and work of the day and listening to the children who were playing duck-on-rock down by the branch.

The Committee drove up in Amos Pease's surrey, but by the back way, leaving the rig at the carriage-house, so that the first sign Jess and Eliza had of visitors was the smell of trodden mint. Amos Pease wasn't a man to note where he put his feet down when duty called.

Eliza smelled it first and stepped over to the west window to see who was coming. She saw, and in a flash she knew why. "It's the Ministry and Oversight," she said, and her voice shook, but when Amos Pease knocked at the door she was sitting in her rocker, her feet on a footstool one hand lying loose and easy in the other.

Jess answered the knock. "Good evening, Amos. Good evening, Ezra. Good evening, Friend Hooper."

The Committee said its good evenings to Jess and Eliza, found chairs, adjusted First Day coat-tails—it wasn't First Day, but they'd put on their best since what they had to do was serious. But before they could even ease into their questions with some remark upon the weather or how the corn was shaping up—Jess heard it—the faint kind of leathery sigh the organ made when the foot first touched the bellows. That sound was like a pain hitting him in the heart and he thought, I've sold my birthright for a mess of pottage. For Jess was a Quaker through and through, no misdoubting that. For two hundred years his people had been Quakers, sometimes suffering for that right, and now he thought, I've gone and lost it all for a wheezing organ.

It was Mattie at the organ and Jess knew her habits there: they were like his own. She never began to play a piece at once, but touched the organ here and there, slowly pumped in the air, then lovingly laid her fingers across upon keys. After that the music. Jess looked across at Eliza and he saw by the way her hands had tightened round each other that she'd heard, too. I'm a far worse man than Esau, he thought, for he sold only his own birthright, and I've sold my wife's as well as my own.

Jess remembered how Eliza loved to bring the Lord's message to the Lord's people and how his own love for pushing air through a set of reeds was going to lose her all this. And before his lips moved his heart began to pray, "Lord, deliver thy servant from the snare of his own iniquity."

By the time Mattie was ready to touch the first key he was on his feet saying, "Friends, let us lift our hearts to God in prayer." This was nothing startling to a gathering of Quakers. They'd any of them take to praying at the drop of a hat. So some knelt and others didn't, but all bowed their heads and shut their eyes.

All except Jess. He stood with face uplifted to the ceiling, facing his God and his sin. By the time Mattie had got into "The Old Musician," and a few faint wisps of music were floating into the room, Jess was talking to God in a voice that shook the studding. He was talking to Him in the voice of a man whose sins have come home to roost. He was reminding Him of all the other sinners to whom His mercy had nevertheless been granted.

He went through the Bible book by book and sinner by sinner. He prayed in the name of Adam, who had sinned and fallen short of grace; of Moses, who had lost the Promised Land; of David, who had looked with desire on another man's wife. He prayed in the name of Solomon, his follies, of Abraham and his jealousies, and Jephthah, who kept his word in cruelty; he made a music of his own out of his contrition; his revulsion mounted up in melody.

He left the Old Testament and prayed for them all, sinners alike, in the name of Paul, who what he would not, he did; and of Peter, who said he knew the Man not, and of Thomas who doubted and Judas who betrayed and of that Mary who repented.

He stood with his red head lifted up while his long Irish lip wrapped itself around the good Bible names. He prayed until the light had left the room and his hair in the dark had become as colorless as Amos Pease's dun thatch. He prayed until all the mint smell had left the room and the only smell left was that of a penitent man seeking forgiveness.

Now Jess was no hypocrite and if his prayer swelled a little, if it boomed out a little stronger when Mattie pulled the fortissimo stop, it was through none of his planning; it was the Lord's doing entirely. And if his prayer wasn't finished until Mattie'd finished playing after going five times through "The Old Musician," that was the Lord's hand, too, and nothing of Jess' contriving.

Finally, when he'd made an end, and the visiting men had taken their faces out from behind their hands and looked around the dark room with dazed eyes, Jess dropped down into his chair and rubbed his forefinger across his lips, the way a man will when he's been speaking. Eliza lit them a candle, then went out to bring in the lamps.

Amos Pease picked up the candle and held it so the light fell on to Jess' face. "Friend," he said, "thee's been an instrument of the Lord this night. Thee's risen to the throne of grace and carried us all upwards on thy pinions. Thy prayer carried us so near to heaven's gates that now and again I thought I could hear angels' voices choiring and the sound of heavenly harps."

And with that he set the candle back down, put his hat on his head and said, "Praise God." Friend Griffith and Friend Hooper said, "Amen, brother. Amen to that," and with great gravity followed Amos Pease out of the door.

When Eliza came back in with the lamp, Jess was sitting there alone in the candlelight. There was a smell of trod-on mint again in the room and the children had stopped playing duck-on-rock and were whooping after lightning-bugs to put in bottles. Jess was huddled over, his eyes shut, like a man who has felt the weight of the Lord's hand between his shoulder blades. But before Eliza could clear her throat to say "Amen" to the edifying sight he made, down from the attic floated "The Old Musician" once again, and Jess' foot began to tap:

> Tap, tap—the riverside,
> Tap, tap—upon its tide.

SHIVAREE BEFORE BREAKFAST

ELIZA always said Labe never put a foot out of bed until he heard her start to scrape the gravy skillet. "Thee won't see Labe," she'd say fondly, "until he hears that sound—knows the gravy's going on the breakfast table." Labe was harum-scarum and Eliza had a tenderness for her son's easy-going ways.

But that morning in September the big cast-iron skillet was still hanging on its nail behind the stove, a light spot if anything in the early morning darkness. There wasn't a smell in the house of dried beef frizzling for gravy, nor of the birchwood smoke which always seeped out a little around the second joint of the kitchen stovepipe. The starling still slept in his wooden cage by the front door, as if the sun were just lost behind the west rim of hills, not almost ready to push his head above the eastern wood lot. And Labe had both feet out of bed.

He wasn't completely awake yet and he was mumbling and complaining—but he was out of bed. His brother Joshua, who was three years older though scarcely any bigger, stood in front of him talking fiercely. But Joshua almost always talked to him fiercely, about something he hadn't done right, so Labe sat on the edge of the bed and swayed back and forth with sleep still as warm and cozy about him as a nest. He didn't want to hear what Josh was saying, be snatched out of the nest, find himself sitting in his unbleached muslin nightgown, the cold September air touching him like little pieces of iron.

Josh was buttoning his last suspender loop to his pants. "Labe," he said, "thee makes me sick. Thee just about turns my stomach. This was thy idea. Thee said to do it. And it's just like always. I'm ready and thee's so dilly-dallyish, it'll be too late. Old Alf Applegate'll be up and out to work before we get there."

Josh sounded the way he felt—as if he'd like to give Labe a good sound smack—but he knew better. Labe would bawl like a bay steer, and their mother would be in, and then there wouldn't be any shivareeing Old Alf now, or any morning.

"I'm going down and wash," he said, "and get the horse fiddle and go on without thee."

Labe knew then he'd have to wake up; Josh would more than likely do what he said. His nightshirt was over his head, and one leg was in his knickerbockers, before Josh was half way down the back stairs.

Labe tip-toed down the front stairs. Josh had gone the back way so's he could wash, but Labe didn't see any sense washing. Nobody'd see him but Josh and Alf, and Old Alf'd be too excited about his new wife to notice such things.

His hand slid along the cool bannister, his feet went slowly along the stairs into the gray room as if into water. Labe always loved the first morning sight of the big sitting-room—to creep up on it when the furniture wasn't ready yet for human eyes. Chair still turned toward chair, clock and grate saying who knows what to each other with tick and tock and little clunks of falling coals.

It was just light enough to see outlines—pa's shoes by the grate, mother's shawl over the back of the rocker, Mattie's knitting where she'd left it on the newel post. It's like a ship, he thought, where the crew'd got the plague and all died in their bunks, with everything left just as they'd last touched it. He stood on the steps, the first man to view that sorry scene after the disaster.

Josh put his head in the front door. "It's almost sunup," he whispered like a hornet, ready to sting. Labe forgot the plague-stricken ship and ran out to shivaree Old Alf.

Josh was washed clean as a pebble and his fine black hair had a part down it straight as a pike. He had the horse fiddle in one hand, and a lard can with pebbles in it for Labe to shake in the other. "Thee carry thy own stuff," he said to Labe.

"Sure," Labe said. "Want me to take the fiddle, too?"

Josh gave him a sharp look out of his black, green-flecked eyes—but Labe didn't know enough to be sarcastic. He was saying something to Ebony, the starling, like he always did before he went any place.

The early hour, the grayness, their secret made them keep their voices low. "I bet thee dreamed it," Josh said. "I bet it was one of thy daydreams, that Old Alf got married and was talking to a woman."

They were cutting across the west forty. From there on they could follow the pike direct to Applegate's. The corn stubble raked the skin rough on their bare feet, but they were used to that. Beyond the river bend, behind the sycamores, the sky that had been gray was getting yellow. A crow slanted in from the woods lot to the open fields ready to start his morning work. The pebbles in Labe's lard can rattled a little as he walked.

"No, sir, Josh," he said, his round face so serious he looked as if he might cry. "No, Josh, honest, I didn't. I heard him. I told thee it was the morning pa took me fishing. And I got tired and sat down on a stump by Alf's place—and then's when I heard him."

"What'd he say?" Josh asked. He knew—Labe had told him a half dozen times—but every time he thought of those words coming out of Alf Applegate's old hickory-nut face, he was so tickled he couldn't wait until he'd heard them again. "What was it he said?"

"First, I could just hear him talking—but not what he was saying. It kind of sounded like he's talking to a baby, at first. Then he said, 'Time to get up, Molly darling. Time to tie up your beautiful black hair, Molly darling. Night's over—time for day and work.' Maybe that ain't it exactly," Labe added conscientiously, "but as far as I can remember, it is."

Josh shook his head. " 'Molly darling, Molly darling.' Did you hear anything—that sounded like—kissing, Labe?" Josh's face burned a little to be asking such a question.

Labe said, "Thee think I'm soft? Sit on a stump and listen to Old Alf Applegate kissing? 'Smack, smack, smack.' Who'd listen to that?"

Josh didn't say what he'd have done. "If he'd got a wife," he said, "why don't our folks know it? Why's he hiding her?"

"Cause he's ashamed to be getting married, he's so old. He's scared folks'll laugh at him."

Labe suddenly stopped. "I got to go to the privy, Josh," he said.

"Thee always has to go to the privy the minute we start any place," Josh said bitterly. "Thee can just go here."

"No," he said, "I'm going back. Thee go on and I'll catch up with thee," and back he ran across the cornfield at a great clip, the stones rattling in his lard pail like hail on a roof.

"Set thy pail down," Josh called after him. "Thee'll wake the dead."

I'll go off and leave him, Josh thought. I'll run and get there first and the shivaree will be over before Labe comes. But as he watched Labe covering the field like a hound with long easy lopes he knew it wasn't any use. He could run until his legs stung like nettles, and the back of his mouth tasted as if he had swallowed a lump of sulphur, and Labe would still catch up with him, breathing easy and talking, even, as he ran. It never seemed fair to Josh. Labe washed about once a week, a rat could live in his white curly hair for all Labe would ever disturb it with a comb; his shirt-tail was always out and his pants flapped almost to his ankles. He was just plain dirty and messy and everybody loved him.

Josh turned and tramped on fast, climbed the snake fence and went at a trot down the pike. Goldenrod and farewell-summer and iron weed bloomed at the pike's edge. The yellow sky was reddening; the dry sharp morning air, just waking up, sent a flurry of maple leaves across the road. Josh trotted right through them, thinking hard. He liked to be clean and neat, to put away things people had left about, to set the chairs in orderly rows, to pull the blinds so they all hung level. And that was right. Cleanliness was next to godliness, he thought stoutly, his pipestem legs methodically measuring off the pike—and he had both—and it was beyond him how Labe, who wasn't any of one, and not so's you could notice it of the other, was always being petted and forgiven. Even by his mother, who was a Quaker preacher and ought to be as fair as God. Maybe God Himself wasn't so awfully fair, he thought bitterly as he heard Labe's bare feet come slapping up the pike behind him, his lard pail rattling.

"I didn't take long, did I?" Labe called cheerfully. Josh looked at him somberly. "Thee set thy hand to the plow, and then thee turned back."

Labe didn't say anything. He was thinking how surprised Old Alf and his wife were going to be when they heard him and Josh outside their window playing the horse fiddle and shaking the lard pail.

"Thee would be salt, now," Josh went on, "if thee was Lot's wife. And thee would be dirty salt, too, because thee don't ever wash."

"How could I be a wife?" Labe asked.

Josh wasn't stumped, "God could do it for a miracle."

But Labe wasn't interested in miracles. "Josh," he asked, "does thee think Old Alf's got some candy on hand ready to give the shivaree-ers?"

"No," Josh said scornfully. "He don't think anyone knows he's married, so why would he be fixed for a shivaree?"

They were almost there. Josh took out his handkerchief and put it in with the stones so they wouldn't rattle and give them away. Old Alf's house set to the left of the pike on a little rise at the end of a long and cypress-framed lane. Not many people went up the lane now that Alf's old English mother was dead, except to use it as a short cut to the fishing pools in the creek which lay behind the house.

When Josh and Labe turned into the lane they began to talk

in whispers again. "We ain't too late," Labe said. "No smoke from the chimney, yet. They're still in bed."

"No credit to thee, we ain't," Josh whispered back.

"I'll show thee the window where I heard the talk coming from."

They tip-toed round the old house that had once been white, but was gray now with age. They walked through flower beds that no longer stayed within their border, and tried to lift their feet above the piles of drifted leaves.

"There it is," Labe whispered, pointing to a window at the back of the house. They pressed themselves along the edge of the house until they stood under the window.

Labe's face was sparkling. Cautiously he got Josh's handkerchief out from around the pebbles. "Thee ready?" he asked, pail poised for action.

"Sh," Josh said, pinching his arm. "Sh. Let's listen to them talk first." They stood there listening, hearing only their own heartbeats. There wasn't another sound to be heard except a scratching in the leaves made by a sparrow celebrating sunup.

Then they heard Old Alf say something. Something they couldn't catch, something in a low soft voice that sounded the way Labe had said—as if he might be talking to a baby. Finally his voice was louder and they could hear what he was saying.

"Molly darling," he said, "I'd ought to get up and light the fire for you. You're a sweet girl to say you'll do it for me—a sweet girl, with your long black hair. But you're plain spoiling me, Molly darling. That's what you are."

There was a pause. "They're kissing now," Josh said. Labe looked at Josh with respect.

Old Alf went on. "I always did say, Molly, there's no sight so pretty as a woman combing out her hair. And when her hair's as black and her arms as white as yours, Molly, it's a pure feast for the eyes. A pure feast." The old fellow sighed contentedly. Labe was getting restive. He wanted to start the shivaree, but Josh gave him another pinch.

"A woman as good as you and as pretty as you, Molly, is more than any man deserves—but that you should be from Tewkesbury —can talk old times with me—" He sounded as if he was going to cry. "Lord, my cup runneth over."

Then he got cheerful again. "Flannel cakes for breakfast, did you say? Flannel cakes and treacle and tea strong enough for a mouse to trot over. That's my girl, Molly. That's the breakfast to get."

"I can't hear her talk," Labe complained.

"Maybe she's dumb," Josh whispered. "Maybe that's the reason he's keeping her a secret."

They heard the cornhusk mattress rustle, the old man's bare feet hit the floor boards. "I'll be downstairs, Molly," he called, "before the cake's on."

"Now," Josh whispered, "now," and he turned the handle of his horse fiddle so that it sounded like a cat with its tail caught in a door. Labe shook his lard pail so hard and fast every inch of space was packed with sound waves. He hopped up and down while he shook it, like an Indian brave. This was what they'd planned and waited for and here they were doing it. Pretty soon Old Alf would bring his wife to the window, and make a little speech, and maybe give them some candy.

But Old Alf didn't bring his wife. He came to the window alone, his night cap still tied under his sharp brown chin, his striped nightshirt hanging from his bony shoulders. He peered out as if he didn't know what his eyes might light on. When he saw the boys under his window he said with more wonderment than anger, "What's the meaning of this racket? This time of day? Under my window? You Birdwell boys taken leave of your senses?"

Labe spoke up. Shivareeing was a polite and thoughtful thing to do. It was a disgrace if you got married and no one shivaree-ed you. So Labe felt proud and honorable about the enterprise. "We was shivareeing thee and thy new wife," he said. "Thee and Molly," he explained as Old Alf continued to stare at them.

"What's that?" the old man said, and he had the same look in his eyes Labe had seen in the eyes of a cotton-tail he had run into a fence corner. For the first time Labe felt a little uncertain about what he was doing.

Josh said, "It's a shivaree for thee and Molly. We found out thy secret and got ahead of everybody else."

"My secret," the old man said, and looked as if his bony shoulders kind of folded up inside his nightshirt.

"We heard thee talking to her," Labe said, "and knowed thee was married."

"Talking to her," repeated Old Alf, and seemed to wake up for the first time. "You heard me talking to her?" He stood there at the window for a long time looking at them. Then he said, "Go round to the back and come in, boys. Door's unlocked. I'll be right down."

The old man was downstairs by the time Josh and Labe opened the kitchen door. "Come in and sit, boys," he said, but the boys felt better standing. He had taken off his nightcap and pulled a pair of pants on over his nightshirt but his feet were still bare. Labe tried to keep his eyes off the bristle of black hair on his big knobby toes. Old Alf kept pinching his lower lip together, and his sad brown eyes still had the rabbit-in-the-fence-corner look.

"Boys," he said, "I ain't married." He went over to the bucket where he kept his corncobs soaking in coal-oil, took a half dozen and put them in the cook-stove.

Labe didn't know what to think. Josh thought, That ain't no way to be talking to a hired girl. He said, "We heard thee, talking. Talking to Molly darling," he added.

Old Alf got his fire going before he said any more. Then he settled himself in a rocking chair and put one bare foot on top of the other.

"How old're you boys?"

"Thirteen," said Josh.

"Ten," said Labe.

"Six or seven of you Birdwells, ain't there?"

"Six," Josh said. "Sarah died."

"Six," the old man repeated. "You don't ever get lonesome over there, do you?" He rocked back and forth and rubbed his bare feet together.

"Neither did I while ma was alive. You boys remember ma?" They nodded. Little dried-up old lady who always came out to talk to them when they cut across the Applegate place to go fishing.

"While she was alive," Old Alf said, "I didn't know the meaning of the word. Ma was a great talker. Nothing she wasn't interested in. She'd call out to me before she got up what'd I think the weather'd be like. Loved to talk about how high the river was—or how much the corn had growed. Didn't matter what it was, she'd have something to say about it. I used to get a little tired of it. Yes, I did," he told the staring boys. "Then after she'd been dead awhile didn't seem as if I could stand it. Getting up and not a sound in the house. Not a sound," he said, and rubbed his feet slowly and sadly together. "Not a single sound," he repeated, and leaned toward the boys trying to make them see how bad it had been.

Josh and Labe backed toward the door.

"Then's when I started talking to Molly," he told them.

Josh asked in a dry voice he couldn't seem to dampen by swallowing, "Who is Molly? Is she," he asked, knowing his Bible, "thy concubine?"

"No," Old Alf said, and sighed. "No, she ain't. She ain't nobody. She don't exist. I just made her up. I talk to her—just to hear my own voice. I just pretend she's my wife. There ain't no harm in it—or none I can see anyways, and besides I never figured anybody'd hear me."

The stove was drawing good now and the kitchen was warming, but Josh felt cold—he felt as if all his blood had got stuck in his heart and made it heavy as a bucket of lead. He looked at Old Alf as if he were part of a nightmare he was dreaming.

But Labe was smiling. Everything was clear to him now. "Thee got anyone else?" he asked.

It was the old man's turn to stare. "Eh?" he asked.

"Thee got anyone else thee talks to? Besides Molly," he explained.

"No," Alf said shortly, "just Molly. I ain't no Mormon."

Labe knew about them. "Thee could have children," he said.

"No," Old Alf insisted. "There's just Molly. At my age children would rile me."

Josh felt his heart getting smaller and smaller, and heavier and heavier. "Thee's crazy," he said. "Thee's gone soft in the head." He had to believe that—not that this was what growing up meant for everyone—for him too. Growing up meant not being worried or scared any more. Meant having things just as they ought to be, the way you liked them, everything neat and happy—at last. If it didn't, what was the use of being alive—taking the trouble to grow up? If you just got scareder and lonesomer—like Old Alf? No, he was loony, crazy as a bedbug.

Old Alf was nodding his head and giving his lip a pull at each nod. "That's what folk'll be saying all right. No misdoubting that. If they get wind of this, 'Old Alf's gone off his head,' they'll say. Not though," he said, "if you boys could manage to keep mum. Hold your tongues. I ain't asking you to. But," he added, "I don't know's your ma, or pa either, for that matter, would much cotton to the idea of you boys eavesdropping. The way you was. And you know yourselves I ain't any more cracked than you are."

Labe was only an inch or two from Alf's bare toes now. Cracked? He'd never seen a grownup act so smart. "I won't tell a living soul, Mr. Applegate," he said. "And don't thee say anything to mother." A hand of bones and leather went round Labe's and gave it a shake.

Old Alf looked at Josh. Josh was flat against the kitchen door; his black eyes seemed to have flowed to points. "Well, Joshua?" he asked.

"Thee's crazy," Josh said, "but thee needn't worry. I won't tell anyone." He turned and flashed out the door.

Labe watched him race round the corner of the house. "I guess I'd better go," he said. "Breakfast'll be over." But he kind of hated to go. The sun was shining through the dusty windows, the tea-kettle was humming, a cat had crawled out of the woodbox. Old Alf was rocking away, his eyes on something Labe couldn't see.

"Good-bye," Labe said.

Old Alf roused himself, and for a long minute the old man and the boy looked at each other.

"Come back again," Old Alf said, smiling.

"Thank thee," Labe answered, "I will," and off he loped after Josh, his lard pail rattling.

THE PACING GOOSE

JESS sat in the kitchen at the long table by the west window where in winter he kept his grafting tools: the thin-bladed knife, the paper sweet with the smell of beeswax and the resin, the boxes of roots and scions. Jess was a nurseryman and spring meant for him not only spirits flowering—but the earth's. A week more of moderating weather and he'd be out, still in gum boots, but touching an earth that had thawed, whose riches were once again fluid enough to be sucked upward, toward those burgeonings which by summer would have swelled into Early Harvests, Permains and Sweet Bows.

Spring's a various season, Jess thought, no two years the same: comes in with rains, mud deep enough to swallow horse and rider; comes in cold, snow falling so fast it weaves a web; comes in with a warm wind blowing about thy ears and bringing a smell of something flowering, not here, but southaways, across the Ohio, maybe, in Kentucky. Nothing here now but a smell of melting snow—which is no smell at all, but a kind of prickle in the nose, like a bygone sneeze. Comes in so various, winter put by and always so welcome.

"And us each spring so much the same."

"Thee speaking to me, Jess?"

"Nothing thee'd understand, Eliza."

Spring made Jess discontented with the human race—and with women, if anything more than men. It looked as if spring put them all in the shade: the season so resourceful and they each year meeting it with nothing changed from last year; digging up roots from the same sassafras thicket, licking sulphur and molasses from the same big-bowled spoon.

Behind him the table was set for supper, plates neatly turned to cover the bone-handled knives and forks, spoon vase aglitter with steel well burnished by brick dust, dishes of jam with more light to them than the sun, which was dwindling away, peaked and overcast outside, his window.

"Spring opening up," he said, "and nobody in this house so much as putting down a line of poetry."

Eliza, who was lifting dried-peach pies from a hot oven, said nothing. She set the four of them in a neat row on the edge of her kitchen cabinet to cool, and slid her pans of cornbread into the oven. Then she turned to Jess, her cheeks red with heat, and her black eyes warm with what she had to say. "Thee'd maybe relish a nice little rhyme for thy supper, Jess Birdwell."

Jess sighed, then sniffed the pies, so rich with ripe peach flavor that the kitchen smelled like a summer orchard, nothing lacking but the sound of bees. "Now, Eliza," he said, "thee knows I wouldn't have thee anyways altered. Thee . . ."

"Thee," Eliza interrupted him, "is like all men. Thee wants to have thy poetry and eat it too."

Jess wondered how what he'd felt about spring, a season with the Lord's thumbprint fresh on it, could've led to anything so unspringlike as an argument about a batch of dried peach pies.

"Eliza," he said firmly, "I didn't mean thee. Though it's crossed my mind sometimes as strange that none of the boys have ever turned, this time of year, to rhyming."

"Josh writes poems," Eliza said.

"Thee ever read what Josh writes, Eliza?"

Eliza nodded.

Ah, well, Jess thought, no use at this late date to tell her what's the difference.

Eliza looked her husband over carefully. "Jess Birdwell," she said, "thee's full of humors. Thy blood needs thinning. I'll boil thee up a good cup of sassafras tea."

Jess turned away from the green and gold sunset and the patches of snow it was gilding and fairly faced the dried-peach pies and Eliza, who was dropping dumplings into a pot of beans. "That's just it, Eliza," he said. "That's just the rub."

Eliza gave him no encouragement, but he went on anyway. "Earth alters, season to season, spring comes in never two times the same, only us pounding on steady as pump bolts and not freshened by so much as a grass blade."

"Jess, thee's got spring fever."

"I could reckon time and temperature, each spring, by the way thee starts honing for geese. 'Jess, don't thee think we might have a few geese?' It's a tardy spring," Jess said. "Snow still on the ground and not a word yet from thee about geese."

Eliza pulled a chair out from the table and sat. "Jess, why's thee always been so set against geese?"

"I'm not set against geese. It's geese that's set against farming. They can mow down a half acre of sprouting corn while thee's trying to head them off—and in two minutes they'll level a row of pie plant it's taken two years to get started. No, Eliza, it's the geese that's against me."

"If thee had tight fences . . ." Eliza said.

"Eliza, I got tight fences, but the goose's never been hatched that'll admit fences exist. And an old gander'd just as soon go through a fence as hiss—and if he can't find a hole or crack in a fence he'll lift the latch."

"Jess," said Eliza flatly, "thee don't like geese."

"Well," said Jess, "I wouldn't go so far's to say I didn't like them, but I will say that if there's any meaner, dirtier animal, or one that glories in it more, I don't know it. And a thing I've never been able to understand about thee, Eliza, is what thee sees in the shifty-eyed birds."

"Geese," said Eliza, with a dreaminess unusual to her, "march along so lordly like . . . they're pretty as swans floating down a branch . . . in fall they stretch out their necks and honk to geese passing overhead as if they's wild. My father never had any trouble raising geese and I've heard him say many a time that there's no better food for a brisk morning than a fried goose egg."

Jess knew, with spring his topic, he'd ought to pass over Eliza's father and his fried goose egg but he couldn't help saying, "A fried goose egg always had a kind of bloated look to me, Eliza"— but then he went on fast. "The season's shaping up," he said. "I can see thee's all primed to say, 'Jess, let's get a setting of goose eggs.'"

Eliza went over to the bean kettle and began to lift out dumplings. "It's a forwarder season than thee thinks, Jess," she said. "I got a setting under a hen now."

Jess looked at his wife. He didn't know what had made him want spring's variety in a human being—nor Eliza's substituting doing for asking. And speaking of it just now, as he had, made opposition kind of ticklish.

"When'd thee set them?" he asked finally.

"Yesterday," said Eliza.

"Where'd thee get the eggs?"

"Overbys'," said Eliza. The Overbys were their neighbors to the south.

"Well, they got enough for a surety," Jess said, "to give a few away."

"The Overbys don't give anything away, as thee knows. I paid for them. With my own money," Eliza added.

"How many?" Jess asked.

"Eight," Eliza said.

Jess turned back to his window. The sun had set, leaving a sad green sky and desolate black and white earth. "Five acres of corn gone," he calculated.

"Thee said," Eliza reminded him, "that what thee wanted was a little variety in me. 'Steady as a pump bolt,' were thy words."

"I know I did," Jess admitted glumly. "I talk too much."

"Draw up thy chair," Eliza said placidly, not contradicting him; "here's Enoch and the boys."

Next morning after breakfast Jess and Enoch left the kitchen together. The sun was the warmest the year had yet produced and the farm roofs were steaming; south branch, swollen by melting snow, was running so full the soft lap of its eddies could be heard in the barnyard; a rooster tossed his voice into the bright air, loud and clear as if aiming to be heard by every fowl in Jennings County.

"Enoch," said Jess to his hired man, "what's thy feeling about geese?"

Enoch was instantly equipped, for the most part, with feelings on every subject. Geese was a homelier topic than he'd choose himself to enlarge upon, not one that could be much embellished nor one on which Mr. Emerson, so far's he could recall, had ever expressed an opinion. "In the fall of the year," he said, "long about November or December, there's nothing tastier on the table than roast goose."

"Goose on the table's not what I mean," Jess said. "I was speaking of goose on the hoof. Goose nipping off a stand of corn, Enoch, goose roistering round, honking and hissing so's thee can't hear thyself think, goose eyeing thee like a snake on stilts."

Enoch gazed at his employer for a few seconds. "Mr. Birdwell," he said, "I think that if they's an ornery bird, it's a goose. Ornery and undependable."

"I'm glad we's so like minded about them," Jess said. "Otherwise, I'd not like to ask thee to do this little job." He pulled a long darning needle from beneath the lapel of his coat.

Enoch eyed it with some mistrust. "I can't say's I've ever been handy with a needle, Mr. Birdwell."

"Thee'll be handy enough for this," Jess said with hearty conviction. "To come to it, Enoch, Eliza's set eight goose eggs. Next year with any luck she'd have two dozen. And so on. More and more. Feeling the way thee does, Enoch, about geese it's no more'n fair to give thee a chance to put a stop to this before it goes too far. One little puncture in each egg with this and the goose project's nipped in the bud and Eliza none the wiser."

"I'm mighty awkward with my hands," said Enoch, "doing fine work. Ticklish job like this I might drop an egg and break it."

"Enoch," said Jess, "thee's not developing a weakness for geese, is thee?"

"It ain't the geese," said Enoch frankly, "it's your wife. She's been mighty clever to me and if she's got her heart set on geese, it'd go against the grain to disappoint her. Whyn't you do it, Mr. Birdwell?"

"Same reason," said Jess, "only more of them—and if Eliza ever asks if I tampered with that setting of eggs I figure on being able to say No." Jess held the needle nearer Enoch, who looked at it but still made no motion to take it.

"Likely no need to do a thing," Enoch said. "Two to one those eggs'll never hatch anyways. Overbys' such a fox-eared tribe they more'n likely sold her bad eggs to begin with."

"Thee's knowed about this," Jess asked, "all along?"

"Yes," Enoch said.

"Here's the needle," Jess said.

"You look at this," Enoch inquired, "not so much as a favor asked as a part of the day's work with orders from you?"

"Yes," Jess said, "that's about the way I look at it."

Enoch took the needle, held it somewhat gingerly, and with the sun glinting across its length, walked slowly toward the chickenhouse.

It takes thirty days for a goose egg to hatch, and the time, with spring work to be done, went fast. The hen Eliza had picked was a good one and kept her mind strictly on her setting. Eliza kept her mind on the hen, and Jess and Enoch found their minds oftener than they liked on Eliza and her hoped-for geese.

At breakfast on the day the geese were due to break their shells Jess said, "If I's thee, Eliza. I wouldn't bank too much on them geese. I heard Enoch say a while back he wouldn't be surprised if not an egg hatched. Thought the eggs were likely no good."

Enoch was busy pouring coffee into a saucer, then busy cooling it, but Eliza waited until he was through. "Did thee say that Enoch?"

Enoch looked at Jess. "Yes," he said, "I kind of recollect something of the sort."

"What made thee think so, Enoch?"

"Why," said Jess, for Enoch was busy with his coffee again, "it was the Overbys. Enoch's got a feeling they's kind of unreliable. Fox-eared, I think thee said, Enoch, didn't thee?"

Enoch's work took him outside almost at once and Jess himself said, "If thee'll just give me a little packet of food, Eliza, I won't trouble thee for anything at noon. I'm going to be over'n the south forty and it'll save time coming and going."

Eliza was surprised for Jess'd usually come twice as far for a hot dinner at midday, but she made him fried ham sandwiches and put them and some cold apple-turnovers in a bag.

"It's a pity thee has to miss thy dinner," she told him, but Jess only said, "Press of work, press of work," and hurriedly departed.

Jess came home that evening through the spring twilight, somewhat late, and found a number of things to do at the barn before he went up to the house. When he entered the kitchen nothing seemed amiss—lamps ruddy, table set, stove humming, and beside the stove a small box over which Eliza was bending. Jess stopped to look—and listen; from inside the box was coming a kind of birdlike peeping, soft and not unpleasant. Reluctantly he walked to Eliza's side. There, eating minced boiled egg, and between bites lifting its beak to Eliza, it seemed, and making those chirping sounds he'd heard was a gray-gold gosling.

Eliza looked up pleasantly. "Enoch was right," she said. "The eggs were bad. Only one hatched. I plan to call it Samantha," she told Jess. "It's a name I've always been partial to."

"Samantha," said Jess without any enthusiasm whatever for either name or gosling. "How's thee know it's a she?"

"I don't," said Eliza, "but if it's a gander it's a name easily changed to Sam."

Enoch came in just then with a load of wood for the kitchen woodbox. "Enoch," asked Jess, "has thee seen Samantha—or Sam?"

Enoch mumbled but Jess understood him to say he had.

"It was my understanding, Enoch, that thy opinion was that all those eggs were bad."

"Well, Mr. Birdwell," said Enoch, "a man could make a mistake. He could count wrong."

"A man ought to be able to count to eight without going astray," Jess said.

Eliza was paying no attention to either of them; she was making little tweeting sounds herself, bending over the chirping gosling. "Does thee know," she asked Jess, "that this is the first pet I ever had in my life?"

"Thee's got Ebony," Jess said.

"I don't mean a caged pet," Eliza said, "but one to walk beside thee. I'm reconciled the others didn't hatch. With eight I'd've had to raise geese for the table. With one only I can make Samantha a pure pet."

A pure pet was what she made of her: Samantha ate what the family ate, with the exception of articles which Eliza thought might be indigestible and would risk on humans but not on her goose. Cake, pie, corn-on-the-cob, there was nothing too good for Samantha. From a big-footed, gold-downed gosling she swelled, almost at once, like a slack sail which gets a sudden breeze, into a full-rounded convexity.

"Emphasis on the vexity," Jess said when he thought of this. Samantha was everything he'd disliked in the general run of geese, with added traits peculiar to herself, which vexed him. Because she was fed at the doorstep, she was always underfoot. No shout, however loud, would move her before she's ready to move. If she's talked to too strong she'd flail you with her wings and pinch the calf of your leg until for some days it would look to be mortifying. She'd take food out of children's hands and the pansies Jess had planted in a circle at the base of the Juneberry tree she sheared so close that there was not a naked stem left to show for all his work. And when not being crossed in any way, Jess simply looking at her and meditating, trying to fathom Samantha's fascination for Eliza, the goose would suddenly extend her snakelike neck, and almost touching Jess, hiss with such a hint of icy disapprobation that Jess would involuntarily recoil.

But she was Eliza's pure pet, no two ways about that, and would lift her head for Eliza to scratch, and walk beside her with the lordly roll of the known elect.

"There was some goddess," Enoch remembered, "who always had a big bird with her." Jess supposed Enoch was thinking of Juno and her peacock, but the reference didn't convince him that a goose was a suitable companion for any goddess—let alone Eliza, and he couldn't honestly feel much regret when one evening toward the end of November Eliza told him Samantha was missing. "She'll turn up," Jess said. "That bird's too ornery to die young."

Eliza said nothing, but next evening she proved Jess was right. "Samantha's over at Overbys'," she said.

"Well, did thee fetch her home?" Jess asked.

"No," said Eliza with righteous indignation, "they wouldn't let me. They said they had forty geese—and forty's what they got now, and they don't think Samantha's there. They provoked me so, Jess, I told them they'd sold me seven bad eggs and now they try to take the eighth away from me."

Jess felt a little abashed at this, but he asked, "How can thee be so sure Samantha's there? She might've been carried off by a varmint."

Eliza was scornful. "Thee forgets I hand-raised Samantha from a gosling. I'd know her among four hundred—let alone forty."

"Whyn't thee buy her back then," Jess asked, "if that's the only way?"

"After what I said about their eggs," Eliza answered sadly, "the Overbys say they don't want any more dealings with me."

Eliza mourned so for the lost Samantha that first Enoch and then Jess went over to the Overbys' but no one there would admit the presence of a visiting goose—forty they had, and forty you could see by counting was what they had now. Short of force there didn't seem any way of getting Samantha home again.

When Eliza heard the Overbys were going to sell geese for Christmas eating she was frantic. "Jess," she said, "I just can't bear to think of Samantha, plucked naked and resting on a table waiting to be carved. She used to sing as sweet as any bird when she was little, and she'd walk by my side taking the air. She's the only goose I ever heard of," Eliza remembered mournfully, "who'd drink tea."

In Jess' opinion a goose'd eat anything at either end of the scale, but he didn't suppose this was a suitable time to mention it to Eliza. "Eliza," he said, "short of me and Enoch's going over there and using force on old man Overby—or sneaking over at night and breaking into their chicken pen, I don't know how in the world we're going to get Samantha back for thee."

"We could sue," said Eliza.

"Thee mean go to law?" Jess asked, astounded. Quakers stayed out of courts, believing in amicable settlements without recourse to law.

"Yes," said Eliza. "I'd do it for Samantha. I'd think it my duty. Going to law'd be a misery for us . . . but not so lasting a misery as being roasted would be for Samantha."

Jess couldn't deny this, but he said, "I'd have to think it over. I've never been to law yet in my life and suing for a gone goose don't seem to me a very likely place to start."

Next morning Eliza served a good but silent breakfast, not sitting herself to eat with the rest of her family.

"Thee feeling dauncy, Eliza?" Jess asked.

"I just can't eat," she said, "for thinking of Samantha."

Labe and Mattie had tears in their eyes. Little Jess was mournfully bellowing. Enoch looked mighty glum. Jess felt ashamed to be swallowing victuals in the midst of so much sorrow. Eliza stood at the end of the stove where the gosling's box had rested for the first few weeks of its life, looking down, as if remembering how it had sung and lifted its beak to her.

Jess couldn't stand it. "Eliza," he said, "if thee wants to go through with it I'll go to Vernon and fee a lawyer for thee. Thee'll have to go to court, be on the witness stand—and even then I misdoubt thee'll ever get thy goose back. Does thee still want me to do it?"

Eliza came to the table and stood with her hand on Jess' shoulder. "Yes, Jess," she said, "I want thee to do it."

Jess went to Vernon, fee'd a lawyer, had a restraining order put on the Overbys so they couldn't sell or kill the goose Eliza said was Samantha, and awaited with misgivings the day of the trial. It came in mid-December.

Eliza, Jess and Enoch rode to the trial through a fall of light, fresh snow. Brilliant sunlight, crisp air, glittering snow, and Rome's spirited stepping made the occasion, in spite of its purpose, seem festive. Eliza made it seem festive. Jess, who did not forget its purpose, regarded her with some wonder. He couldn't say what it was about her—dress and bonnet appeared to be simply her First Day best—but she had a holiday air.

He considered it his duty to warn her. "Eliza," he said, "thee understands thee's not going to Meeting? They're not going to sit silent while thee tells them how much thee loves Samantha and how she sang when young and drank tea. Old man Overby'll have his say and he's got a lawyer hired for no other purpose than to trip thee up."

Eliza was unimpressed. "What's our lawyer fee'd for, Jess?" she asked.

Jess took another tack. "Eliza," he told her, "I don't figger thee's got a chance in a thousand to get Samantha back."

"This is a court of justice, isn't it?" Eliza asked.

"Yes," Jess said.

"Then there's no need for thee to fash thyself, Jess Birdwell. I'll get Samantha back."

Not getting Samantha back wasn't what fashed Jess—he reckoned he could bear up under that mighty well. What fashed him was the whole shooting match. . . . In some few cases, matters of life and death, going to court might be necessary, and he could imagine such. But a suit over a goose named Samantha wasn't one of them. And poor Eliza. Law to her was all Greek and turkey tracks . . . and here she was bound for court as chipper as if she was Chief Justice Taney himself. Jess sighed and shook his head. Getting shut of Samantha would be no hardship for him, but he was downcast for Eliza's sake and the way she'd have to turn homeward empty-handed.

In the courtroom hard, clear light reflected upward from the snow fell onto what Jess thought were hard faces: courthouse hangers on; farmers whose slackening work made the diversion of a trial an inviting possibility; lovers of oddity who figured a tilt between a Quaker female, preacher, to boot, and an old sinner like Milt Overby over the ownership of a goose ought to produce some enlivening quirks. They stared at Eliza, exchanged salutes with Milt Overby and inspected Samantha who in her crate awaited the court's decision.

The two lawyers, Jess considered to be on a par. Nothing fancy either one . . . old roadsters both, gone gray in service and with a knowledge of their business. The circuit judge was something else, unaccountably young, jug-eared and dressed more sprightly than a groom for his own wedding. A city whipper-snapper, born and trained north of the Missisinewa, and now, in Jess' opinion, setting a squeamish foot in backwoods provinces, and irked to find himself trying so trifling a case. Didn't know a goose from a guinea hen, like as not, and would consider tossing a coin a more suitable manner of settling such a matter—just as near right in the end—and his valuable time saved.

Eliza, Jess saw, was of no such opinion. She, too, was scanning the young judge, and Jess, who knew her, saw from the look on her face that she was taken by him. A neat, thin, pious boy—far from home—he looked, no doubt to her; a young man who could do with better cooking and more regular eating.

The young man rapped the court to order. Spitting and shuffling slackened and in a high, precise voice he read, "Birdwell versus Overby. Charge, petty larceny. Appropriation and willful withholding of goose named Samantha." The name Samantha seemed to somewhat choke him, but he got it out.

"Ready for Birdwell," said Mr. Abel Samp, Eliza's lawyer.

"Ready for Overby," said the defendant's lawyer.

Eliza was the first witness on the stand. Jess sometimes forgot what a good-looking woman Eliza was, but the interest shown on lifted faces all about him refreshed his memory.

"Swear the plaintiff in," the judge said.

Eliza, in her sweet voice, spoke directly to the judge. "I don't swear," she said.

The judge explained that profanity was not asked for. "I understood," said Eliza, "that thee wasn't asking for profanity. No one would think that of thee. But we Quakers do not take oaths in court. We affirm."

"Permit Mrs. Birdwell to affirm," said the judge. Eliza affirmed.

Mr. Samp then proceeded to question Eliza as to Samantha's birth and habits.

"Judge," Eliza began.

"Address the judge," Mr. Samp said, "as Your Honor."

"We Quakers," Eliza told the judge, gently, "do not make use of such titles. What is thy name? I think thee'll go far in our state and thy name's one I'd like to know."

The judge appeared somewhat distraught, undecided as to whether to make the tone of the court brisk and legal (if possible) or to follow Eliza's lead of urbane sociability.

"Pomeroy," he said and made a slight bow in Eliza's direction.

Eliza returned the bow, deeper and with more grace. "Friend Pomeroy," she said, "it is indeed a pleasure to know thee."

Samantha's story as Eliza told it to Friend Pomeroy was surprisingly terse. Affecting, and losing nothing by Eliza's telling, but to the point.

"Mrs. Birdwell," said Samp, "how long have you had an acquaintanceship with geese and their habits?"

"Since I was a child," Eliza said. "My father was a great fancier of geese."

"And you think you could identify this goose Samantha, which you admit in looks was similar to the defendant's?"

"I could," Eliza said with much authority.

Mr. Samp, to Jess' surprise, left the matter there. "Take the witness," he said to Overby's lawyer—but the counsel for the defendant was in no hurry to cross-examine Eliza. Instead he put his client on the stand.

"Farewell, Samantha," Jess said to Enoch.

"You relieved?" Enoch asked.

"Putting Eliza first," Jess said, "as I do, no."

Milt Overby, whose natural truculence was somewhat stimulated by a nip he'd had to offset snappy weather, bellowed his way through his testimony. At one juncture he set the judge aright when he asked some elementary questions concerning the habits and configurations of geese. "Where in tarnation you from?" he snorted. "What they mean sending us judges down here who don't know Toulouse from Wyandotte, or goose from gander?"

The young judge used voice and gavel to quiet the guffawing which filled the courtroom and the trial proceeded. A number of witnesses for both sides were brought to the stand and while it was shown that Overbys had maybe eaten a goose or two and neglected out of pure fondness for the creatures to count them as among the departed, still nobody had been able to positively identify Samantha.

Mr. Overby's lawyer seemed somewhat loath to cross-examine Eliza, but he put her on the stand. She'd said she knew geese and her testimony had been direct and positive. "Mrs. Birdwell," he said, "how can you be so sure your goose was with my client's geese?"

Eliza's black eyes rested confidingly upon the judge. "Friend Pomeroy," she said, "I raised Samantha from a gosling."

Jess sighed. "Here it comes," he said, "how that goose could sing and drink tea."

Eliza continued, "And there's one thing about her that always set her apart from every other goose."

"Yes, Mrs. Birdwell," said Judge Pomeroy, who was inclined to forget, with Eliza on the stand, that he was in a courtroom.

"Samantha," said Eliza, with much earnestness, "from the day she was born had a gait unlike any other goose I ever saw and one that set her apart from all her Overby connections. I picked her out at once when I went over there, because of it. Thee couldn't've missed it, Friend Pomeroy."

"Yes, Mrs. Birdwell," said the judge with interest in his voice.

"Samantha," said Eliza, "was a born pacer. Thee knows what a pacer is?"

"Certainly," said Judge Pomeroy. "A pacer," he repeated with no surprise—and with obvious pleasure that Eliza'd hit upon so clear and differentiating an aspect of her goose and one that made identification possible.

A titter was mounting through the courtroom—Judge Pomeroy lifted his head. He had no desire to be further instructed as to the history, habits and breeds of geese, and he liked to see a trial settled by some such little and too often overlooked subtlety. Judge Pomeroy brought down his gavel. "The court awards decision in favor of the plaintiff. Case dismissed." While the silence that followed on his words still prevailed Judge Pomeroy stepped briskly and with obvious pleasure out through the rear door.

Jess was also brisk about departure. No use lingering until friend Pomeroy had been more thoroughly informed as to gaits in general and geese in particular. Mid-afternoon's a quiet time in any season. In winter with snow on the ground, no leaves to rustle and bare limbs rigid as rock against a cloudless sky, the hush is deepest of all. Nothing broke that hush in the surrey, except the squeak of leather and snow, the muffled footfalls of Rome Beauty. Jess and Eliza, on the front seat, rode without speaking. Enoch, in the back, seemed to meditate. Even Samantha in her crate at Enoch's feet was silent.

Maple Grove Nursery was in sight before Jess spoke. "Eliza," he said, "would thee mind telling me—did thee ever see a trotting goose?"

Enoch ceased to meditate and listened. He had been wondering about this himself.

"Certainly not," said Eliza. "Thee knows as well as I, Jess Birdwell, an animal can't trot without hind feet and forefeet."

"So far, Eliza," Jess said, "we see eye to eye. Now maybe thee'd tell me—did thee ever see a goose that didn't pace?"

Eliza was truly amazed, it seemed. "Why, Jess," she said, "an ordinary goose just walks—but Samantha paces."

Jess was silent for a spell. "What'd thee say the difference is?"

"It's the swing, Jess Birdwell," said Eliza, "same as in a horse that nature's formed for a pacer . . . it's the natural bent, the way the spirit leads the beast to set his feet down. Samantha's a natural pacer."

That seemed as far as they'd likely get on the subject and Jess joined Enoch in meditation. In the barnyard, before she went up to the house, Eliza said, like an old hand at the business, "Attending court whettens the appetite. It's a little early but I thought if thee'd relish it"—and she looked at Jess and Enoch, never sparing a glance for Samantha, as if her menfolk's welfare was her sole concern—"I'd stir us up a bite to eat. Hot tea and fresh sweetcakes, say. Might fry a little sausage and open some cherry preserves. If thee'd relish it," she repeated.

Jess wasn't taken in, but he'd relish it, and so would Enoch, and they both said so. They hustled with the unhitching so they could uncrate Samantha and note her progress with eyes newly instructed as to what made a pacer. Jess dumped her in the snow, and Enoch tapped her with his hat. Samantha made for the back door.

"By sugar," said Jess, "Eliza's right. She paces." Samantha had the smooth roll of a racker—there were no two ways about it. At heart she was a pacer, and what two legs could do in that line, Samantha accomplished.

"With four legs," Enoch said, "you could enter her in any county fair—rack on," he cried with enthusiasm. As they followed Samantha to the house, Enoch, for whom any event existed chiefly in its after aspects as a cud for rumination, asked, "How you feel in respect of court trials, now, Mr. Birdwell?"

"I'm still against them," Jess said, "though they's three things this trial's taught me I might never otherwise have learned. Two's about women."

Enoch revered all knowledge and he had a notion that information on this subject might have a more than transcendental value. "What's the two things you learned about women, Mr. Birdwell?"

"Well, Enoch, I learned first, dependability's woman's greatest virtue. Steady as a pump bolt, day in, day out. When thee finds a woman like that, Enoch, don't try to change her. Not even in spring."

"No, sir," said Enoch, "I won't."

"Second, when it's a case of woman and the law—thee don't need to waste any worry on the woman."

"No, sir," said Enoch again.

When they reached the back steps, Enoch asked, "I understood you to say you'd learned three things, Mr. Birdwell. What's the third about?"

"Hired men," said Jess.

Enoch was taken aback, but he'd asked for it. "Yes, Mr. Birdwell," he said.

"Never hire one," Jess told him, "till thee finds out first if he can count to eight. Save thyself a lot of trouble that way, Enoch."

"How's I to know the eighth'd turn out to be Samantha?" Enoch asked.

Samantha herself, who was waiting at the doorstep for an expected tidbit, reached out and unhampered by either boots or work pants nipped Enoch firmly through his thin Sunday best.

"Thee say something, Enoch?" Jess asked.

Enoch had but he didn't repeat it. Instead he said, "Pacer or no pacer, that's Samantha," and the two of them stepped out of the snow into the warm kitchen, scented with baking sweetcakes and frying sausage.

LEAD HER LIKE A PIGEON

IT was deep in May. Fingers had lifted the green strawberry leaves and had found fruit beneath them. Wheat was heading up. Cherries, bright as Christmas candles, hung from the trees. The bees had swarmed twice. The wind was from the south and sent a drift of locust blossoms like summer snow—Mattie thought—through the air.

She left her churn on the back porch and stood for a minute by the spring-house with uplifted face to see how locust-snow felt; but the wind died down and no more blossoms fell, so she went back to her churning.

She counted slowly as she moved the dasher up and down. She was keeping track of the least and most strokes it took to bring butter. This at any rate was not going to be a least-time. "Eighty-eight, eighty-nine . . ." Little Jess was putting horsehairs in the rain barrel to turn into worms. Enoch stuck his head out of the barn door, saw her and directly pulled it in again.

"Mattie," called her mother, "get finished with thy churning and ride over to the Bents' with some rocks."

Mattie could smell the rocks baking: raisins and hickory nuts all bedded down together in sweet dough.

"Lavony Bent's as queer as Dick's hatband," her mother called above the slap and gurgle of the dasher, "half Indian and a newcomer. She needs a token to show she's welcome."

Listening, Mattie slowed her churning. "Bring that butter humping," her mother said. "Thee'll have to get a soon start or it'll get dark on thee." She came to the kitchen door, rosy from the oven's heat, bringing Mattie a new-baked rock. "Day fading so soon," she said.

Mattie looked at her mother because of the sadness in her voice, and felt uncertainty and sorrow herself.

"There'll be another to match it tomorrow," her mother promised. "Its equal or better, Mattie. That red sky's a sure sign."

The butter was slow coming, only five strokes short of the most she'd ever counted. "Thee'd best go as thee is, Mattie."

"In this?" said Mattie.

"Who's to see?" asked her mother. "None but Bents and hoot-owls at this hour."

Mattie wouldn't've named them together—hoot-owls and the black-haired, brown-faced boys she'd watched walking riverward with fishing poles over their shoulders.

"Once thee starts combing and changing it'll be nightfall."

So Mattie rode as she was to the Bents', barefooted and in her blue anchor print which had faded until the anchors were almost as pale as the sea that lapped about them.

She carried the rocks in a little wooden box her mother was fixing to make into a footstool. So far, it was only painted white, with cranes and cattails on each side. The brown cattails were set onto the box with so much paint that they curved up plump as real ones beneath Mattie's exploring thumb.

Old Polly walked like a horse in a dream . . . slow . . . slow . . . with forever to arrive. Tonight, a short way on the pike and then across the wood lot. Mattie ate a rock, pulled down a limb to see it spring back in place . . . remembered what she'd heard about the Bents . . .

"Never seen a more comfortable sight in my life," her father called one day, and there on a padded chair was Jud Bent riding down the pike in his manure wagon sitting and reading like a man at ease in his parlor. "Wonderful emancipation," her father said. "Thee mark it, Mattie. The spirit of man's got no limitations."

Jud Bent read and farmed. His boys, all but Gardiner, fished and farmed. "Gardiner's a reader like his pa," said Mattie's father, "off to Normal studying to be a teacher. He figures on getting shut of the manure wagon and having just the book left."

But the day she rode through was more to Mattie than her destination. In the woods it was warm and sheltered and the sun, setting, lay like butter on the new green leaves.

At the far edge of the woods she stopped for a minute at the old Wright place. A little white tumbling-down house, empty for years, stood there. A forgotten house, but flowers still came up about it in the patterns in which Mrs. Wright had planted them. It was a sad, beautiful sight, Mattie thought, to see flowers hands had planted, growing alone in the woods with not an eye to note whether they did well or not: the snowball bush where the front gate had been, spice pinks still keeping to their circle by the steps and white flags, gold-powered now at sunset, by the ruined uppingblock. A pair of doves, as she watched, slid down from the deep shadows of the woods and wheeled about in the sunlit clearing as if coming home.

Mattie stretched a hand to them. "You don't act like wildings," she said.

She slipped down from fat old Polly and carrying her box of cookies went to pick some flags. These flowers and buildings have known people for too long, she thought, to be happy alone. They have grown away from their own kind and forgotten the language of woods and doves and long to hear household words again. To hear at bedtime a woman coming to the door for a sight of stars and saying, "There'll be rain before morning. A circle round the moon and hark to that cock crowing. It's a sure sign."

Or a man at morning, scanning the sky as he hitches up his suspenders, "A weather breeder. Have to hustle the hay in."

Mattie talked for the house and flowers to hear as she gathered the flags and laid them across the top of the cookie-filled footstool.

"If it's a dry summer I'll bring you some water," she said. "I couldn't bear to lie abed a hot night, and you parching here. I'll carry buckets from the branch if the well's dry, and some night I'll come and light a candle in the house so it'll look like olden times. I'll sing a song in the house and it'll be like Mrs. Wright playing on her melodeon again."

"Sing now, why don't you?"

She was bending over the flags, but she wasn't frightened—the voice was so quiet. It was a young man's voice though and she dropped the flags in her hand onto her bare feet before she turned to face him.

"No human would enjoy my singing . . . only maybe an old house that can't be choosy."

"I'm not choosy, either."

"No, I'm on an errand to take some rocks to Lavony Bent. I only stopped to pick some flags."

"Well, I'm Gard Bent," the boy said, "and I'll walk along home with you. What's your name?"

"Martha Truth Birdwell. Only I'm mostly called Mattie."

"Martha Truth Birdwell. That's as pretty as any song. If he'd a known you," and Gardiner Bent held up the book he was carrying, "he'd written a poem called Martha Truth."

Mattie saw the name on the book. "He mostly writes of Jeans and Marys," she said. Now maybe this Bent boy wouldn't think she was a know-nothing, barefooted and talking to herself. "Thee take the rocks on to thy ma. I've dallied here so long it'll be dark going home through the wood lot."

"No, I'll walk back with you to the pike. Ma'd never forgive me if I let you go home with your box empty. The boys've been on the river this afternoon. They'll have a fine mess of catfish. Can I help you onto your horse?"

Mattie would dearly have liked being handed onto her horse had she been rightly dressed and old Polly saddled, but that would have to wait for another time. She would not be hoisted like a sack of meal, plopped barefooted onto a saddleless horse. She stood stock still, the flags covering her feet, and said nothing.

"I'll get the rest of my books," the boy said.

While he was gone Mattie led old Polly to the upping-block and settled herself as sedately as if she were riding sidesaddle, one bare foot curled daintily beneath her.

Old Polly stepped slowly along in the dusk down the back road that led to the Bents' and Gard walked beside her. There wasn't much Indian about him, Mattie thought, unless it was his black hair and his quiet, toed-in walk. But his hair wasn't Indian straight, and his eyes weren't black at all but the color of the sandstone in a go-to-meeting watch fob. It was a pleasing face, a face she did not tire of regarding. Her eyes searched its tenderness and boldness in the May dusk.

"I thought thee was away at Vernon, studying at the Normal."

"I was—but it's out. Now I'm studying to take the teacher's examinations. I've got the promise of the school at Rush Branch when I pass. That's why I come to Wrights'—to study where it's quiet. If it gets dark on you, you could see your way home by the fireflies, they're so thick," he finished, as if ashamed of telling so much of himself.

"Fireflies. Is that what thee calls lightning bugs?"

"Elsewhere they're known as fireflies."

It was full sunset before they reached the Bent place. Lavony Bent was cleaning fish on a stump at the edge of the yard. Jud Bent was on the back steps getting the last of the light on to the book he was reading. Two black-haired boys were rolling about on the ground wrestling; a third was trying to bring a tune from a homemade-looking horn. There weren't any flowers or grass about the Bents' house, but the yard was trodden flat and swept as clean as a palm.

Gard called out, "Ma, this is Martha Truth Birdwell come to bring you some cookies."

Mrs. Bent didn't stop her fish cleaning, but looked up kindly enough. "Light down, Martha Truth, light down. I knowed your folks years ago when we's all younger than you are now."

Jud Bent closed his book on his finger and walked over to

Mattie. He was a little plump man with a big head of red hair and a silky red mustache. "If it isn't Spring," he said. "Spring riding a white horse and with flowers in her hands."

Mattie was too taken aback to answer, but Gard laughed. "She's got a box of cookies under the flowers, pa."

Mattie handed the box of cookies and the white flags to him. "Spring for looks and Summer for gifts," said Jud Bent and took a rock in two bites, shaking the crumbs from his mustache like a water-drenched dog.

Mattie was afraid to talk to this strange man who carried a book as if it had been a pipe or a jack-knife, and spoke of her as though she were absent, or a painted picture.

Mrs. Bent took the head from a still quivering catfish with a single, clean stroke. The boy with the horn started a tune she knew, but he couldn't get far with it. "Lead her like a pigeon . . . Lead her like a pigeon . . ." he played over and over. Mattie's ears ached to hear the next notes, have the piece played through to its ending, not left broken and unfinished. "Lead her like a pigeon . . ." Mattie's mind hummed the tune for him . . . "Bed her like a dove . . . Whisper when I'm near her . . . Be my only love . . ." but the horn could not follow. "Lead her like a pigeon," it said once more, then gave up.

The wrestlers groaned and strained. They turned up the earth beneath them like a plow. A catfish leaped from the stump and swam again, most pitifully, in the grass.

"I'll have to be turning homewards," Mattie spoke suddenly. "Could I have my box? Ma's fixing to make a footstool of it."

Mrs. Bent sent Gard into the house to empty the cookies, then she lined the footstool with leaves and filled it with fish.

"There's a mess of fish for your breakfast," she said. "Tell your ma she's so clever at sharing I can't hope to keep pace with her."

As they went out of the yard, Mattie once more on old Polly and Gard walking beside her, Jud Bent called after them, ' Persephone and Pluto. Don't eat any pomegranate seeds, Martha Truth "

"What does he mean?" asked Mattie. What Mr. Bent had said didn't sound like English to her.

"Persephone was a girl," Gard said, "the goddess of Spring, and Pluto, another god, stole her away to live underground with him. And while she was gone it was winter on earth."

"She's back on earth now, isn't she?" Mattie asked, watching the fireflies light themselves like candles among the dark leaves.

"Yes, she's back again," Gard said.

They parted at the edge of the woods where Mattie could see the lights of home glimmering down the road. Supper was over when she brought her box of catfish into the kitchen, and the dishes half washed.

"Sit down, child," her mother said, "and have thy supper. What kept thee?"

"The Bents all talk a lot," said Mattie. "It didn't seem polite to go and leave them all talking."

"They'll not be hindered by thy leaving . . . never fear. Eat, eat. Thy food will lose its savor."

"I can't eat," Mattie said. "I don't seem to have any relish for victuals." She got the dishtowel from the rack and started drying.

"Was thee fanciful," asked her mother, who never attributed fright to aught but fancy, "crossing the wood lot?"

"No. Gardiner Bent came with me."

"The Normal School boy?"

"Yes," said Mattie. "He's learned. Flowers, Fireflies. Poetry. Gods and goddesses. It's all one to him," she declared ardently. "He can lay his tongue to anything and give thee a fact about it. Oh, he's full of facts. He's primed for an examination and knows more than he can hold in."

Mattie made the plates she dried fly through her hands like thistle-down—as if they were weightless as thistles and as imperishable. Her hands were deft but they had not her mother's flashing grace, and they were silent; they could not play the tune she envied, the tinkling bell-like song of her mother's wedding ring against the china; the constant light clatter of gold against glass and silver that said, I'm a lady grown and mistress of dishes and cupboards.

Behind were the dark woods, shadows and bosky places and whatever might slide through them when the sun was set. Here, the kitchen, the stove still burning, sending a wash of light across the scrubbed floor boards, the known dishes in their rightful stacks, and ma's ring sounding its quick song of love.

Mattie hummed a little.

"What's thee humming?" her mother asked. "Seems like I've heard it."

" 'Lead Her Like a Pigeon,' " Mattie, smiling, said.

"Play-party tune." Her mother held her hands above the soapy water and looked far away. " 'Weevily Wheat.' Once I was tempted to lift my foot to that."

Lift her foot. . . . Mattie looked at her mother . . . the Quaker preacher, whose foot now never peeped from beneath her full and seemly skirts. Once tempted . . . the wedding-ring music began again, but Mattie was watching, not drying. A long time ago tempted, yet there was something in the way her mother'd bury her face in a cabbage rose, or run to the door when father's spring wagon turned off the pike that showed her the black-haired girl who once listened to that music.

"Who's the Bent boy favor, Mattie?"

"His mother, I reckon. But handsomer. He's got a face to re-member," Mattie said earnestly. "A proud, learned face. He's got eyes the color of sandstones. When he walks there isn't any up and down. It's a pleasure to watch him walk."

Mattie's mother put a washed skillet on the still warm stove to dry. "After a good heart," she said, "the least a woman can do is pick a face she fancies. Men's so much alike and many so sorry, that's the very least. If a man's face pleasures thee, that doesn't change. That is something to bank on. Thy father," she said, "has always been a comely man."

She turned back to her dishpan. "Why, Mattie," she said, 'what's thee crying about?"

Mattie would not say. Then she burst out. "Pushing me off. Pushing me out of my own home. Thee talking about men that way . . . as if I would marry one. Anxious to be shut of me." She cried into her already wet dishtowel. "My own mother," she sobbed.

"Why, lovey," her mother said and went to her, but Mattie buried her face more deeply in her dishtowel and stumbled up the back stairs. "My own mother," she wailed.

"What's the trouble? What's Mattie taking on about?" Mattie's mother looked up at her husband, filling the doorway from the sitting-room like a staunch timber.

"Well, Jess," she said. "I think Mattie got a sudden inkling of what leaving home'll be like."

"Leaving home?" asked Jess. "Getting married? Thee think that's a crying matter, Eliza?"

Eliza looked at the face that had always pleasured her. "Thee knows I don't, Jess," she said.

Jess smiled. "Seems like," he said, "I have a recollection of some few tears thee shed those first . . ." But Eliza would have none of that. "Tsk, tsk," she said, her wedding ring beating a lively tattoo against the last kettle, "tsk, tsk, Jess Birdwell."

"Thee happy now?" Jess asked, smiling.

Eliza wouldn't say, but she hummed a little raveling of a song.

"Seems as if I know that," Jess said. "A long time ago."

"Like as not," Eliza agreed and handed him the pan to empty.

Jess went out with it, trying the tune over. "Tum-te-tum-te-tum. I can't name it," he said when he came back, "but it runs in my mind I know it."

"Thee know it, Jess, never fear," Eliza said. She took the empty pan from him, her wedding ring making one more musical note.

THE BATTLE OF FINNEY'S FORD

Except for the name of Morgan the morning of the eleventh opened up like any other in July: clear, with promise of heat to come. Overhead arched the great cloudless sky of summer, tranquil above the reports, the rumors, the whisperings, the fears. And above the true evidence. The evidence brought in by the eye witnesses; by the boy who had hid himself and horse in the thicket while Morgan's outriders galloped past; by the girl who had waded along the branch and was not seen; the stories of the burnings, the shootings, the looting.

The mind knew Morgan's name had altered the day, yet the untutored eye could find no difference, either in it or the horizon which framed it. Eliza, standing in the doorway of the summer kitchen, breakfast bell in hand, searched every crevice of the landscape, but in so far as she could see there was no shred of alteration in it. The cows, milked early, stood in the shade along the banks of the south branch; heat waves already rippled above the well-tasseled corn; the windmill turned round three or four times with considerable speed, then stopped, as if forever.

Eliza lifted her breakfast bell to ring, then let arm and soundless bell drop to her side. She felt a profound reluctance to disturb in any way the morning quiet. She had a conviction unreasoning, but deep, that the sound of her bell might be all that was needed to shatter tranquillity, call up from out of the wood lot, or across the river side, John Morgan himself.

Jess looked down at his wife. "Thee want me to ring it?" he asked.

"No," Eliza said. "I'll ring it. The boys need to be called up for their breakfasts." But she did not raise her arm nor sound the bell. "All's so quiet," she said. "It gives me the feeling I'd oughtn't disturb it. As if ringing the bell might be the beginning . . . as if hearing it, John Morgan might ride up and say, 'Has thee any horses . . . any silver . . . any blankets?' "

"He don't ask, from what I hear," Jess said. "He takes."

"Ride up and take," Eliza said, as if digesting the fact. "Well, that's a happen-chance. Flood or fire could do the same. One bolt of lightning's enough if it's the Lord's will. Talking's not my concern. It's what the boys would do."

"The boys?" Jess asked.

"Joshua," his wife answered.

Jess nodded.

"If hearing the name alone's enough . . ." Eliza began, "if the very sound of it's strong enough . . ."

"Yes," Jess said, nodding again.

Morgan's name had been heard in the southern counties before July, but it was in July that it began to be heard above everything else: above the rustle of the growing corn, the clack of mills, the plop of the big bass in the deep pools. Women churning stopped their dashers to listen, children stayed away from the wood lots, men worked quietly behind their horses, foregoing all talk lest their words muffle the approach of Morgan's scouts.

But it was the young men who listened most intently, the skin tightening across their cheek bones. Not with apprehension or fear so much as with wonder. What would they do? If the hoof-beats along the wood's trace were made by John Morgan's men? If the press-gang said, "Unhitch your horses, bub, bring out your hams and bacon, show us where the old man keeps his silver." Would they unhitch, the young men wondered . . . hand over Prince and Dolly, walk up through the fine dust of the field-path, lay the meat and silver on the outstretched hands? Would they? The young men did not know. They had no way of knowing.

Since childhood they had dreamed of resistance, but the foes they had resisted were mythical: the vanished Indian, the unseen highwayman, the long-gone river pirate, figures who fled easily, whose bullets ricocheted from resolute hearts. Morgan's men were not mythical, they did not flee, their bullets pierced even the most steadfast hearts. The young men at dusk on the river road, where the banks were shoulder high and fox-grapes, thick as curtains, hung between the shadowy trees, did not look back, nor hasten. But they listened. And wondered. And hearing nothing, were not reassured. Silence also was ominous.

Eliza once again lifted the breakfast bell. "Thee think I should ring it?" she asked.

"Ring it," Jess told her. "I got no mind to meet John Morgan on an empty stomach."

Breakfast was almost over when Joshua came in. He noted with astonishment the nearly empty gravy bowl, the meat platter with its single egg, the plates crusted with jam and biscuit crumbs. It was a wonder to him that people had been able on such a morning to sit down to the table, put gravy onto biscuits, spear slices of ham and then opening and shutting their mouths, chew such things with relish. Such eating, such self-concern, seemed, when their neighbors were dying, calloused and unspiritual.

It was not only that these men were their neighbors nor that their deaths were in a sense for them, since they had died defending beliefs Joshua and his family held dear: it was the whole matter of death to which Joshua was not yet reconciled. Nor was he reconciled to the apathy of his elders in the face of death, their indifference and mild acceptance. They said Amen and God's will be done. This he could have borne, had he been convinced that they really suffered, that God's name and the Amen had not come easy. Old people, and for Joshua all who were somewhat advanced beyond his own eighteen years were old, did suffer when they lost a member of their own households. This, Joshua was ready to admit.

But Josh sorrowed over death as an abstract fact: he resented it for unknown men and women. He went without meals because of an item in The Banner *News* about a woman dead in a mill-pond in another county; because of a man dragged to death behind his team. He made himself forego all one fall—in so far as he was able—any sight of the frosty, autumnal constellations in which he delighted because of a conversation of his mother's which he had overheard. After a long sickness stretching through more than a year (his mother had told a visitor) a young woman, whose name was Lydia, had said, "I know I must die, but I wish I could live long enough to see Orion outside my window once more." This girl (unknown to him) named Lydia had died, his mother said, in early August, long before Orion had come near her window. All that fall Joshua had kept his eyes off the evening sky, saying stubbornly, "I won't take anything she can't have. I won't look since she can't."

For the most part Josh kept these feelings to himself, for when they burst out, as they occasionally did, what his mother and father had to say about them angered him.

"Thee should rejoice, son," Eliza had once said when he had spoken sorrowfully of the death of a young boy who had gone through the ice and drowned. "Thee should rejoice. Young Quincy's in heaven, spared all this world's misery."

"Quincy didn't think this world was a miserable place," Joshua, who had known the boy, said.

"He'll find heaven a better place, Josh," his mother had insisted.

"He's cheated," Josh had flashed out. "He's cheated."

"Thee's not to question the Lord, Joshua," his mother said.

Ordinarily he was able to hear his father speak about death with more tolerance than his mother. His father was not so sure as his mother. Joshua saw that possibilities his mother had never laid an eye on opened their long avenues of chance to his father's sight. But his father had a kind of calm, a tolerant pliability which sometimes set Joshua's teeth on edge. Old people, Josh thought, get so eroded by time and events that they are as slippery as a handful of wettened stones at a branch bottom. Rolling and tumbling against each other, slippery as soap, not a single rough, jagged spot left with which to hold on—or resist, or strike out.

"Thee'll find a lot of things worse than death, Josh," his father had said to him one day—more as if reading his mind than answering anything Josh had spoken.

Joshua had answered his father sharply. "Death was a curse, wasn't it? A curse put on man for his disobedience?"

"Well, yes," Jess had said. "In a way thee can . . ."

But Joshua had not waited for qualifications. "What's worse than the Lord's curse? If the Lord put a curse on thee, thee'd be wrong to find anything worse, wouldn't thee?"

This logic seemed inescapable to Joshua, but his father, with his usual suppleness, escaped it. "The Lord's curses," he said mildly, "can usually be borne. There are some few man devises for himself that bite deeper."

Joshua never spoke of these things to his brother, Laban, but Labe once asked him, incuriously, Josh thought, and in his usual sleepy way, "Is thee afraid to die, Josh?"

Josh had not known what to answer. He was opposed to dying . . . was he afraid of it? He didn't know. He remembered being frightened, years ago, by sounds at night which he couldn't account for, being so frightened that the thumping of his heart had stirred the bed covers like a hand. Then he had been able to calm himself by thinking: What's the worst that can happen to me? Nothing but this: the burglar will creep nearer and nearer, finally give me one hard clunk on the head and I'll be killed. This had always calmed him, had seemed so insignificant a thing that he would cease listening and fearing and sleep.

That was imagined death, though, and imagined danger; the sounds he heard, perhaps mice in back of the studding or nails snapping in a heavy frost. If the death were real death—the sounds of danger real sounds? The click of the breech-lock in the musket before firing, a man's sucked-in breath as he pressed the trigger? He didn't know.

"I don't know, Labe," he said. But like the other young men he wondered.

Now Josh stood with hands tightly clenched over the rounded top of the chair in which his brother, Little Jess, sat. He knew, in his self-conscious way, that his family was looking at him, and he made a strong effort to control his feelings. He was particularly aware of Labe's calm, cool gaze, and he supposed that Labe, in what he thought of as Labe's belittling way, was enumerating his own physical shortcomings (Labe who was muscular, smooth-jointed, supple): Built like a beanpole, black hair like a wig, high, burning cheekbones, a lopsided mouth that trembles when he's in earnest.

"What kept thee, son?" his father asked.

"I went over to Whiteys'," Josh said.

"Sit, sit, Josh," his mother bade, bustling up from her place. "I'll cook thee fresh eggs."

"I couldn't swallow an egg," said Josh.

"What do they hear at the Whiteys'?" asked his father.

"Morgan's heading this way—he's following the railroad up from Vienna. He's making for Vernon. He'll be there today or tomorrow."

"Vernon," said his mother. She put the two eggs she had in her hand back in the egg crock. Vernon was home. Josh had as well've said the Maple Grove Nursery. Or the south forty.

"How they know so much over at Whiteys'?" his father asked. "Morgan didn't cross the Ohio till evening of fourth day. Morgan's lost out there in the woods . . . got guerrillas trained to stay out of sight. Yet people'll sit at their breakfast tables and say just where John Morgan is. Tell you whether he's shaved yet this morning . . . and where he'll be this time tomorrow."

Josh felt, many times, like a stone beneath the cold waves of his father's detached unconcern. As if in spite of all he knew, and burningly believed, he would in time be worn down, effaced by all that ceaseless, quiet questioning.

"People at breakfast tables . . ." he began angrily, then stopped. "Ben Whitey was in Harrison County when Morgan crossed over. He's been riding ahead of him for three days."

"Did thee talk to Ben?" asked his father.

"Yes."

"What did he say?"

This shift of approach, this willingness to learn, cutting from beneath his feet ground for reasonable anger, angered Josh anew.

"Nothing about whether Morgan'd shaved yet, or not, this morning."

"Son," said his father, "sit thyself down and tell us. Get up, Little Jess. Give thy brother thy chair."

Little Jess went around the table to Eliza's chair and hung over his mother's shoulder, awaiting Josh's word. Josh himself, without intending to do so, sat suddenly in the chair that was pushed out for him—and also without conscious intent, began to chew hurriedly on a cold biscuit. His mother made a gesture toward passing him butter and jam, but Jess shook his head and said, "Well, Josh?"

Josh spoke rapidly, his voice a little muffled by dry biscuit crumbs. "Ben Whitey passed a dozen of Morgan's out-riders last night camped down this side of Blocher. Not more'n twenty miles from Vernon. They're following the railroad. They'll raid Vernon."

"Raid Vernon," said his mother. "What does that mean?" It was a word whose meaning on the page of any book she knew perfectly well. But, "Raid Vernon"—the town where she sold her eggs, the church town, the county fair town, with its whitewashed brick houses, its quiet, dusty streets, its snowball bushes dangling their white blossoms over the unpainted picket fences—what did that mean? "Raid Vernon," she said once again as if the words themselves might somehow suddenly focus, as a stereoptican glass did when given just the proper shove, to show a landscape, lifelike in its dimensions, distances—and ruin.

Josh knew what the word meant. Ben Whitey had told him. "Raid means," he said, "burn, kill, take what you want."

"Are Morgan's men killing people?" Eliza asked.

For a second the world his mother saw flickered before Josh's eyes: a world of such loving companionableness that the word war had no other meaning for her than murder; where deliberate killing was unthinkable as though in her own household son should turn on son; but it flickered for a second only, then disappeared, leaving him angry again.

"Doesn't thee know there's a war?" Josh asked with intensity. "Doesn't thee know what a war is?"

"Thy mother knows there's a war, Josh," his father reminded him, "but she don't know what a war is. Let alone what a war in Vernon'd be like. She's more used to think of caring for people than killing them."

"John Morgan thinks of killing them," Josh said. "He shot a boy through the legs who didn't run fast enough. He shot an old man in the back. I don't know how many's dead in Harrison County. Ben Whitey said he could smell the smoke of Morgan's burnings the whole way up. He said he didn't think there was a mill left standing in Harrison County. He said the country's scoured of horses—and anything else in any house a trooper wanted and could carry across his saddle-bow."

Eliza leaned across the table. "The earth," she said, "and the fullness thereof, is the Lord's. What's Morgan's men but a ruckus of boys with their pants in their boots? Trying to get something they've never had a taste of before? We've got more'n we need here. High time we're called on to share it with someone. If John Morgan's men came here," Eliza said—and Josh saw his mother's eyes turn toward the door of the summer kitchen as if she saw there a dusty, slouch-hatted trooper, "I'd offer them the best I had on hand. No man's my enemy," she said.

Josh stood up, crumbling in one hand the biscuit he had been quickly munching. "Some men are my enemies," he said. "Any man's my enemy who kills innocent men and makes slaves. They're my mortal enemies."

Josh felt his sister Mattie's hand, long-fingered—and cold for so warm a morning—touch, then feel its way into his clenched fist, and he gave way to its insistent downward pressure and sat again. "I will share with my friends," he said. "If thee gives all thee's got to a thief, thy friends will have to go hungry—there's not enough to go round. What's good about that?" he asked.

No one answered his question, but Jess said evenly, "Tales like these are always a part of war times."

Tales were lies. Josh picked up a case-knife and tried to ease off some of his feelings in clenching it. "Ben Whitey don't lie . . . some he saw with his own eyes . . . some was told him. He saw the fires . . . he heard the people whose horses were stolen. He saw an outrider with a bird-cage and bird looped to his saddle. They said he'd been carrying that bird all the way from Maukport."

Josh was interrupted by his mother. She had started up, taken two steps toward the kitchen window where Ebony, the starling, hung in his cage. There, after the two steps, she stopped, stood stock still in her tracks, as if just then aware of what she'd been doing. "This is thy chance," Josh told himself, "to keep thy mouth shut, not shove a contradiction down thy own mother's throat." But he could not do it. He wrapped his hand round the cutting edge of the case-knife, but there was not enough pain in its blunt edge to divert him.

"I thought thee said," Josh told his mother, his mouth trembling with scorn for himself, "that this was our chance to share? Thee's got a good chance now to share Ebony. Thee's had that bird a long time and every single man riding with Morgan's never had him once in his life time."

Eliza turned back facing the table and her family. Josh gazed at his mother's neat, dark head, saw her black eyes move for a moment toward the head of the table where his father sat, then turn resolutely toward himself. "I was thinking he might be mistreated," she said. "I've grown over-fond of the particular."

"Mistreated," Josh shouted, ignoring her admission. "Thee can worry about a bird's being mistreated while men are being shot. Thee'd try to save it and not turn thy hand to help the men. No man's thy enemy . . . unless he tries to take thy bird. Every man's enemy is my enemy. I'd do as much any day for a man as a bird."

Jess and Labe both started at once to speak, but Eliza held up her hand, as if she were in meeting. "I was wrong, Joshua," she said. "I'd give Ebony to any man who'd care for him."

"Care for him," Josh again shouted. "Thee was right the first time. Thee think that bird Ben Whitey saw's alive now? Its neck's been wrung long ago. If it was a big bird it's been boiled and eat. Ebony'd end up in no time on a forked stick over a fire."

Joshua leaned across the table toward his mother, gesturing with the case-knife, making Ebony the whole issue of war and peace, of life and death; talking to Eliza, but for his whole family . . . for Labe . . . to hear and contradict. "Thee has responsibilities. Thee can't just take birds and make them tame. Slit their tongues and fatten them so's they can't fly. Then let anybody grab them. And cook them. Thee don't have any right to be good and generous to such a price. A price thee don't pay. Old Ebony's got to pay that price. And that old man. And the boy shot in the legs. And the Harrison County Militia. And the Vernon Militia. I'd rather die," Josh said.

There was a long silence about the breakfast table. Eliza reseated herself. Little Jess looked from face to face with nervousness. He was embarrassed when grown-ups showed emotion. He thought it did not suit their faces. He saw it break the smooth surface of authority and knowledgability with which they were accustomed to front him. And without that where were they? And where was he? Lost, not a thing to fall back on, floundering from notion to notion.

Mattie gazed at Ebony, jauntily cracking sunflower seeds in his wooden cage. She saw there both her mother's bird, who was first of all God's bird, and now was no man's bird, but belonged to all, and she saw Joshua's bird, the defenseless pet who would be plucked like a chicken and eaten unless they were willing to fight and die for him. And because she oscillated between the two ways of seeing Ebony, she suffered: when she was generous and peaceful, as was her mother, she thought herself a coward, and when she was, like Joshua, ready to fight (she supposed) she felt herself a renegade, an outcast from faith and scriptures.

Only Labe sat quietly at the table, his calm face touched neither by sorrow nor eagerness. One way only opened before him, and except that he believed this to be a matter between his mother and brother, and presently his father, he would have spoken, and said better words, he thought, for loving all men than his mother had said. And he would have gotten that bird from out the center of the conversation, where its feathers, its litter, its long periods of sulky quiet muffled and strangled the thing they should be really speaking of.

In the long silence . . . while there was no talk, sounds of great clarity filled the room. All, except Little Jess, harkened to them as if they were omens; as if each, properly apprehended, might carry some kind of a revelation: the slow grating start of the windmill easing into rhythmic clicking as the wind freshened; two distant notes as old Bess the bell-cow reached forward toward uncropped grass; the prolonged, sweet morning trill of a warbler, who, uncaged and undesired either by raiders or raided, flew, singing, near the windows, then flipped out of sight.

Jess, from his place at the head of the table, looked down toward his eldest son. He bent upon him a face of so much love and regard—and good humor, too, as if behind this talk of war there were still a few reasons to laugh—that Josh thought he might be unable to bear his father's gaze, would have to lay his arms across the table and bury his face in them, and so hidden, say, "Yes, pa," or "No, pa," to whatever his father had to say. But as his father continued to gaze, quizzically and lovingly, Josh knew that he had left behind him forever the happy time of freedom from decision and sat very straight, back teeth clamped together, lips trembling, waiting his father's word.

"Thee knows, Josh," his father said, "dying's only half of it. Any of us here, I hope"—and Jess included Little Jess and Mattie in the nod of his head—"is ready to die for what he believes. If it's asked of us and can be turned to good account. I'm not for dying, willy-nilly, thee understands," Jess said, his big nose wrinkling at the bridge. "It's an awful final thing, and more often and not nobody's much discommoded by it, except thyself, but there are times when it's the only answer a man can give to certain questions. Then I'm for it. But thee's not been asked such a question, now, Josh. Thee can go out on the pike, and if thee can find John Morgan, die there in front of him by his own hand if thee can manage it, and nothing'll be decided. He'll move right on, take Ebony, if he's a mind to, though I give John Morgan credit for being a smarter man than that and thee'll be back there on the pike just as dead and just as forgotten as if thee'd tied a stone round thy neck and jumped off Clifty Falls. No, Josh, dying won't turn the trick. What thee'll be asked to do now—is kill."

The word hung in the air. A fly circled the table, loudly and slowly, and still the sound of the word was there . . . louder than the ugly humming. It hung in the air like an open wound. Kill. In the Quaker household the word was bare and stark. Bare as in Cain and Abel's time with none of the panoply of wars and regiments and campaigns to clothe it. Kill. Kill a man. Kill thy brother. Josh regarded the word. He explored it, his hand tightening again about the knife.

"I know that," he said. "I am ready to fight." But that wouldn't do. He could not pretend that he was ready for the necessary act so long as he flinched away—from even the word. "I will kill these men if I have to."

"No, Josh," Eliza said.

Josh was glad to be relieved of the need of facing his father and regarding death abstractly. He turned to his mother. "Yes," he said. "I will. I'm going to meet Ben Whitey at eight. Soon as he's had two hours' rest. The Governor's made a proclamation. Every man's to join the Home Guard and help defend his town. We're going right down to Vernon and join. Morgan'll be there any time. I'd ought to've gone a week ago."

"Joshua, Joshua," cried his mother. "Thee knows what thee's turning thy back on? On thy church. On thy God. Thy great-grandfather came here with William Penn to establish ways of peace. And he did," Eliza declared passionately. "With savage Indians. Men of blood. Now thee proves thyself to be worse than the Indians. They kept the peace."

Josh felt better. The picture of himself as bloodier than a savage Indian was so fantastic it hid for the time such savagery and blood-thirstiness as he did possess—and hid too, what Josh felt to be, perhaps even worse, his lack of these qualities. "The Indians," he said, "weren't dealing with John Morgan."

Jess spoke. First that bird, now William Penn and the Indians. The human mind could move, if it moved at all, only from symbol to symbol and these so chosen that sharp and even final issues were padded enough to make them more tolerable. "Josh," he said, "those who take the sword shall perish by it."

They were back to dying: only a nicer word. "I am ready to perish," said Josh.

But Jess wouldn't let them stay there. " 'Thou shalt not kill,' " said Jess.

There it was. "But He said, 'Render unto Caesar the things that are Caesar's,' " Josh said desperately. "I live here—in Jennings County. My town is Vernon. The Governor said to defend it. My body is my country's."

"Thy soul, son, is God's."

"God won't want it," Josh said, "if I don't do what I think's my duty." He was standing again, half crying, a horrible way for a man to be starting to war. "Thee can live with God now, maybe. I can't. I don't want to die . . . and I don't even know if I could kill anyone if I tried. But I got to try," he said, "as long as people around me have to. I'm no better'n they are. I can't be separated from them."

He left the table and ran toward the kitchen stairway. "I'm going," he said. "I'm meeting Ben Whitey at eight."

As he went up the stairs he heard his father say, "No, Eliza, no."

In his room Josh said, "Packing to go to war," but it didn't mean much. He scarcely believed it; though the pain that started at the bottom of his throat and seemed to run the whole length of his chest told him this was no ordinary departure. There wasn't much packing to do. Extra socks, Ben Whitey said. Spare hand-kerchiefs—good in case of a wound. Stout shoes—he had them on. A heavy coat—no telling how long they'd be in the field; they might have to chase Morgan the length of the state. Musket—his musket was always oiled, cleaned, ready; shot—he didn't know whether he had enough or not. He didn't know how many . . . He didn't know how good he'd be at . . . Knife—yes. Cup—he'd get that downstairs, and the tin plate. Two blankets to roll round all the stuff, saddle old Snorty—Morgan'd have to be a pretty slow runner if old Snorty was ever to catch up with him.

He was finished. Getting ready for war was a short horse and soon curried, it seemed. There was nothing to do now but go. He'd keep that a short horse, too, but it'd be a horse of a different color. Josh marveled at himself. Cracking jokes, for that was what it was even though there was no one to hear. Ten minutes ago he'd been crying, his mouth full of death, duty and the scriptures and here he was, dry-eyed, a pain in his chest, to be sure, but somewhat outside the whole matter, far enough apart, anyway, to say it was like this or that. It was very peculiar—but the pain itself lay like a bar between him and what had gone before. There was the pain, wide, heavy, real, and he needn't, indeed he couldn't, cross over it to explore its causes.

He looked about the room—his and Labe's—neat, orderly, the bedcovers tossed back to air, the way his mother had taught them, clothes on pegs, chest drawers closed. He felt as if he wanted to say a prayer of some kind . . . God, take care of this room, or something like that, but he thought perhaps he'd better not. He wasn't sure God was with him in this move, in spite of what he had said downstairs, and there was no use involving Him in something He wouldn't approve. He'd picked up his bed-roll to go when Mattie came in. He would rather have seen almost anyone else.

As far as Josh could tell Mattie acted parts from morning to night: very delicate and fainty at one hour like she's too fine-haired to live on a farm, the next loud and yelling as if she had Comanche blood and a quarter section wasn't big enough to give her scope. She'd help him with a piece of work, doing more than her share, one time—the next sit half a day on a tree-stump, breathing, Josh supposed, but giving no sign of it.

"Oh, Joshua," said Mattie.

Josh held onto his bed-roll. Mattie'd been crying and Josh wasn't sure who he was seeing: sister Mattie or actress Mattie. A little of both, maybe, but when she threw her arms around his neck he thought he knew which one was clasping him most warmly.

"Oh, Joshua," said Mattie again.

"I've got to go, Matt," Josh said. "I'm late now."

Mattie took her arms down. "Josh," she said, "I want thee to take this." She had a little New Testament in her hand and she reached up and slipped it gently into Josh's shirt pocket. "There," she said. "Over thy heart it will guard thee from all harm." Then in her natural voice she added, "I read about two soldiers who'd've been shot through the heart except for their Bibles." Then sister Mattie was hidden away again, lost behind inclined head and folded hands.

Josh couldn't help laughing, so long and loud he was surprised.

"What's so funny?" Mattie asked. "Thee setting up to be an atheist?

"No," Josh said, "I ain't. I'll take it, and read it, too, maybe." He put the little book in his hip pocket.

"Thee going to sit on it?" Mattie asked.

Josh shouldered his bed-roll again and went to the door. "It's the one sure foundation," he said.

"Why, Josh Birdwell," said Mattie. She had come upstairs expecting a pious and tearful farewell, and here was Josh laughing and joking, and not very reverently, either. Outside the door Josh turned back to reassure his sister. "Thee don't sit on thy hip pockets," he said. "Thee sits between them."

Mattie said feebly, "Good-bye, Josh."

The rest of the good-byes, Josh figured, had been said, in as far as they could be said, downstairs about the breakfast table. He went quietly out the front door and to the barn without seeing anyone. Not until he had saddled and tied his bed-roll to the saddle and led old Snorty out into the sunny barnyard did he see his mother and Little Jess standing at the bottom of the lane waiting for him. Seeing them, he was glad they were there.

Eliza's face was very serious but she wasn't crying. She held up a package to Josh. "Here's food, Josh. You'll have to eat. I didn't know what was best. This's mostly meat and cold biscuits."

Thinking of food Josh remembered the forgotten tin cup and plate.

"Run fetch them, Little Jess," Eliza said. "Be lively," she called after him. "Josh mustn't be late."

Josh let old Snorty's reins hang and laid his arms about his mother's shoulders, hugging her tight.

"Good-bye, Joshua," his mother said, and then not a word about his coming home safe, only, "I hope thee doesn't have to kill anyone." Joshua shut his eyes for a minute. "If thee has to die that's thy own business and thee won't anyway unless it's the Lord's will—but, oh, son," Eliza said, "I hope thee don't have to kill."

Josh opened his eyes and smiled. That was just the right thing to say . . . the words he would've chosen for her. He patted his mother's shoulder. Sticking by her principles and not getting

over-fond of the particular—even when it was her own son. Josh
bent and kissed her. He could not have borne it if she had broken
down, put his safety first.

"Good-bye," Josh said. "Don't thee worry. I'll be shaking too
hard to hit or get hit." He kissed his mother and got into the
saddle. Eliza made a gesture toward him of love and farewell and
walked resolutely back up the lane.

Little Jess trotted along the pike beside Josh for a way. Before
turning homewards he held onto the stirrup for a minute and
whispered fiercely up to his brother, "Thee shoot one for me,
Josh." Josh then, looking down into Little Jess' drawn face and
lips thinned with whispering, saw that no man acted to himself.

Josh was to meet Ben Whitey at the Milford cut-off, but even
now, riding alone, he supposed he was a soldier and he tried to
carry himself, through the warm morning and down the dusty
road, like a Home Guardsman: scanning the horizon for signs of
smoke or dust, keeping an eye out for single horsemen. There was
no telling; if outriders of Morgan's were only twenty miles away
last night, they could easily be in this neighborhood now.

In spite of his conviction that his intentions made him a militia-
man, sworn to hunt down and stop or kill John Morgan, Josh
would fall into looking at the farmland with a country man's eyes:
sizing up a field of wheat unaccountably left standing, or noting
how the apples were shaping up in an orchard. To offset this he
stopped and loaded his gun. If he were to meet or sight a raider it
would be his duty to shoot. He tried to think how it would be to
come upon a man, emerging from the woods, say, or around a
sharp turn, not speak, not pause to pass the time of day, but instantly with raised musket fire and hope to blow the stranger's
head off. The idea made Josh sweat. My God, Josh thought or
prayed—he didn't know which—I hope it's no boy nor old man.
I hope it's some hard, old slave-driving bugger. Thinking of this
hard old slave-driving bugger Josh remembered that he might be

a man handy with firearms himself, and he settled deeper into the saddle and listened more intently.

The pain he had felt in his chest after breakfast was gone: in its place he now had in his middle a curious, dry, empty, swollen feeling. As if he carried something inside him, hollow, but beyond his size and growing bigger.

Ben Whitey was waiting for him at the Milford cut-off, impatient, fuming. "You're half an hour late," he yelled.

"I know it," Josh said. "We'll make up for it now," but they were only fairly started when Ben, looking back down the pike, said, "Looks like Labe on Rome Beauty. He joining too?"

"No," Josh said, "he's got convictions the other way."

"Well, you forgot something then," Ben Whitey said, "and your ma's sending it you." He rode on while Josh turned back to meet Labe.

Labe came up at a long trot, the only kind Rome Beauty had, dismounted and said, "Get on. Father said for thee to take Rome."

Josh sat atop old Snorty, unmoving, unbelieving.

"Get down," said Labe. "If thee's going to fight Morgan, fight him. Don't set there like a bump on a log."

"Father's against my going," said Josh.

"He's against it, but that didn't stop thee. Now get on. He says as far as he knows, Rome's no Quaker. From all he can tell thee and Rome think about alike. Get on."

Josh got off Snorty, transferred his bed-roll to Rome's saddle and stood in the dusty road beside his brother. He was taller than Labe but Labe's shoulders and stance made him feel small.

"Tell father," he began, but Labe interrupted him.

"Father said to tell thee most killing's caused by fear. . . . Rome's being under thee ought to help a little. He don't send thee Rome because his mind's changed about anything."

"Labe," Josh asked, "thee don't think about going?"

"No," said Labe, "I don't."

"I got to," said Josh. "Otherwise I'd always think maybe it was because . . ."

"Get on," said Labe, giving him no time to finish.

Astride the big red horse Josh rode after Ben Whitey, but before he overtook him he finished his sentence. "I am afraid," he said.

"You got a fine mount now," Ben Whitey told him when he drew alongside. "If you can just keep his nose headed the right direction you ought to make out."

"Never thee fear," Josh began . . . but he shut his mouth at that point. "Thee don't know," he told himself.

They rode into Vernon together; a roan, and a claybank, two rawboned farm boys: Ben Whitey, a born fighter, and Josh who was trying to do his duty. They entered Vernon and saw it the way a man who thinks he has been dreaming wakes and sees the landscape of his dream lying all about him, the disaster real, hard and unmelting as sunlight—and dreaming the only means of escape. Deep in the country, on the farms they had believed—and not believed. To come here with loaded guns had been an act of faith and now their faith was justified. Morgan was true; he existed; he was killing and looting; he would be here at any hour. There were tens of mouths to tell them.

The town blazed under the July sun; it throbbed with the heat of the season—and the heat of fear and excitement and wonder and resolution. At first Josh thought it was alive as he had seen it for an August fair or Fourth of July celebration. And there was something of a holiday spirit in the plunging, headlong activity. As if fifty years of seeing the Muscatatuck rise and fall, the crops ripen and be harvested, the summer rains harden and whiten into winter's snow and hail, were enough for Vernon, as if tired now of this placid punkin-butter existence, they would turn to something with sharper flavor.

That was the surface: the movement, the shouts, the numbers of horses in the street, the vehicles, the laughter even. That was what Josh saw when he saw everything at once and heard everything at once. A medley in which all the sounds, blending, were a holiday roar; all the sights, the excess movements of celebration when steps reach higher and higher into the air, bows go lower and lower toward earth and smiles strain at the limitations of a single face.

When he saw the sights, one by one, there was no holiday in them. There were spring wagons full of women, children and bedding headed for back country farms and supposedly greater safety.

"No sense in that," Ben Whitey said. "That way a couple of outriders can pick up the best any household has to offer without being put to the bother of ripping up the feather ticks and taking the insides out of clocks."

But in spite of what Ben Whitey thought, they were there: spring wagons, democrats, gigs, buckboards, all filled with women, children and valuables, and headed for back country and the hills. There were men throwing shovelfuls of earth out of deep holes, preparing to bury silver, money, keepsakes: whatever they and their wives cherished and thought a raider might fancy. There were boys barricading doors, boarding up windows, reinforcing bolts. There was a man who had turned his house into a store and was now busy ripping down his sign and trying to make his store look like a house again. There was an old fellow atop the gable of his house, peering off to the south through a long spy-glass. The voices, too, when Josh listened were not celebrating anything; they rasped; they started even, then broke; a man began yelling, looked around, ended whispering.

"Let's get out of this," Ben Whitey said. "Let's find the Home Guard."

They pulled up beside a one-legged man calmly taking his ease on a street corner.

"Where's Morgan?" yelled Ben Whitey.

"Don't know for sure. Reports are thicker'n toads after a rain, but he's near. Hear tell the old boy slept in Lexington last night."

"We're here to join the Home Guard," said Ben.

" 'Bout a week late," said the one-legged man, sucking on a cold pipe.

"We know that," Ben told him, "but we come up as fast as we could. We're here now. We got prime horses and we'll give good accounts of ourselves. Where's the commander?"

"Not sittin' on his pratt recruiting."

Ben Whitey put his heel in his horse's flank. "Come on back," yelled the one-legged man. More quietly he said, "You johnnies rile me, through. Every drumstick of a boy comes in here from back country, brasher'n a parched pea, and ready to spit in old Johnnie Morgan's eye. It'll take more spit'n you got, bub, or I miss my guess. Morgan's clear grit, ginger to the backbone and no more fear in him than a rifle."

"Which side you on?" Ben asked.

"Our side. I'm for whipping Morgan but you ain't gonna do it by . . ."

"Save thy breath to cool thy broth," Josh said. "Where's the Home Guard?"

"Well, God kiss me," said the peg-legger. He took his pipe from his mouth and elevated his weather-beaten chops as if awaiting the salutation. "A Quaker sure's the Lord made Moses. What's thee planning to do, sonny? Pray for the boys?"

"Come on," said Ben and the two rode on down the street.

"How we going to get any place with men like that?" Josh asked.

"They ain't all like that," said Ben.

From across a picket fence an old man beckoned to them. "Want to mix in it?" he asked.

"That's what we're here for. Where's the Home Guard?"

"Everywhere," said the old man. He picked up the end of his long beard and used it to point with. "Spread thin, but mostly to the south. Morgan could circle us—but reports are he's hitting us solid from the south. Coming up the railroad from Vienna. They got companies posted at every ford, road and bridge south of town."

"Where you figger we could do the most good?"

"The bridge below the Forks. I been thinking about this for two days. I figger John Morgan being the man he is will come straight in, cross the bridge and bust into town from there. If you want to get in some telling licks that's the place I'd head for."

"That's the place we want," Ben said.

The Muscatatuck where it is bridged below the forks flows between banks of considerable height. Here the Home Guard Commander had massed as many men as could be spared from the other approaches to Vernon. Of these, the majority and among them the men Colonel Williams considered most steady and level headed were stationed on the west bank of the stream ready to fall upon the raiders should the smaller force which was holding the approaches to the bridge be overpowered. The Colonel hoped to stop by show of force, if possible, if not, by force itself any thrust the raiders might make before they reached the bridge. Failing this the guard on the west bank would have a fine chance to pick off the men as they debouched from the bridge and headed toward town.

That was the plan. The captain in command of the river could use as many men as he could get and when Ben and Josh showed up, well mounted, he sent them at once to join the company beyond the bridge.

"They're headed this way," the captain told them. "Some of them," he said, pointing, "are sitting right there on top of that hill. Them, we fooled. Our men marched across the cliff road and then out of sight of Morgan—if he's there—a half dozen times over. Musta looked like quite an army to him. But there's likely others and they may be here soon. If we don't stop them nothing will. Once they're past us, it will be Maukport and Salem and Lexington all over again. Keep your guns handy. Dismount and rest your horses, but stay by them and keep them quiet. I'm glad you're here. I need you."

Overhead the July sun had weight as well as heat. It lay across

Josh's shoulders like a burning timber. Though Ben was on one side of him, and big Gum Anson, a beefy farmer, was on the other, still Josh felt bereft of shelter, unshielded and alone—a naked target.

For a long time he scanned the road before him with rigid and unrelaxing vigilance. There was not much to be seen: the dusty road, the lush growth of summer, dock, volunteer oats, some daisies, a small field of shoulder high corn, and beyond these a thicket and the road curving out of sight around it. Above earth and river and the river's rank growth were the heat waves, the massive clouds of noon skies, the burning sun. Josh, who felt as if the whole duty of seeing and apprising rested with him, inspected every leaf and shadow. When a sudden movement of air fluttered the leaves of the elders up the road and rasped through the corn he lifted his gun, then put it down shamefacedly. He would feel the sweat trickle down the sides of his chest, then drop to his middle and soak in around his belt.

"Have some cherries," said Gum. "You can't keep that up all afternoon." He held out a big bag. The cherries were cool and firm and Josh took a handful.

"When Nance brought these out this morning," Gum said, "I'd've thrown 'em down except to please her. Goin' off to fight Morgan with a bag of cherries tied to my saddle like a doggone picnicker." He munched away and spat pits. "Looks like they might be the handiest article I brought."

"Wait'll Morgan gets here, Gum," somebody yelled. "It's gonna take more'n cherry-stones to stop that old shite-poke."

"I got more'n cherry-stones," Gum called back and the men around him laughed.

Josh shifted in his saddle and looked about. He was amazed at the sound of laughter, amazed that men waiting to kill or be killed should laugh and joke. He scanned the faces of those who were laughing: old fellows, middle-aged farmers, boys younger than himself. Sweating, chewing tobacco, some lolling in their saddles. Most, dismounted. Some in uniform, others not.

Mounted on farm plugs. Mounted on fast animals he had seen at county fairs. Every kind of fire arm. One man with a bayonet even. The sight of that lifted Josh up in his saddle again. Did the raiders carry bayonets? His sweating which he had not noticed for a while had started up once more.

"Have some more cherries?" asked Gum.

Josh took another handful. "Thanks," he said. "I was awful dry. And hungry, too. I can't remember when I had anything to eat last."

"Go kinda slow on them cherries, then. They don't set too good on'n empty stomach."

"They're setting good on mine," Josh said, chewing and spitting, but keeping his eyes up-road.

"Take it easy," advised Gum. "You'll be petered out before Johnnie gets here. They's scouts up ahead. They'll let us know if anything's twitchin'."

Josh felt a fool not to have thought of that before rearing up till his backbone was petrified, and staring till his eyes popped, acting like he was scout, trooper, captain, everything; the other men were relaxed, guns dangling or laid across their bed-rolls; some smoking; a man behind him was having a nip of something that didn't smell like switchel.

"Old Morgan'll never come this way," one bearded farmer was saying. "That boy's shiftier than a creased buck. He ain't never goin' to fight his way in the front door when the back door's open."

"Back door ain't so all-fired wide open's you might think."

"Open or shut—what's it to Morgan? With five thousand men you go in where it pleasures you and don't wait for the welcome mat to be put out."

"Five thousand," somebody yelled. "What the hell we doing here? Why ain't we making a good hickory for Indianapolis?"

"Indianapolis, boy? You better stay clear of there. Morton's waitin' for you there with a writ."

"Five thousand or ten thousand," said a quiet voice, "I'm going to stay right here. I'm going to give Morgan the butt-end of my mind if nothing else before he busts over that bridge and into my store."

"Me too. Only I'm goin' to talk with lead. My folks live down in Harrison County."

"Did you hear about old man Yardell?"

"Ya—shot in the back."

"Not doin' a thing—just come to his door to see what the ruckus was about."

"Did you hear about 'em down at Versailles? Had the cannon loaded, ready to let go smack dab in the middle of the rebs."

"What happened?"

"Cannoneer dropped his coal and before they could get another the rebs took the gun."

"Oughta court-martial the feller who done that."

"'Fore the afternoon's over, Grogan, you'll likely change your tune as to that."

The afternoon wore on. To the funky smell of the river and of lush river growth was added that of sweating men and horses. Josh eased Rome's girth and hoisted his blankets so a little air could flow under them. Back in the saddle he felt light-headed and detached. Gum had been right about the cherries; they weren't setting right. He felt kind of sick but happy. He'd got here, he was all right, he was where he belonged. By twisting about he could see a curve of the Muscatatuck where it flowed in shallow ripples across a sandbar, then darkened as the channel deepened near the bridge. It was three or four o'clock. The sun went through the water and onto the sandbar, then flashed, pulsing with the movement of the water in his temples. He could see the silvery glint of the little minnows, like bullets; a dragon-fly ran its darning needle in-and-out—in-and-out of the flowing water. It was July . . . a summer afternoon . . . the cool water . . . the hot sun . . . the darting . . . the silver bullets.

Josh's neck stiffened, his head snapped up, his hand closed

round the stock of his gun. A horseman was pounding up the road.

"It's one of our scouts," said Ben Whitey.

The rider, a little fellow in uniform on a lathered black, pulled up beside the captain. Josh couldn't hear what he was saying, but after a minute the captain turned and told them, his voice quiet but with an edge to it that let them know that this was it, the time had come.

"Boys," he said, "they're closing in. They're up the road a couple of miles. Less of 'em than we figured. I expect them to charge. There's just two things to remember: first, stand steady. Second, don't fire till I give the word." He stood in his stirrups and pounded the words home. "Don't fire till I give the word. If you fire before you can make your shots good, it's all over. They'll ride you down. Hold it. Your guns carry just as far as theirs, and you're better shots. Those men've been in the saddle for weeks now, and it's telling on them. Shoot low so's if you miss a man you get a horse. But don't miss."

The scout went on past them at a gallop and Josh could hear the black's hooves ring on the bridge planking, then quiet as he hit the dust of the road on the west bank where the men in hiding were waiting the news. The captain himself wheeled round to await the attack with his men.

Josh reached for his gun. Waves of something, he didn't know what, were hitting his chest. It's like riding through the woods and being hit by branches that leave thee in the saddle, but so belabored thy chest aches, he thought. Other waves, or perhaps the same ones, pounded against his ears, broke in deafening crashes as if he were deep under water, buffeted by currents that could break bones, could rip a man out of his flesh and let him run, liquid, away. Then, in the midst of the pain and crashing, Josh thought, It's thy heart beating. Nothing but thy heart.

Gum said, "Fix those lines, boy." And again, "Get those reins fixed. If your horse jerks his head he'll spoil your aim."

Josh saw that Gum was right. He got his hand out of the reins and rubbed it along Rome's neck. "Good boy," he said. "Good old Rome. Thee'll be all right." He knew he was encouraging himself. Rome didn't need cheering—he stood solid as a meeting house, only his big head moving up and down a little.

They were all waiting. Ben Whitey was cussing, a long line of words as if he was dreaming, or singing, in a kind of funny way. But they were mostly quiet—listening. Something came down, or perhaps it came up, out of the earth itself, something very thin and fine, like a spun web, and held them all together. Josh could feel it. Anybody could break away from it, if he liked, but while they headed the same way, waited the same thing, it held them. You could lean against it like steel. Josh felt its support . . . the waves beat against him, but he leaned against that fabric and it held him.

It held him until he heard the first sounds: a rebel yell from up the road, beyond the elder thicket—then another. Josh never knew a man could make a sound like that. It was a screech such as an animal might make—only it was in a man's voice, a voice that could say "Farewell" or "Rain tomorrow" . . . and that made it worse. It sounded crazy . . . it sounded as if the tongue that gave it could lap blood. It broke the web that held them together, it left Josh alone.

He could hear far away the thud of hooves and the waves that had beat against his ears before began now to say words: Rome's fast, Rome's mighty fast. Run for it, run for it. The minute they turn the curve, run for it.

He looked around, he picked out the likely path. "Sure wish I had a cherry-stone to suck on," said Gum Anson. "Sure am parched."

Gum's words drowned out the others. The hoof beats came nearer. What's the worst can happen to thee? Josh asked himself. Get a bullet in thy gizzard. Get killed. Nothing else. . . . It was all right. He settled down to wait.

"Hold it, hold it," the captain was calling. "Wait for the word. Hold it. Hold it."

From around the bend, very slowly, came a single man, carrying a white flag. A few paces behind him were perhaps twenty or thirty other mounted men.

"It's a trick, it's a trick," the Home Guardsmen were yelling. "Watch it, captain. It's funny business."

"Don't shoot," shouted the colonel who had ridden up. "Don't fire on a white flag. But watch 'em. Keep 'em covered."

He rode forward a couple of paces. "Are you surrendering?" he called.

The man with the white flag called back, "No. No surrender. We want to parley."

"Come on in," said the colonel. "You," he yelled. "You with the white flag. The rest of you stay back."

"Trying to get up inside our range and ride us down," said Gum.

The flag-bearer came up alongside the Home Guard colonel and saluted.

"Keep your guns on those men," the colonel called back, then lowered his own. Josh couldn't hear his words, but could see that the raider was talking fast and earnestly.

"Could be your brother," said Gum.

It was so. The rebel doing the talking was tow haired and young, a gaunt brown-faced boy, very broad shouldered and supple in the saddle. Josh's gun, which had been leveled on him, wavered, but he brought it to bear, once again.

The Guardsmen were getting restless. "Tell him to make up his mind. Surrender and talk—or shut his mouth and fight."

"What's he doin'? Preachin'?"

"Lectioneering for Jeff Davis."

"Shut him up, colonel. Shut him up."

"We'll make him talk outa the other corner of his mouth."

"You the one shot old man Yardell?"

The colonel turned his back on the raiders and rode up to his own men. "Don't take your guns off them," he told them. "He says we're surrounded. He says they've cut in back of us—that they've got five thousand men circled around Vernon and it's suicide to resist. He says every bridge and ford can be rushed. He says surrender and save bloodshed. He says if we surrender no-body'll be harmed. Provisions and fresh mounts taken only. What do you say?"

The storekeeper who had wanted to give Morgan the butt-end of his mind rose now in his stirrups and delivered a piece of it. "He's lying. Men don't start talking until they're past fighting."

"If he had five thousand men they'd be in Vernon now. Blood shed, so long's it's your blood, ain't nothin' to a reb."

"Horses and provisions, eh? Who appointed us quartermaster corps to the Confederate Army?"

Ben Whitey gave the final answer. He yelled. His yell wasn't practiced like the rebel screech; it hadn't the long falsetto mid-night quaver which could raise the hackles and slide between the bones like cold steel, but it was very strong and it lifted toward the end with a raw, unsheathed resonance of its own. It seemed what they had waited for—it seemed the only answer to give. It drained away the uncertainty, the distrust, the fear of the long wait. Above the quiet river it rose in great volume and flowed in a roiled and mounting current across the summer fields. Josh's musket quivered with the violence of his own shouting.

The colonel regarded his men quizzically, then shrugged his shoulders as if to say to the raiders, What can I do with such fire-eaters? and rode back to the rebel leader. There was another conference shorter than the first one, after which the raiders turned, cantered back down the road up which they had just ridden.

"They give us two hours," the colonel said, "to get our women and children out of town. After which, they attack."

At eight that evening they were still waiting, drawn up, ready. The new moon had set and the night was very dark and warm, filled with soft summer stars which seemed to escape from set star shapes and let light shimmer fluidly—and it almost seemed, moistly—across the sky. Some time later the captain with a militia-man came up to the group Josh was in.

"Count off here," he said. "I'm sending twenty of you men to Finney's Ford. The rebs could come through there as well as here if they know the crick. There's a company there now—but no use having any if you don't have enough." He turned to the militia-man. "Let some of your men sleep," he said, "but keep a heavy guard posted."

Josh rode with the twenty men slowly and quietly through the night, back across the bridge and to a bank above the river where any party attempting to use the ford could be fired on while in the water. He rode among strangers. Gum and Ben Whitey had been left behind, and he thought, as he had been thinking all day, Now it begins.

In the darkness the company at the ford seemed very large; the men dismounted, speaking in muffled voices, their horses tethered and resting behind them.

"The crick takes a turn here," the new men were told. "Twenty feet down to the bottom here, so keep your eyes peeled. I'm going to let you men have a couple of hours' sleep, then you can relieve some of us. Get out of your saddles and get some rest—but don't rest so hard you can't hear a raider crossin' that branch."

Josh dismounted and felt his way along the bank in the layered darkness. He felt rather than saw the stream below him, smelled it, really, he believed, though he could hear the occasional lap of a little eddy against a stone, and see here and there a prick of light reflected from a star. He ate cold biscuit with dried beef, gave Rome a biscuit, then stretched out on his blankets, some-what withdrawn from the main body of the militia and near the bank of the stream. Rome stood behind him snuffing at the scent of the strange men and horses about him, mouthing the already cropped-over grass in search of a neglected tuft.

War, Josh thought, seemed a hard thing to come at. The dying and killing he had declared himself ready for at the breakfast table, and which he had imagined he would meet face to face as soon as he'd gotten out onto the road, seemed always to lurk round another corner. He had fortified himself for so many encounters with either or both that there were now almost no breast-works he could fling up, or armaments he could assemble. His supply of anticipation was about used up. War appeared to consist not of the dramatic and immediate sacrifice, either of his body in dying, or his spirit in killing, as he had foreseen it at the breakfast table, but of an infinite series of waitings and postponements.

This is it, he had said, and it was only Ben Whitey waiting at the cut-off. This is it, and it was Vernon as much like Fourth of July as war. This surely is it, he had said, and it was the wind in the elder clump. This, this: a man with a white flag. And now in the dark night to defend the vulnerable ford—and this was not it either, but simply lying at ease on his blankets, his cherry-addled stomach settled with good beef and biscuit, Rome munching by his side and the Milky Way banding the sky familiarly. Except for the gun under his hand it could be any summer night, lying outside for a time to cool off before bed time. And if John Morgan himself, lantern in hand, should bend over him, prod him with his toe and say, "This is it, bub," he didn't know whether he'd believe him or not. Maybe John Morgan was waiting and hunting, too, no more an authority on *its* arrival than he. Getting ready for war might be a short horse and soon curried, but war itself was a horse liable to stretch, so far as he could see, from July to eternity . . . head at Maple Grove and hocks in Beulah Land.

Josh closed his eyes to sleep; but beneath his lids there flowed not only the remembered sights of the day, the faces, attitudes, gestures he had seen and noted, but the multitudinous sights that there had been in daylight no time to name, or space within the crowded mind to delineate. Now in darkness, behind shut lids, they lived again. He saw the L-shaped rip in the pants of the raider who had carried the white flag, and beneath the rip, the long, improperly healed wound which reddened the man's calf from knee to ankle. He saw now, what he had missed then, the downward motion of the raider's hand toward his gun when Ben

Whitey's yell lunged unexpectedly toward him. He saw now, trying to sleep, the controlled drop of a spider, delicately spinning, from the spire of an unblooming head of goldenrod to the yellowed grass beneath it. He heard Gum Anson's answer to someone who asked him, "What you doing here, Gum?" "I'm a farmer," said Gum, "and you can't farm unless you keep the varmints down." He heard another voice—the storekeeper's, he thought—say, "I'm a man of peace—but there ain't any peace when your neighbors are being killed. And if it's a question of good blood, or bad, on my hands, by God, I choose bad."

At last he slept—and continued to see and hear . . . a raider was trying to take Ebony . . . he had ridden his horse inside the summer kitchen, and overturned the table, trampled the crockery and was snatching at Ebony, who above the sounds of confusion was screaming, "Wake up, wake up."

Josh woke up. He found himself in the center of a great, bubbling cauldron of noise: men shouting, screaming advice, cursing, horses neighing; and in the creek below the splash and clatter of men and animals crossing the ford. There was a spattering of shots. Someone was calling over and over, "Mount, mount, mount."

Josh stepped cautiously, felt for Rome in the dark, said his name, doubled his hands hoping to feel them close upon horse flesh, harkened to the billowing roll of sound. Then suddenly the sound fanned out, burst inside his head, roared against the bones of his skull and breaking through bone and tissue, trickled out by way of mouth and nose; it fluttered a few last times against his ear drums, then left him in quiet.

It was daylight before he was sure what had happened: he had gone over the cliff, through the branches of a willow which grew almost parallel with the stream, and now lay within hand's reach of the creek itself. At first he had tried to call out, but the sound of his own voice had detonated like gun fire inside his head and he was afraid that his skull, which he reckoned was broken, might fall apart with the effort. He was half-conscious, and wholly sick, but between bouts of retching he thought: This is it. I've come to it at last. This is war. It's falling over a cliff, cracking thy skull and puking.

It was just after sunup when Labe found him. He had about given up when he heard sounds from beneath the willow.

"Josh," he cried, "thee's alive, thee's all right."

"No, I'm not," said Josh morosely.

"Oh, Josh," Labe said again, and knelt beside him, "thee's all right."

"I wish thee'd stop saying that," Josh told him. "It makes me feel sicker. I'm not all right. My head's split, I think."

Labe looked at it. "It does kind of look that way," he said, "but if thee's not died yet I reckon thee's not going to."

Josh moaned.

"Why didn't thee call out—get some help?" Labe asked.

"At first," Josh said, "because I didn't know anything. Then when I did, if I even opened my mouth to whisper, my whole head like to fell off. Then I got so's I could talk—but if I did, I puked. I still do," he said, and did. "I wish thee'd go away," he told Labe finally, "and leave me alone. I was beginning to get a little easy." He lay back for a while, then painfully lifted himself on one elbow. "Did we get Morgan?"

"They didn't come this way."

"Didn't come this way?" asked Josh. "I heard them. They crossed the crick last night."

"That wasn't Morgan," Labe said. "That was some cotton-headed farmers over'n the south bank who took a freak to drive their stock across so's the rebs wouldn't get 'em."

"I thought it was Morgan," Josh said. "I was fooled."

"Thee had plenty of company," Labe said. "They's all fooled."

"Where's Morgan now?"

"Dupont, they say. He gave Vernon the go-by."

Josh lay back again. "We stood them off," he said proudly. "We kept Morgan out of Vernon."

There was nothing Labe could say to that. Presently he asked, "If I get some help does thee think thee could move, Josh? They're worried about thee at home."

"How'd thee come to find me?" Josh asked.

"Rome came home without thee."

"I'd just as lief stay here," Josh said bitterly. "Go to war and fall off a cliff."

"Thee needn't let that fash you," Labe said. "More did than didn't."

With the help of Guardsmen who were still lingering about the ford, discussing the night's events, Labe got Josh, unwilling and protesting, up the bank and into Rome's saddle. Labe rode behind and let Josh lean against him, and thus supported Josh was able to travel.

"Am I bleeding?" Josh asked weakly after they'd covered a mile or so. A thin trickle of blood was coming across his shoulder and down his shirt front.

"No," Labe said, "that's me."

"Thee?" asked Josh, for whom the events of the past twenty-four hours were still uncertain. "Thee wasn't fighting, was thee?"

"Well, I was a little," Labe admitted.

"In the Guard?" Josh asked.

"No," Labe said, "just kind of privately."

"Why?"

"Well," said Labe, "when I's hunting thee a man sung a song."

"I wouldn't fight anybody about any song," Josh said.

Labe didn't say anything.

"I purely hate fighting," Josh said. "Don't thee, Labe?"

"Not so much," Labe answered.

"I hate it," Josh said. "That's why I got to."

"And I got not to," Labe said, "because I like it."

Josh wanted to be with them, so they carried the sofa out of the sitting-room into the summer kitchen, and he lay on it, a cool wet towel wrapped round his head. He felt as if his skull had been peeled away and his brain left so exposed that even the changed cadence of a voice could strike it like a blow. He pushed the towel a little way off his eyes. Labe was in a chair, head back, wet cloth across his nose, and broken hand in a bucket of hot water. They were both awaiting a doctor if one could be found who was not busy. His mother was changing cloths and minding breakfast, stepping very light so's not to jar his head. His father was at the table where he'd been the morning before. There was a mingling of looks on his face.

"Well," Jess said, "I never had a First Day morning like this before and never hope to again. Though I reckon everybody's done what had to be done. Josh anyway. I'm not so sure about Labe."

Labe lifted the cloth which covered mouth as well as nose. "Mine was kind of an accident," he admitted.

Jess turned toward his eldest son. Their eyes met and Jess nodded. "Well," he said again, "no reason why we can't eat, is there, Eliza? Have a sup of hot coffee and some biscuit and gravy?"

Josh groaned.

"I can't chew," Labe muttered.

Jess seemed to be feeling better and better. "I ain't been doing any fighting," he said, "in the militia or on the side. I got a good appetite. If you boys don't mind, and thy mother'll set it forth, I'll have a bite. So far's I can remember there wasn't much eating done here yesterday. Eliza," he asked, "won't thee sit and eat?"

"Thee go ahead, Jess," Eliza said. "I'm busy with the boys just now."

"Mattie?"

"No," Mattie said delicately, ". . . all this blood and broken bones . . ."

"Little Jess?"

"Thee don't need to wait for me," said Little Jess.

"Well, then," Jess said heartily, "let us eat. But before we eat let's return thanks. This is First Day morning and we've much to be thankful for."

Josh listened to his father's words . . . they were a part of his happiness. When he had first come to, found himself lying at the edge of the crick, he had thought he would hate coming home, admit he'd been hurt, not by gun or saber, but by falling over a bank onto his head. Now it didn't matter. Yesterday morning and his talk of dying and killing seemed almost a life-time away . . . the past twenty-four hours a prolonged campaign from which he had emerged, a veteran, with mind much cleared as to what mattered and what did not.

Next time . . . he wouldn't talk so big . . . about fighting . . . and dying. But that didn't matter either, now. What mattered was that he had stood there . . . he had been afraid, but he had stood at the bridge. He had thought of running . . . but he hadn't done it . . . he had stood in the front line, not knowing but that Morgan himself might bear down upon them . . . he had stood at the crick's edge in the darkness and confusion and had been hunting gun and horse when he had fallen.

And there were the things he had learned . . . that talk beforehand is no good . . . that in darkness on a twenty-foot cliff it is best not to hurry . . . that death, when you moved toward it, seemed to retreat . . . that it was only when you turned your back on it . . . and ran . . . that it pursued.

With these thoughts the words of his father's grace mingled very well. . . . "Eternal Father . . . blessed Son . . . life everlasting. . . ."

He had thought his father was still praying, his tone was still so prayerful. But the words had changed. Josh once more cautiously pushed the towel away from his eyes. Jess was looking about the sunlit kitchen now, inspecting his family. "All here," he said, "right side up and forked end down." But then, maybe he was still praying, for he said next, "Amen, amen." Either way it was all right with Josh.

THE BURIED LEAF

MATTIE was sitting on the upping-block, murmuring, she thought. Muttering, was what Labe called it, passing by. Talking to herself, poor child, her mother noted going to the spring-house on an errand for supper which Mattie should have run. "Playing possum," was Josh's opinion as he drove to the field for a last load of clover. Only Little Jess, hunting eggs with side trips pretty far afield, gave her no thought. He didn't see her. She was a part of his landscape, African at the moment, and the sounds she made were animal: tiger or rhinoceros as the fortunes of stalking demanded.

It was an in-between time: afternoon bygone, night not yet come, neither summer, nor fall. Leaves had had a six months' term, but still they hung, dusty and frayed, to the trees. Blooming was past, though. A rose that very morning, round and firm to the eye as an apple, dropped its petals at Mattie's feet as suddenly as if winter had exploded in its heart. Days began brisk, were finger-cold in the mornings, as Jess said, but by noon there was June heat and coats were a nuisance; and now, Mattie thought, luke-warm, with a funky taste like the last cracker at the bottom of the barrel.

"Gladys," Mattie said in a soft lingering voice. There was a flutter of yellow across the driveway in the orchard, a butterfly, Mattie supposed, but no, it was a leaf falling from the Rambo tree. Good, she thought, summer is ending.

" 'Gladys,' " she murmured again, in a voice she believed to have broken accents, for it was thus he had spoken, "his voice breaking on the sweet syllables of her name. 'Gladys, do not do this thing to me.' "

"No," Mattie said, lifting her face to the scorned and lukewarm air, "I will not."

Behind the barn she heard her father's voice, quite unbroken, very strong and clear. "Pigee, pigee," he was calling, "here, pigee, pigee. Sooy, sooy," he shouted, enjoying, Mattie knew, the sight of his animals fattening toward butchering time.

A man who could do that, call to his pigs like friends, scratch them behind their ears until their pink eyes closed and with no other thought in his mind than butchering, what could thee expect of such a person? It was horrible. I will never eat meat again, Mattie decided instantly. Pork anyway, she amended, thinking twice.

"Hey, pigee, pigee, pigee," her father called.

"And he won't let me change my name to Gladys." A pig killer and quibbling about a name. Mattie clenched her hand until her short nails hurt her palm to help her to remember that her father was an unfair man. "Thy own father," she told herself, for she was easy-going and believed she forgave too quickly. She intended to forgive. Not to do so would be un-Christian; but she did not intend to do so soon, nor to forget how much she had to forgive.

"Batty," she said dispiritedly. "Catty. Fatty," she wailed after a little pause, and then as if really suffering, "Ratty." Except for those who were used to her name that was how "Mattie" sounded —and what it might as well have been. "Tatty," she said with disgust.

Little Jess, eggs delivered to the house, paused beside the upping-block. He had left Africa and needed company. "What's thee talking to thyself for?" he asked.

"I'm not," Mattie said.

"Who's thee talking to, then?" he asked, peering about like an old man with failing sight.

"Thee looks simple-minded, doing that," Mattie said tartly.

"Staring at empty space. A stranger passing by'd think thee was crazy."

"He'd think it run in the family then," Little Jess told her promptly. "Thee talking to thyself."

"I was talking for anyone to hear. Anyone who wanted to. It's not my fault nobody wants to hear me."

"Other people," Little Jess said, "are working."

"What's thee doing?" Mattie asked. "Thee don't look very busy to me. Carrying a pick around don't make thee a worker."

"I'm going to dig," Little Jess said.

"Dig a hole," Mattie said. "That'll be a great help. Catch rain water. Break horses' legs. Undermine things."

Little Jess was undisturbed. "Who said dig a hole? I'm going to unearth something in the ruins."

The ruins was what Little Jess called the cellar, which, since the log house had burned at the beginning of summer, still stood, unfilled, beyond the carriage-house.

"I had a dream last night," Little Jess told her, but would say no more, hastening off, pick across one shoulder like a man late for work and with no time to spare.

Mattie believed in dreams, her own dreams anyway, but she had scant faith in anything Little Jess might do in that line. What would he dream of finding? Money, she supposed, or a buried map, or even a skeleton; some far-fetched pirate dream. What would she dream of finding? A ring, a heart-shaped brooch, "thine" engraved upon it and a lock of crisp hair curling inside. What would Little Jess find? A button maybe, a tarnished spoon or the handle from some broken cup.

Since she could remember the log house had been used as a store place, filled with sacks of grain, old furniture, unused gear, boxes of keepsakes; but before the "big white house" had been built it had been "the little white house," raised by her grandparents when trees had to be felled to make a clearing in which it could stand. Two rooms, a loft and a lean-to were the whole of it, but Mattie had heard her grandmother speak of it with pride, a show-place in the woods, whitewashed, with puncheon floors, sound chinking, a clapboard roof overhead and a dry cellar beneath. Mattie would see it as her grandmother spoke: there in the great, dark woods, the small house with red honeysuckle at the door and morning-glories laced through the snake fences, so that a stranger, her grandmother said, coming upon it could not believe his eyes, and would sniff the honeysuckle and pat the whitewashed logs, as if to make sure his three-day fever hadn't returned, causing him to imagine the house and its flowers.

The thuds of Little Jess' pick, few at first, and far between, his dream telling him, Mattie guessed, not only dig, but dig easy, were quickening as if he had come upon a toe of the skeleton, or a coin from the treasure. Mattie slid from the upping-block without seeming to hurry, yet moved with speed enough to fan the lukewarm air into some freshness about her face. On the rim of the ruins she paused and watched Little Jess probing into the gray, dead-looking earth of the cellar. He had scratched here and there but was now sticking to one spot, not swinging his pick but prying with it.

"Thee coming to something, Little Jess?" she asked.

Little Jess' freckles were shining with sweat, the effort to combine speed with care telling on him. "Just a hole for rain water," he said. But Mattie could hear as well as Little Jess the strange hollow sound his pick made against the earth and she jumped into the cellar.

"Give it to me," she said, taking hold of the pick. "I'm stronger."

"Thee hold thy taters," Little Jess said. "Strength ain't needed now."

Mattie dropped onto her knees and though the touch of the dry, gritty earth shivered nerves as distant as her teeth, she thought, she lifted away handfuls Little Jess had loosened. "There's something here," she said. "A stone maybe, but not more dirt." Scrabbling, prizing, she was coming to something. "Did thee really dream to dig here, Little Jess?"

"No," said Little Jess, full of confidence, as always, "down by the branch is what I dreamed, but this seemed likelier."

"Here," said Mattie, tossing dirt to each side, "here it is. Here's something anyway."

Both scraping, both lifting, they got it out, and both held it as if its weight might be too great for one person, though what they held was only a small box, book-shaped, weathered and earth-colored but still solid, unrotted and firm; each glad the other was there so he could say when questioned, "It's just the way I'm telling thee. Mattie (or Little Jess) was watching when I dug it out."

Little Jess stared with round eyes, humbled by his own powers. "It was put here," he said. "Buried on purpose, not lost. No telling what. Pa," he cried with great urgency, "pa, come quick."

"Pa," Mattie screamed in a voice which spoke no longer to herself alone, but asked a whole township to harken. "Pa, hurry, hurry."

Jess, feeding pigs, dropped a full bucket and ran. A copperhead snake was his first thought, then locating the source of the noise, he said, "Fallen into the old cellar. Backs and legs broken. A judgment on me for not filling it."

On the rim of the cellar he paused. "Is thee hurt?" he asked first one, then the other. Then seeing so much noise could not come from anyone seriously harmed, he said, "Hush that yippering, Mattie. Thee'll wake the dead. Rouse the neighbors."

Mattie hushed and Little Jess held up the box. "We unearthed it, pa. I dreamed to dig, and here it is."

"Thee dig that out of the cellar?" Jess asked.

"Right here," said Little Jess, lifting the loosened dirt with his toes.

Jess leaped down into the cellar, took the box, turned it round and round. "An old-timer," he said. "A box of the kind they used to carry maps and deeds in, a place of safe-keeping for what was treasured."

Open it, open it, Mattie was saying to herself, but her father fondled the box as gently as if it had life, turning it slowly from side to side.

"Call thy mother," he told Little Jess. "Call the boys. This is no happen-chance. This is something buried a purpose for our later having. Something set in the earth with foresight."

"Don't screech," he commanded, as Little Jess sped, screeching, toward the house. "Don't frighten thy mother out of her pleasure."

"What's thee think it is, father?" Mattie asked. "Money?"

"Not money," Jess said. "The little they had them days was needed."

"Letters?" Mattie asked. "Love letters," she said before thinking but her father took no note of it.

"Why, yes," he said. "Letters, it could be, though not many. This is mighty light." He tapped the box. "Has an empty sound."

"Oh, pa," said Mattie. "Who'd bury an empty box?"

"A man might," Jess said. "In those days a man might do so. Times was hard enough them days to make a man do strange things."

"Hard," Mattie repeated.

"Thee don't think this grew?" Jess asked, nodding toward the farm and all its paraphernalia. "Buildings sprout like toadstools and seeds plant themselves? Trees die away without being deadened and windmills rise up and flap? No," Jess said, turning the box like a wonder in his hands, "this could be empty, set here by a man, his mind touched by work without end." He tried the little catch on the box, and moved it, Mattie could see. "I ain't so far from those days not to know a man plowed the earth then with his heart as well as his hands. It ain't always been ingrain carpets and celery vases, Mattie, and thee's not to forget it." He moved the catch again.

Mattie, watching, said, this time out loud, "Open it," but her father answered, "We'll wait for thy mother and the boys."

When they were all about him, standing where the first house in all that stretch of virgin forest had once stood, Eliza looking solemn, Labe and Josh with their hands in their pockets to keep them from the temptation of helping their father in his slow opening, Jess moved the catch, lifted the lid from the buried box. Mattie tried hard to see reflected in her father's face whatever it was he bent his gaze so steadily upon; but there was nothing to be read there except calm pleasure. Jess lifted from the box a little roll, something wrapped close about in oiled silk, or waxed cloth, then handing the box to Eliza he unwound the cloth.

"A leaf," he told them. "A buried leaf. A page from the Bible," and putting it between his hands he smoothed it slowly and carefully flat.

A leaf from the Bible, Mattie thought . . . who'd want to bury that? A book they all had, Bibles for each person in the house and copies to spare for strangers. Mattie hoped she wasn't going to cry. A brooch, a lock of hair, a heart, engraved, now nothing but a buried leaf: Abraham begot Isaac, Isaac begot Jacob, Jacob begot Joseph. What kind of treasure was that? But her father was saying in a joyous voice, "Fifty years this has lain beneath our feet. Half a century."

He held the page low so that all might see the faded writing on the margin. " 'Laid here on the twelfth of August by Jordan Birdwell, aged 74.' Well, well," said Jess, "thy Great-Uncle Jerd. Signed his name and age and set it in the ground. Left it as a legacy for us to come."

What kind of legacy was that, Mattie asked, looking upward out of the cellar where against the darkening sky swallows were hunting their supper—a page fallen from some old Bible, set in the earth like a seed.

"Light the trash heap, boys," Jess said. "Build us up a bonfire. Bring down a seat for thy mother. Let's celebrate a little, let's have a look at what we've heired."

The boys lit the trash heap in a corner of the cellar, they ranged the makeshift seats about the fire; only Mattie stayed aloof, not sitting in the circle with the others, watching her father as he stood feasting his eyes upon the page he held.

"Old Jordan Birdwell," he told them in a voice that sounded as if he were recounting a miracle. "Thy Great-Uncle Jerd. When the Friends in South Carolina came to see they'd hit upon a poor unfertile spot they moved westward, all of a body. Sold their farms and set forth in a wagon train together. Thy Uncle Jerd was taken sick on the day of leaving, he a widower with one unmarried daughter. The wagon train waited two days and he worsened, so there was naught for it, the season growing late, but to leave him behind."

"Alone," Little Jess asked, "without a home?"

"Why, no," Jess said, "his daughter caring for him, and well lodged with neighbors. Well taken care of, only sorrowing at being left behind."

"Did he die?" asked Little Jess.

"Die," Josh rebuked his brother. "How'd he bury this page if he died?"

"No," Jess said, "he didn't die. By spring he was fluting and flying again, sprightly as ever. Anxious to be heading west. And head west he did, he and his daughter aged sixteen."

Mattie moved nearer the fire. She leaned against the box her mother sat on. "They said he'd never make it. One old man, one girl. A team of middlin' oxen, a second-rate wagon and a fair-to-middlin' saddle horse. Leaving South Carolina they was bid good-bye like they's heading for a graveyard. They was baptized with tears and parted from as if the next meeting place would be Beulah Land."

"Was there Indians?" Little Jess asked.

"Not Indians," Jess said, "but every other let and hindrance. Swamps, ague, broken axles, meal turned bad, fords washed out, unmarked crossings, torrential downpours. And the forest so thick them days it was like traveling in a cave."

Mattie saw it all, her father's words making pictures that opened one into another like rooms giving onto rooms beyond. The fire

of trash burning in the cellar becoming for her the fire of this girl
one year older than herself, burning at night in the unending forest, only it between her and whatever animals—or Indians, unseen
—lurked in the deep shadows. She moved nearer the fire and
looked back across her shoulder, but there was only lessening light
and the familiar outlines against the streaked sky: house and windmill, sheds and barn. Buildings, she reminded herself, that had not
sprouted.

"It'd rain all day," Jess said, "and they'd be soaked to the skin,
the old man and his daughter, and at night the wood so wet they'd
be hard put to coax a blaze."

Mattie could feel her dress, cold and wet, cling to her, and
could see the fire die down to a heatless steaming.

"Thy Uncle Jerd was at all times a high-flyer, paying no heed to
his years. Following a deer he went head foremost over a log, and
tore something loose in his leg, so he was wagon-bound for the
rest of the trip."

"How'd they make out for food?" Labe asked. "Meal gone bad,
Uncle Jerd laid up?"

"The girl," Jess said, "thy Cousin Mattie, turned out a prime
shot. Kept fresh meat on hand and didn't break her leg in doing
so."

Mattie listened, came nearer, settled onto a corner of her
mother's upturned box. She held one hand toward the fire and
looked about the circle of faces: her father, standing, holding the
buried leaf, the others seated, looking upward as he spoke; Little
Jess, winding his fingers through his red hair, eyes shining; Josh,
dark and serious; Labe's round face smiling; her mother, gazing
up at Jess as if she'd never heard such fine words as those he
spoke.

Overhead the sky had faded to a cold, gray green and three large
birds flew swiftly across it, silent now, no longer hunting, bound
for their night's resting place. . . . "Thy Cousin Mattie" . . .
the girl's name had been Mattie. . . .

"Well," her father said, "they made it. Man and beast they

made it, pulled in when all hope had been given up . . . they'n another wagon they'd met up with." He smoothed the page he held in his hand. "And when they come to build the house that stood here I can see just how it was. Thy uncle wanted to make a kind of offering . . . say a kind of thank you to the Lord for leading them . . . and make a prayer for this house."

"What'd he bury, Jess?" Eliza asked. "What page did he choose?"

"Couldn't have chosen a fitter," Jess said heartily. "Kind of flighty old fellow I've always heard, but wise-hearted. A better heritage than a farm," he told them, his eyes running along the page. "I'd rather unearth this in my backyard than spade up a crockful of rubies."

"Read it, Jess," Eliza said. "We can't see it, the way thee can. Read it out to us."

Jess' eyes followed the lines. The fire the boys had lit was burning low, but there was still enough light to read by. "This is what he left for us," he said. "What he picked out for us to read. 'And the Lord brought us forth out of Egypt with a mighty hand,'" he read in a strong and proud voice, " 'and with an outstretched arm and with great terribleness and with signs and with wonders. And he hath brought us into this place and hath given us this land, even a land that floweth with milk and honey.' Yes, yes," Jess said, "even then, even in the wilderness the old man saw how it was to be. Laid this leaf in the earth as a remembrance of what'd been done for us and given to us."

"Read on," bade Eliza. "It's like the dead speaking to us."

" 'Look down from thy holy habitation, from heaven,'" Jess read, " 'and bless thy people, Israel, and the land which thou hast given us, as thou swarest unto our fathers, a land that floweth with milk and honey.' There's more," he said, "there's more," but he seemed not inclined to read further, looking down for a spell into the embers.

The fire had sunk now and coldness seemed to be gathering in the cellar as it will in low places. There was a rustling of dry leaves in the gum tree, and the wind, newly sprung up, sent a few leaves over the edge of the cellar and one into the dying fire where it burned suddenly, lighting all their faces. Fall has come, Mattie thought. It is here. It came while pa was reading. Then, not thinking of Great-Uncle Jerd or the Bible, she asked, "The girl . . . what became of the girl? Did she take care of her father . . . be an old maid?"

Jess blew his nose. "Wind coming up, blows the smoke in my face," he told them. He handed the buried leaf and its wrapping to Josh. "Thee handle this carefully," he said. "It's precious. Thee'll never happen on anything more valuable." Then he turned to Mattie. "Most juberous lot of young uns I got. I declare, I don't know where they get it. 'Did he die?' says Little Jess. 'Was she an old maid?' says thee. Far from it, far from it," he said. "Married Seth Jenkins, the driver of the second wagon, and a blade he was, too. Married out of the church, a non-Quaker, but later Seth seen the light, was a Friend by conviction. Married right here in this house on her seventeenth birthday and headed west next day."

In this house, on the floor boards that had rested overhead, this girl who had come overland, driving the oxen . . . bone wet . . . bringing in the meat . . . fording the streams . . .

"She was of a dark turn," Jess said, "chunky, but handsome to look at, I always heard."

She had met this driver, this blade, Seth Jenkins. "Mattie," he had said. "Mattie," he had whispered. What had he said then, what further words, this blade, this traveler, a reckless man?

"This Seth Jenkins could hold a pole, I've always heard tell," Jess said, "a hand at either end and leap backwards and forwards over it twenty-five times without once breathing hard."

Had they stood, after the wedding, on the doorstep, Seth and Mattie? Was the honeysuckle planted yet, did the bleeding-hearts run then, as her grandmother had told her, in a double line to the lane? Did they walk between them for a last look at the stars overhead? Seth and Mattie . . .

"Young people," Jess said, "deep in love, they headed west next morning."

Mattie rose from the box where she sat with her mother; she ran quickly round the last embers of the fire and took her father's hand in both of hers. "Oh, pa," she said, "I do forgive thee. With all my heart I do." Then she flashed up the cellar steps and was only a gray blur, speeding toward the house in the dark.

Jess gazed after her in astonishment. He looked down at Eliza for explanation. "What's come over the girl?" he asked. "What's she forgiving me for? Thy daughter addled?" he asked.

Eliza, too, arose, faced Jess, and smiled. "It's just her Birdwell blood, I don't misdoubt. Just her flighty Birdwell blood," she said. Then she followed Mattie toward the house, walking quickly at first, then slowing her steps so Jess had no trouble overtaking her.

The three boys, left alone, sat for a time looking at the last of the coals. Then Little Jess took up his pick and going to another corner of the cellar began, once more, to dig. "Might be lots of things buried here," he said.

Josh stirred the gray embers with the toe of his boot. "Fifty years ago, they headed west," he said. "And we still here. Sitting in a cellar they dug."

Labe threw a handful of twigs onto the dying fire. They caught and blazed so that finger-shaped points of light wavered uncertainly across the dark floor of earth, almost but not quite reaching him. " 'Look down from thy holy habitation and bless thy people.' " He wrapped the buried leaf, once more, with its covering. "This is a thing I'd like always to keep," he said to Josh—or Little Jess—or anyone who cared to listen.

A LIKELY EXCHANGE

IT was an October morning, and in the kitchen on the lamplit table an October breakfast was set out. Jess gazed at the meal of leave-taking; the red tablecloth gone rosy with many washings, the food itself, ham and quince jelly, cream gravy and soda biscuits, rosy beneath the clear flame of the lamp.

The kitchen was sweet with the smell of wood smoke. It was dark in the kitchen, but the light from the fire in the cookstove moved like a morning tide across the scrubbed floor-boards. The lamplight deepened the wide-awake gleam of Eliza's black eyes, and put a kind of hoarfrost glitter on Enoch's straw-colored stubble.

Jess smelled and looked. He chewed and swallowed. He gave the table a lick that lifted the half-filled cups out of their saucers. He gazed from wife to hired man.

"Tell me," he asked of each, "what makes a man leave home? What'll I find in Kentucky better'n here? What's the sense of traipsing off? Leaving my home? Crossing the boundaries of my own state? A fool notion. I've a mind to stay."

Eliza knew this was a way her husband had of being two places at once; of keeping his knees under the breakfast table, and at the same time feeling wheels moving him along some lonely pike. But she could never answer him from a like duality. Her feet, and mind too, were one place at a time. Here, this October morning, they were in the kitchen of the Maple Grove Nursery.

"Jess," she reminded him, "thy valise is packed. Thee always goes to Kentucky this time of year. How'd we make out if thee didn't sell thy nursery stock?"

"Make out?" asked Jess affronted. "Why, when the Lord made me, I hope He didn't say, 'Here's Jess Birdwell, a little nurseryman.' The Lord," said Jess, taking a fine long draught of Eliza's good coffee, "said, I don't misdoubt, when He made me, 'Here's Jess Birdwell, a man.'"

Eliza looked about with dismay. This talk of what the Lord had or hadn't said could, and like enough would, last till midmorning. Jess, perhaps, didn't have any set time for reaching Kentucky, but time for a woman was no such pliable commodity as it was for a man; time for a woman was rigid, and marked with the names of duties.

The hired man reared back in his rush-bottomed chair, squinted his green eyes. This was a fine way for a morning to start: a little speculation, a little tossing about before you settled down to the hog wash and wood splitting.

"The Lord," Enoch said, addressing Eliza, but squinting beyond the lamplight as if Omniscience itself might be planted just a little to the left of the cookstove, "brings forth possibilities. A raw lump —a man. But whether a nurseryman or not, He don't say."

Eliza loved the name of the Lord, but hearing it in Enoch's mouth at this time of the day didn't add a thing to it. Jess picked his hired men for two reasons: to help with the work and to forward the talking. Sometimes he'd get a man who could do both, but mostly they favored one or the other. Enoch leaned considerably toward talking.

"Jess," worried Eliza, "if thee didn't sell thy nursery stock—"

Enoch interrupted her. "Play on a flute," he told her. "He's got a wonderful turn for music. Raise silkworms. Concoct pieces for the paper. Train horses."

Jess looked at his hired man. "Train horses." Was it a dab? A reminder? Was the fellow laughing up his sleeve at the way Reverend Godley's Black Prince had run circles round Red Rover?

"Train horses," repeated Eliza, happy to have the conversation veer, without her turning it, to a point where she could put in, off-hand-like, further advice about that animal Red Rover. "Jess is finished with fast horseflesh," she told Enoch. "Red Rover gave him his fill of that."

"Red Rover wasn't so plaguy fast," Enoch reminded her.

"Fast-looking," said Eliza. "A constant temptation." She turned to Jess. "Thee keep thy eyes open for a likely exchange," she told him once again.

Jess grew restive. What Red Rover had done wasn't a thing that chewed well early in the morning. He pushed back his chair. "It's getting on," he said. "I ought to be to the Ohio by noon. Sunup," he complained, "and my chin still in the gravy bowl. Enoch, thee hitch while I get my traps together."

"Thy traps," said Eliza firmly, who hadn't finished on the subject of Red Rover, "are together. Thee promised," she began, and her husband nodded soberly.

Jess aimed to please his wife whenever it was humanly possible, and getting shut of Red Rover would be one of the most satisfying ways of doing so he'd been offered in a coon's age. Ever since he'd disgraced himself, after that unseemly brush with the Reverend Marcus Augustus Godley's Black Prince, by lighting into Red Rover with his hat in front of all the Bethel congregation, the sight of Red Rover in his stall was no salve for his eyes, either.

And for another thing, he didn't plan always to move up the pike a tail to Godley's comet. But if he was ever to get out in front of that procession it would take another animal than Red Rover to do it. No horse had ever looked so much like traveling and had traveled so much like standing still. With one trade (exchange, Jess called it, talking to Eliza) promising thus to give two people so much pleasure and for such different reasons, Jess didn't have, as far as he could see, the slightest call for considering himself married to Red Rover.

Outside, the big red gelding let forth his great conceited neigh. Jess listened wryly. "Never knew a nag promise so much and perform so little."

"Thee get shut of him," Eliza urged again. "There'll be no end of brushings and clockings so long as thee's got such a racy-looking animal."

"He can clock," Jess conceded, "but he sure can't brush. Got a sup more coffee, Eliza?"

"Thee won't reach the Ohio till doomsday, at this rate," Eliza said, but poured the coffee.

"Banks of the Ohio on doomsday morning," Jess ruminated. "Couldn't pick a prettier place to be. The Indiana side just below Madison."

Eliza put an end to that. She leaned across the table and blew out the lamp. It was no longer night in the kitchen now. Together, Jess and Eliza walked out into the gray fall morning, laden with paraphernalia of the journey.

Jess journeyed Kentuckyward talking—talking to himself, talking to his horse, remarking on this and that to the absent Enoch and Eliza.

Saying to Eliza: A clump of Chiny asters set in star shape, deep colors in the center and lessening toward the edges—just outside of Madison; there's something thee would fancy.

Saying to Enoch: This Red Rover's nothing to depend on, I grant thee. Running against Reverend Godley's Black Prince, he had less get-up than a gourd vine. But he carries me along like a chip now, nobody pressing him.

Saying to himself: Landscape foams up round about me like a painted picture where every brush stroke's got meaning. Meaning bursting out of weeds and fence rails. Full of meaning I can't read. What's the message? What're they saying?

Saying to the horse: Friend, thee's taught me a lesson: come to say to me, "Jess, don't let appearance be thy god."

He traveled through the tissue-fine day, through sunshine, fine but thin. Lean against it and it would give way, he thought. But it was real. No alloy. Pure gold leaf.

He crossed the Ohio a little after noon and thought of doomsday and smelled fried ham. In midafternoon he still could hear the whistle of the steamboats passing down the broad Ohio, and as he drove between rows of shocked corn saw, instead of the corn, that great surge of water and the boats it bore: white-pillared swans, floating verandas.

He turned in at driveways, sent the buckboard up known lanes and under admired trees. Patted growling dogs until porch floor-boards resounded beneath their thumping tails. Talked to women churning outside at the close of day, tasting the last of sunshine. Rang the bell that brought the farmer up from the fields. Spread out his order books and showed them the pictures. The churn, with the butter half-come, and the wagon, half-filled with husked corn, waited while he showed the pictures and said the names.

"Shaffer's Colossal—bids fair to eclipse anything in the raspberry line. Gooseberries—Smith's Improved, grown from the seed of the Houghton; sweet. May Duke—fine for dwarfs and pyramids. Flemish Beauty. Grimes Golden. Fall Wine."

"Give me five of those," they'd say. "Nothing so pretty as a cherry in bloom, fruit or no fruit."

"And the fruit, too," the wife would add, leaning on the churn dasher. "Puts me in mind of home—in Pennsylvania. Cherries on each side the driveway, red among the leaves."

They'd shake his hand at leave-taking. Friend Birdwell—a good man, notional, a Quaker, a plain-speaker.

He drove on. At nightfall he pulled up his big red gelding at a driveway he'd never turned down before. Not that it didn't look to be a likely place for selling first-class stock; a fine, big farm well kept up, mostly corn and tobacco, but some thrifty fruit trees, too. What had kept him from turning in was the sign on the barn. A man who'd spread his history out so publicly went against Jess's grain, both as Quaker and as man.

But that gold evening Jess let the reins go slack and leaned forward peering at the red barn and the white painted sign that ran from gable to gable above the big double doors.

"Otto Hudspeth," the sign said. "I was borned in 1807. I was married in 1837." Jess read the sign aloud, tickled to think of the big know-nothing farmer who'd had it painted.

"Know-nothing," he said to himself after a while. "By sugar, thee's come to let appearances be thy god, Jess Birdwell, for sure. Judging a man without ever setting eyes on him." He slapped the lines lightly across Red Rover's glossy rump. "Thought thee'd cured me of that, friend," he said, and turned the red horse into the driveway.

The big farmhouse was set at the end of a long double line of locusts, and there wasn't a thing about the layout that wasn't up to Maple Grove standards. Before Jess could light down, the Hudspeth hired man came out. The family, he said, was off to a shindig, but Jess had better stay the night. Mrs. Hudspeth had just bought a forty and she was figuring on putting in some orchard stock.

"Mrs. Hudspeth?" Jess asked.

"The old man passed on a couple of years back," said the hired man, who looked himself to be straight out of Genesis—certainly no nearer than Leviticus or Deuteronomy. "Mrs. Hudspeth and the girls run the place."

Jess was staring up at the sign.

"Yep," said the hired man, "the old man had that painted there."

"Mite touched?" asked Jess.

"No more'n you," said the hired man. "Not as much, maybe. I ain't acquainted with you, mister." The evening wind parted his beard. "What's the most important thing's happened to you, mister? Getting born. Without that, where'd you be?" He paused to let it sink in. "What's next? Getting married. If you married the right woman. Maybe you didn't—like me." His look got more humane, quite full of fellow feeling.

"Thee's wrong there," Jess said, not wanting any slight put on Eliza. "I married the right woman. Pretty as a Summer Sweeting. A Quaker preacher."

The hired man gave a squint and moodily combed his patriarchal fringe with his fingers. "Well, every man to his fancy," he continued. "You agree them's the first things. Gettin' born. Gettin' married. Got any objection to a man's saying so with his own paint on his own barn? Got any remarks you'd like to make to me about it?"

"Nope," said Jess, fighting being against his principles as a Quaker and, Quaker or no Quaker, not being of a mind to be laid out by a hired man over a sign painted on a Kentucky barn.

Calmed, the hired man was as clever as could be: helped put up Red Rover, cooked a tasty supper of fried grits and side meat, and out of pure courtesy, having eaten earlier himself, kept Jess company at the table with a jug of corn whiskey.

Jess had a fine night of sleep in the spare chamber on a feather bed six hands high, but was awakened early next morning by a sound he couldn't place. Clack, clack, bang . . . bang, it went. Jess knew farm noises inside and out, forward and backward, but this one stumped him. Clack, clack, bang . . . bang. It was too much for his curiosity. He scamped his morning prayers to get down to see what was taking place. The minute he opened the back stairs door into the kitchen he saw what it was.

An old lady sat at the kitchen hearthside—a big old lady, thin as a siding, but wide in the shoulders and so tall her head stuck up above the tidy of the rocker she was sitting in. The old lady was smoking a pipe, and she kept her makings in the Dutch oven which was built in one side of the fireplace. Every so often she'd knock her pipe out on the side of the fireplace, open up the iron door of the Dutch oven, get out her tobacco, bang the door shut, fill her pipe, open the door, bang it shut. Clack, clack, bang . . . bang.

Jess went up and paid his respects to her. Mrs. Hudspeth was an old lady like a stove poker, stiff, straight, and black; but she had the same look the stove poker has of having spent a life near the fire and of being tempered by it.

Jess breakfasted with Mrs. Hudspeth, the hired man, Jacob, and Mrs. Hudspeth's four daughters.

"Make the acquaintance of my girls, Mr. Birdwell," Mrs. Hudspeth said. In respect of sex, Jess allowed, they were girls, but in respect of age and size he couldn't have found a more unlikely name for them.

"Meet Opal, Ruby, and Pearl, Mr. Birdwell," said Mrs. Hudspeth. Fifty-carat jewels, every one of them, Jess calculated.

"Meet Bertha," said Mrs. Hudspeth, "my baby." Jess wondered at the shift in naming. After three, he figured, girls maybe didn't seem so precious.

The girls were all so big, so hearty, and such powerful smokers that before breakfast was over Jess felt himself wizening up like a cabbage leaf under a hot sun.

He was the first one at the door when Mrs. Hudspeth said, "Let's have a look at my forty, Friend Birdwell, and see what stock you think'd do best there."

As they stepped toward the barn Mrs. Hudspeth announced, "We'll drive my mare Lady. Give your animal a rest after traveling. I had a look at him this morning. As pretty a looking horse as I recollect seeing. Got style."

"Well," said Jess, giving Red Rover his due, as he would the devil, "he's a treat to the eyes, that's certain."

He saw why Mrs. Hudspeth was so appreciative of handsome horseflesh when her hired man came out leading Lady. Jess looked that mare up and down, and being a man with a pretty turn for words, he began assembling some that might do justice to her when he came to recount the meeting to his hired man, Enoch.

Lady! She didn't look like any lady and it was much as a bargain to say she looked like a horse. It wasn't that she was poor or run-down or spavined or wind-broke, or bloated or had the heaves or was wall-eyed or balky, or was a stump sucker or blind in one eye, or sway-backed or galled or tree-shy. No, Enoch, she was none of these things—nothing so easy to lay the tongue to. It wasn't anything thee could say in one word, or two.

But that mare wasn't hung together right. She looked like she had cow blood in her, or moose blood, or buffalo blood. She was an oddity and she looked like she knew it. She had a long thin neck with a head hung on the end of it like a club. Had a body like a barrel, with muscles on shoulders and haunches like clumps of sweet potatoes. When they worked she looked like she had moles burrowing under her hide. She was rangy for a Morgan; for that's what she was—half Morgan. Thee couldn't miss the Morgan color of her, nor the Morgan look out of her eyes, gentle and proud all at once—and kind of shamefaced, too, for being put together the way she was. Looking in her eye, thee was all for her —otherwise not. Otherwise, Enoch, like seeing something in a distorting glass.

Putting together this how-it-looked for Enoch in the future, Jess forgot to be civil then and there. The old lady reminded him.

She said to him sharp, after watching him stare a spell, "Ain't you people over'n Indianny ever seen a Morgan mare before?"

Jess saw the staring didn't set well, but the best he could say was: "Morgans. Thee's a favored woman, Mrs. Hudspeth. Morgan's always been my favorite breed. Never had the good fortune to own one, but I always hankered to."

That smoothed Mrs. Hudspeth over so that when they started for the forty she was in a good humor, smiling broad, and holding the reins like a born driver.

Soon as that mare Lady struck her hooves to the pike, Jess knew the Lord was going to particular pains to teach him a lesson he needed learning: not to judge man or beast by outward show. He reckoned the world turned round a mite faster when that mare swung into her stride, started pushing the pike from underneath her big, ugly feet. She stepped out like Going was her mammy's name, and Fast her pappy's.

Jess kept his talk where it ought to be—on nursery stock—and he found the old lady mighty near as knowledgeable as himself. When he talked Maiden Blush, Grimes Goldens, and Wealthies, she came right back with Winesaps, Winter Pearmains, and Rome Beauties. When Jess mentioned the Pewaukee, Mrs. Hudspeth matched him with facts about its pedigree; knew it was a seedling from the Duchess of Oldenburg.

They were talking fruit at a 2:40 clip when a rig drew up from behind them. Jess looked around and saw a big roan hitched to a light spring wagon with his driver urging him on like he was Boston himself with the record at stake. Jess figured the man's wife must've had a sudden seizure and he was off hell-bent for the doctor.

But the old lady muttered, stiffened her arms, and leaned back on the reins. "Can't get out on the road without this happening," she said. "It ain't dignified. Gives the men the idea my girls ain't nothing but jockeys in skirts."

Mrs. Hudspeth planted her long, bony legs against the dashboard and leaned back hard, but Lady took the bit in her mouth and lit out. Her long neck stiffened like a ramrod, the muscles started running up and down her hams as smooth as sap, her stride lengthened until she was skimming the road like a swallow.

Jess was gathering up information faster than he could salt it down.

"Let her out," he yelled. "Thee's holding her in. Loosen thy grip. Thee's hanging round her neck like a millstone, Mrs. Hudspeth," he bellowed. "Loosen up, loosen up."

"I got no mind to," the old lady snapped, still leaning back, and still sawing. "I'm going to learn this mare she's got no call to be always out in front. She's a good beast, but she's got to learn to be passed. She's got a fancy she's Lexington. Me and my girls always hittin' it down the pike like the devil's on our tails. No style. It don't appeal to the men."

Lady was running like she'd rather split her mouth in two than be passed, and Mrs. Hudspeth was leaning back like she'd rather have her arms pulled out of their sockets than not have her way, and the wind was whistling past Jess's big Quaker hat like he was riding the whirlwind. But the roan was gaining. Jess hung on to his hat and ventured a backward look. The roan looked to be a natural runner, and he was getting encouragement from a buggy whip.

That decided Jess. It went against his principles to see an honest-trying horse so punished: it would encourage the spread of evil in the world to let a man win by any such means.

He took the reins from Mrs. Hudspeth's hands. The old lady was strong, but so was Jess and he had the considerable advantage of knowing what was up. He had the reins and was doing the driving before she'd got the lay of the land.

Soon as Jess had loosened Lady's reins and spoken to her with admiration, she distanced the roan; she sped away from him like she was the arrow and he the bow. With the roan behind her, Lady settled down to a nice Sunday pace. You could see she was feeling mighty good.

Jess wasn't. It would have pleased him greatly to have got the reins back in Mrs. Hudspeth's hands—but he didn't see any way of doing that without reminding her of how she'd lost them in the first place.

He figured the tactful thing to do was to go on talking fruit, as if nothing had happened. "Thee's a wide choice of apples, Mrs. Hudspeth," he said. "Thy soil and the climate hereabouts would be favorable for Jonathans or Winesaps." But the old lady was of no mind to talk apples.

"For a man," she said, "that's a suitable thing to do—best another man in a race on a public road. But it ain't a fitting action for a woman. Not for a marriageable woman like one of my girls, anyway. Men ain't got any heart for courting a girl they can't pass —let alone catch up with."

"Thee say this mare's never been passed?"

"One time only," the old lady answered truthfully, "with two of my daughters on the reins at once. They couldn't stop her, but they slowed her down enough to get passed—but the man who distanced them was Sheriff Bascom. A married man. Grandpappy to boot. It didn't get 'em any place. I been figuring for some time to get a fitting animal for those girls of mine to drive. Something a degree more maidenly acting."

Jess drove in silence, thinking.

"You own a stylish animal, Mr. Birdwell," said Mrs. Hudspeth finally. "It got racing notions?"

Jess shook his head. "No, ma'am," he said. "Nothing to worry about on that score. Not that it can't pick up its heels, but racing's a thing it's got no stomach for. None whatever," he said with the emphasis of remembering.

They were both thinking the same thing, but the old lady said it first, as a woman will.

"How'd a trade strike you, Mr. Birdwell?"

It struck Jess as being well-nigh providential. "It's something could be thought on," he replied cautiously.

"Lady ain't got but that one fault," Mrs. Hudspeth told him, "and you seen that. A forceful man like yourself, Mr. Birdwell, could learn her better in no time if you's a mind to."

Jess agreed. "If I's a mind to," he said.

"She won't be passed. Otherwise she's fault-free—half Morgan, a prime healthy animal, just turned four and a willing worker."

Jess hemmed and hawed to hide the way his heart was beating.

"Thee'd oughtn't be hasty, Mrs. Hudspeth. Thee's never seen my gelding in action."

"I'm a judge of horseflesh," said Mrs. Hudspeth.

"Thee can't rightly say," said Jess, feeling for his words and trying to be delicate, "that thy marc's a handsome animal."

"Well, no," the old lady allowed. "There might have to be a little to boot."

That finally was the way it was. Next morning Jess had Lady, and he had a little to boot and an order for nursery stock that filled three pages in his neat account-book handwriting. He drove out under the big sign he'd stared at so many times in passing. "Otto Hudspeth," he said. "Thee's done me a good turn, Otto I wish thy daughters well—and if getting passed will help them, they've got the right animal."

The fine weather held right through the trip home, cloudless and serene. Jess proved more than once, and to his pleasure, the rightness of Mrs. Hudspeth's claims that Lady wouldn't be passed. She wouldn't and she wasn't—not by anything Jess encountered homeward bound, anyway.

As he was drawing near the Ohio once more, Jess began to think of Eliza. He'd just had a satisfying little brush with a fast iron gray—nothing very lasty, but satisfying—and he was recalling Eliza's parting words.

"Thee get shut of that racy-looking animal," she'd said, and here he was coming home behind a mare who had more racing sense in one of her lop ears than Red Rover'd had in his four legs, two hams, and handsome mulish head. Racy-looking, he thought. That's what Eliza said. That's what she's set against.

Jess slapped the reins over Lady's back. "Thee may not," he told her, "fulfill the spirit of the law, but Eliza can't say thee don't fulfill the letter. Never saw an animal less racy-looking in my life."

Jess was smiling very contentedly when from a hilltop he caught sight beneath him of a shining loop of the Ohio, and beyond it saw the blue hills of Jefferson County.

"Home tonight, Lady," he said, and Lady moved along as if the words pleased her.

FIRST DAY FINISH

"THEE'S home, Lady," Jess told his mare.

They had made the trip in jig time. The sun was still up, catalpa shadows long across the grass, and mud daubers still busy about the horse trough, gathering a few last loads before nightfall, when Lady turned in the home driveway.

Jess loosened the reins, so that on their first homecoming together they could round the curve to the barn with a little flourish of arrival. It was a short-lived flourish, quickly subsiding when Jess caught sight of the Reverend Marcus Augustus Godley's Black Prince tied to the hitching rack.

"Look who's here," Jess told his mare and they came in slow and seemly as befitted travelers with forty weary miles behind them.

The Reverend Godley himself, shading his eyes from the low sun, stepped to the barn door when his Black Prince nickered.

Jess lit stiffly down and was standing at Lady's head when the Reverend Marcus Augustus reached them.

"Good evening, Marcus," said Jess. "Thee run short of something over at thy place?"

"Welcome home," said the Reverend Godley, never flinching. "I was hunting, with Enoch's help, a bolt to fit my seeder," he told Jess, but he never took his eyes off Lady.

He was a big man, fat but not pursy, with a full red face preaching had kept supple and limber. A variety of feelings, mostly painful, flickered across it now as he gazed at Jess' mare.

He opened and shut his mouth a couple of times, but all he managed to say was, "Where'd you come across that animal, Friend Birdwell?"

"Kentucky," Jess said shortly.

"I'm a Kentuckian myself." The Reverend Godley marveled that the state that had fathered him could have produced such horse-flesh.

"You trade Red Rover for this?" he asked.

Jess rubbed his hand along Lady's neck. "The mare's name is Lady," he said.

"Lady!" The preacher gulped, then threw back his big head and disturbed the evening air with laughter.

"Friend," Jess said, watching the big bulk heave, "thy risibilities are mighty near the surface this evening."

The Reverend Godley wiped the tears from his face and ventured another look. "It's just the cleavage," he said. "The rift between the name and looks."

"That's a matter of opinion," Jess told him, "but Lady is the name."

The preacher stepped off a pace or two as if to try the advantage of a new perspective on the mare's appearance, clapped a handful of hoar-hound drops into his mouth, and chewed reflectively.

"I figure it this way," he told Jess. "You bought that animal Red Rover. Flashy as sin and twice as unreliable. First little brush you have with me and my cob, Red Rover curdles on you—goes sourer than a crock of cream in a June storm. What's the natural thing to do?"

The Reverend Godley gave his talk a pulpit pause and rested his big thumbs in his curving watch chain.

"The natural thing to do? Why, just what you done. Give speed the go-by. Say farewell to looks. Get yourself a beast sound in wind and limb and at home behind a plow. Friend," he commended Jess, "you done the right thing, though I'm free to admit I never laid eyes before on a beast of such dimensions. Have some hoar-

hound drops?" he asked amiably. "Does wonders for the throat."
Jess shook his head.

"Well," he continued, "I want you to know—Sunday mornings
on the way to church, when I pass you, there's nothing personal
in it. That morning when I went round you and Red Rover, I
somehow got the idea you's taking it personal. Speed's an eternal
verity, friend, an eternal verity. Nothing personal. Rain falls. The
stars shine. The grass withereth. The race is to the swift. A fast
horse passes a slow one. An eternal verity, Friend Birdwell. You're
no preacher, but your wife is. She understands these things. Nothing personal. Like gravitation, like life, like death. A law of God.
Nothing personal.

"The good woman will be hallooing for me," he said, gazing
up the pike toward his own farm a quarter of a mile away. He
took another look at Jess' new mare.

"Name's Lady," he said, as if reminding himself. "Much obliged
for the bolt, Friend Birdwell. Me and my cob'll see you Sunday."

Enoch stepped out from the barn door as the Reverend Godley
turned down the driveway.

"Figure I heard my sermon for the week," he said.

"He's got an endurin' flock," Jess told his hired man.

"Cob?" Enoch asked. "What's he mean always calling that
animal of his a cob? He ignorant?"

"Not ignorant—smooth," Jess said. "Cob's just his way of saying Black Prince's no ordinary beast without coming straight out
with so undraped a word as stallion."

The two men turned with one accord from Godley's cob to
Jess' Lady. Enoch's green eyes flickered knowingly; his long
freckled hand touched Lady's muscled shoulder lightly, ran down
the powerful legs, explored the deep chest.

"There's more here, Mr. Birdwell, than meets the eye?"

Jess nodded.

"As far as looks goes," Enoch said, "the Reverend called the
turn."

"As far as looks goes," Jess agreed.

"She part Morgan?"

"Half," Jess said proudly.

Enoch swallowed. "How'd you swing it?"

"Providence," Jess said. "Pure Providence. Widow woman wanted a pretty horse and one that could be passed."

"Red Rover," Enoch agreed and added softly, "The Reverend was took in."

"He's a smart man," said Jess. "We'd best not bank on it. But, by sugar, Enoch, I tell thee I was getting tired of taking Eliza down the pike to Meeting every First Day like a tail to Godley's comet. Have him start late, go round me, then slow down so's we'd eat dust. Riled me so I was arriving at Meeting in no fit state to worship."

"You give her a tryout—coming home?" Enoch asked guardedly.

"I did, Enoch," Jess said solemnly. "This horse, this Morgan mare named Lady's got the heart of a lion and the wings of a bird. Nothing without pinfeathers is going to pass her."

"It's like Mr. Emerson says," said Enoch earnestly.

Jess nodded. "Compensation," he agreed. "A clear case of it and her pure due considering the looks she's got."

"You figure on this Sunday?" Enoch asked.

"Well," Jess said, "I plan to figure on nothing. Thee heard the Reverend Marcus Augustus. A fast horse goes round a slow one. Eternal law. If Black Prince tries to pass us First Day—and don't— it's just a law, just something eternal. And mighty pretty, Enoch, like the stars."

"A pity," Enoch said, reflecting, "the Reverend's young'uns all so piddling and yours such busters. Pity Steve and Jane's so well set up and chunky. It'll tell on your mare."

"A pity," Jess acquiesced, "but there it is. Eliza'd never agree to leave the children home from Meeting."

Enoch ruminated, his fingers busy with Lady's harness. "What'll your wife say to this mare? Been a considerable amount of trading lately."

"Say?" said Jess. "Thee heard her. 'Exchange Red Rover for a horse not racy-looking.' This mare racy-looking?"

"You have to look twice to see it," Enoch admitted.

"Eliza don't look twice at a horse. I'll just lead Lady up now for Eliza to see. She don't hold with coming down to the barn while men's about."

Jess took Lady from the shafts and led her between the rows of currant bushes up to the house. Dusk was come now, lamps were lit. Inside, Eliza and the children were waiting for their greeting until the men had had their talk.

"Lady," Jess said fondly, "I want thee to see thy mistress."

The rest of the week went by, mild and very fair, one of those spells in autumn when time seems to stand still. Clear days with a wind which would die down by afternoon. The faraway smoke-colored ridges seemed to have moved up to the orchard's edge. The purple ironweed, the farewell summer, the goldenrod, stood untrembling beneath an unclouded sky. Onto the corn standing shocked in the fields, gold light softer than arrows, but as pointed, fell. A single crow at dusk would drop in a slow arc against the distant wood to show that not all had died. Indian summer can be a time of great content.

First Day turned up pretty. Just before the start for Meeting, Jess discovered a hub cap missing off the surrey.

"Lost?" asked Eliza.

"I wouldn't say lost," Jess told her. "Missing."

Odd thing, a pity to be sure, but there it was. Nothing for it but for him and Eliza to ride to Meeting in the cut-down buggy and leave the children behind. Great pity, but there it was.

Eliza stood in the yard in her First Day silk. "Jess," she said in a balky voice, "this isn't my idea of what's seemly. A preacher going to Meeting in a cut-down rig like this. Looks more like heading for the trotting races at the county fair than preaching."

Jess said, "Thee surprises me, Eliza. Thee was used to put duty before appearance. Friend Fox was content to tramp the roads to reach his people. Thee asks for thy surrey, fresh blacking on the dashboard and a new whip in the socket."

He turned away sadly. "The Lord's people are everywhere grown more worldly," he said, looking dismally at the ground.

It didn't set good with Jess, pushing Eliza against her will that way—and he wasn't any too sure it was going to work. But the name Fox got her. When she was a girl she'd set out to bring the Word to people, the way Fox had done, and he'd have gone, she knew, to Meeting in a barrow, if need be.

So that's the way they started out, and in spite of the rig, Eliza was lighthearted and holy-feeling. When they pulled out on the pike, she was pleased to note the mare's gait was better than her looks. Lady picked up her feet like she knew what to do with them.

"Thee's got a good-pulling mare, Jess," she said kindly.

"She'll get us there, I don't misdoubt," Jess said.

They'd rounded the first curve below the clump of maples that gave the Maple Grove Nursery its name when the Reverend Godley bore down upon them. Neither bothered to look back; both knew the heavy, steady beat of Black Prince's hoofs.

Eliza settled herself in the cut-down rig, her Bible held comfortably in her lap. "It taxes the imagination," she said, "how a man church-bound can have his mind so set on besting another. Don't thee think so, Jess?"

"It don't tax mine," Jess said, thinking honesty might be the only virtue he'd get credit for that day.

Eliza was surprised not to see Black Prince pulling abreast them. It was here on the long stretch of level road that Black Prince usually showed them his heels.

"Thee'd best pull over, Jess," she said.

"I got no call to pull out in the ditch," Jess said. "The law allows me half the road."

The mare hadn't made any fuss about it—no head-shaking, no fancy footwork—but she'd settled down in her harness, she was traveling. It was plain to Eliza they were eating up the road.

"Don't thee think we'd better pull up, Jess?" Eliza said it easy, so as not to stir up the contrary streak that wasn't buried very deep in her husband.

"By sugar," Jess said, "I don't see why."

As soon as Eliza heard that "by sugar" spoken as bold-faced as if it were a weekday, she knew it was too late for soft words. "By sugar," Jess said again, "I don't see why. The Reverend Godley's got half the road and I ain't urging my mare."

It depended on what you called urging. He hadn't taken to lambasting Lady with his hat yet, the way he had Red Rover, but he was sitting on the edge of the seat—and sitting mighty light, it was plain to see—driving the mare with an easy rein and talking to her like a weanling.

"Thee's a fine mare. Thee's a tryer. Thee's a credit to thy dam. Never have to think twice about thy looks again."

Maybe, strictly speaking, that was just encouraging, not urging, but Eliza wasn't in a hairsplitting mood.

She looked back at the Reverend Marcus Augustus, and no two ways about it: he was urging Black Prince. The Reverend Godley's cob wasn't a length behind them and the Reverend himself was half standing, slapping the reins across Black Prince's rump and exhorting him like a sinner newly come to the mourners' bench.

This was a pass to which Eliza hadn't thought to come twice in a lifetime—twice in a lifetime to be heading for Meeting like a county fair racer in a checkered shirt.

"Nothing lacking now," she thought bitterly, "but for bets to be laid on us."

That wasn't lacking either, if Eliza had only known it. They'd come in view of the Bethel Church now, and more than one of Godley's flock had got so carried away by the race as to try for odds on their own preacher. It didn't seem loyal not to back up their Kentucky brother with hard cash. Two to one the odds were—with no takers.

The Bethel Church sat atop a long, low rise, not much to the eye—but it told on a light mare pulling against a heavy stallion, and it was here Black Prince began to close in; before the rise was half covered, the stallion's nose was pressing toward the buggy's back near wheel.

Jess had given up encouraging. He was urging now. Eliza lifted the hat off his head. Come what might, there wasn't going to be any more hat-whacking if she could help it—but Jess was beyond knowing whether his head was bare or covered. He was pulling with his mare now, sweating with her, sucking the air into scalding lungs with her. Lady had slowed on the rise—she'd have been dead if she hadn't—but she was still a-going, still trying hard. Only the Quaker blood in Jess' veins kept him from shouting with pride at his mare's performance.

The Reverend Godley didn't have Quaker blood in his veins. What he had was Kentucky horse-racing blood, and when Black Prince got his nose opposite Lady's rump Godley's racing blood got the best of him. He began to talk to his cob in a voice that got its volume from camp-meeting practice—and its vocabulary, too, as a matter of fact—but he was using it in a fashion his camp-meeting congregations had never heard.

They were almost opposite the Bethel Church now; Black Prince had nosed up an inch or two more on Lady and the Reverend Godley was still strongly exhorting—getting mighty personal, for a man of his convictions.

But Lady was a stayer and so was Jess. And Eliza, too, for that matter. Jess spared her a glance out of the corner of his eye to see how she was faring. She was faring mighty well—sitting bolt upright, her Bible tightly clasped, and clucking to the mare. Jess couldn't credit what he heard. But there was no doubt about it— Eliza was counseling Lady. "Thee keep a-going, Lady," she called. Eliza hadn't camp-meeting experience, but she had a good clear pulpit voice and Lady heard her.

She kept a-going. She did better. She unloosed a spurt of speed Jess hadn't known was in her. Lady was used to being held back, not yelled at in a brush. Yelling got her dander up. She stretched out her long neck, lengthened her powerful stride, and pulled away from Black Prince just as they reached the Bethel Church grounds.

Jess thought the race was won and over, that from here on the pace to Meeting could be more suitable to First Day travel. But the Reverend Godley had no mind to stop at so critical a juncture. He'd wrestled with sinners too long to give up at the first setback. He figured the mare was weakening. He figured that with a strong stayer like his Black Prince he'd settle the matter easy in the half mile that lay between the Bethel Church and the Quaker Meeting House at the grove. He kept a-coming.

But one thing he didn't figure—that was that the slope from Bethel to the Meeting House was against him. Lady had a downhill grade now. It was all she needed. She didn't pull away from Black Prince in any whirlwind style, but stride by stride she pulled away.

It was a great pity Jess' joy in that brush had to be marred. He'd eaten humble pie some time now, and he was pleasured through and through to be doing the dishing up himself. And he was pleasured for the mare's sake.

But neither winning nor his mare's pleasure was first with Jess. Eliza was. There she sat, white and suffering, holding her Bible like it was the Rock of Ages from which she'd come mighty near to clean slipping off. Jess knew Eliza had a forgiving heart when it came to others—but whether she could forgive herself for getting heated over a horse race the way she'd done, he couldn't say.

And the worst for Eliza was yet to come. Jess saw that clear enough. When Lady and Black Prince had pounded past Godley's church, a number of the Bethel brethren, who had arrived early and were still in their rigs, set out behind the Reverend Marcus Augustus to be in at the finish. And they were going to be. Their brother was losing, but they were for him still, close behind and encouraging him in a wholehearted way. The whole caboodle was going to sweep behind Jess and Eliza into the Quaker churchyard. They wouldn't linger, but Jess feared they'd turn around there before heading back again. And that's the way it was.

Lady was three lengths ahead of Black Prince when they reached the Grove Meeting House. Jess eased her for the turn, made it on two wheels, and drew in close to the church. The Bethelites swooped in behind him and on out—plainly beat but not subdued. The Reverend Marcus Augustus was the only man among them without a word to say. He was as silent as a tombstone and considerably grimmer. Even his fancy vest looked to have faded.

The Quakers waiting in the yard for Meeting to begin were quiet, too. Jess couldn't tell from their faces what they were feeling; but there was no use thinking that they considered what they'd just witnessed an edifying sight. Not for a weekday even, that mess of rigs hitting it down the pike with all that hullabaloo— let alone to First Day and their preacher up front, leading it.

Jess asked a boy to look after Lady. He was so taken up with Eliza he no more than laid a fond hand on Lady's hot flank in passing. He helped Eliza light down, and set his hat on his head when she handed it to him. Eliza looked mighty peaked and withdrawn, like a woman communing with the Lord.

She bowed to the congregation and they bowed back and she led them out of the sunshine into the Meeting House with no word being spoken on either side. She walked to the preacher's bench, laid her Bible quietly down, and untied her bonnet strings.

Jess sat rigid in his seat among the men. Jess was a birthright Quaker—and his father and grandfathers before him—and he'd known Quakers to be read out of Meeting for less.

Eliza laid her little plump hands on her Bible and bowed her head in silent prayer. Jess didn't know how long it lasted—sometimes it seemed stretching out into eternity, but Quakers were used to silent worship and he was the only one who seemed restive. About the time the ice round Jess' heart was hardening past his enduring, Eliza's sweet, cool, carrying voice said, "If the spirit leads any of you to speak, will you speak now?"

Then Eliza lowered her head again—but Jess peered round the Meeting House. He thought he saw a contented look on most of the faces—nothing that went so far as to warm into a smile, but a look that said they were satisfied the way the Lord had handled things. And the spirit didn't move any member of the congregation to speak that day except for the prayers of two elderly Friends in closing.

The ride home was mighty quiet. They drove past the Bethel Church, where the sermon had been short—for all the hitching racks were empty. Lady carried them along proud and untired. Enoch, Steve and Jane met them down the pike a ways from home and Emanuela waited on the doorstep, but Jess could only nod the good news to them; he couldn't glory in it the way he'd like because of Eliza.

Eliza was kind. but silent. Very silent. She spoke when spoken to, did her whole duty by the children and Jess, but in all the ways that made Eliza most herself, she was absent and withdrawn.

Toward evening Jess felt a little dauncy—a pain beneath the ribs, heart, or stomach, he couldn't say which. He thought he'd brew himself a cup of sassafras tea, take it to bed and drink it there, and maybe find a little ease.

It was past nightfall when Jess entered his and Eliza's chamber, but there was a full moon and by its light he saw Eliza sitting at the east window in her white nightdress, plaiting her black hair.

"Jess," asked Eliza, noting the cup he carried, "has thee been taken ill?"

"No," Jess said, "no," his pain easing off of itself when he heard by the tones of Eliza's voice that she was restored to him—forgiving and gentle, letting bygones be bygones.

"Eliza," he asked, "wouldn't thee like a nice hot cup of sassafras tea?"

"Why, yes, Jess," Eliza said. "That'd be real refreshing."

Jess carried Eliza her cup of tea walking down a path of roses the moon had lit up in the ingrain carpet.

He stood, while she drank it, with his hand on her chair, gazing out the window: the whole upcurve and embowered sweep of the earth soaked in moonlight—hill and wood lot, orchard and silent river. And beneath that sheen his own rooftree, and all beneath it, peaceful and at rest. Lady in her stall, Enoch reading Emerson, the children long abed.

" 'Sweet day,' " he said, " 'so cool, so calm, so bright, The bridal of the earth and sky.' "

And though he felt so pensive and reposeful, still the bridge of his big nose wrinkled up, his ribs shook with laughter.

Eliza felt the movement of his laughing in her chair. "What is it, Jess?" she asked.

Jess stopped laughing, but said nothing. He figured Eliza had gone about as far in one day as a woman could in enlarging her appreciation of horseflesh; still he couldn't help smiling when he thought of the sermon that might have been preached that morning in the Bethel Church upon the eternal verities.

"YES, WE'LL GATHER AT THE RIVER"

IT was toward evening of a day in spring, after a long dry spell. A cold wind was blowing dust along the pike, shivering windows in their frames, sending puffs of smoke from the fireplace out into the sitting-room. Eliza, who was braiding rags for a rug, heard at the front door a loud and somehow solemn knocking. She put her work down, laid a shawl across her shoulders and went to the door. If the man she saw there had come to the back instead of the front of the house, she would have thought he was a tramp . . . as it was she wasn't certain.

"Mrs. Birdwell?" the man asked.

"Yes," said Eliza.

"I'm Lafe Millspaugh," the old fellow standing before her said, "come to bring you a little gift of eggs."

Eliza saw the eggs, and she recognized the name. Old Lafe Millspaugh—his name was Lafayette, though no one ever called him that—lived down the pike about a mile south of Maple Grove Nursery. He was an oddity in a neighborhood that had time and space for oddness, appreciated its varieties and did nothing to discourage a full and early blooming. He had been born in the neighborhood but had left early to practice his trade of carpentry in the north of the state and was only now returned since his father, long a widower, had died leaving the family farm to Lafe.

"That's real kind of thee, friend Millspaugh," Eliza said, having placed him in her mind. "Won't thee come in out of this wind and warm thyself?"

"I was waiting to be asked," Old Lafe said frankly, and entered.

Eliza closed the door and turned to look at her caller. He suggested so many things at once to her that she gazed somewhat longer than politeness required.

Old Lafe laughed, his long, ginger-colored mustaches framing his empty (so far as Eliza could see) mouth in the way she'd seen grapevines garnish the edges of a limestone cave.

"Reckon you're going to know me next time you see me, ma'm," he said.

Eliza didn't feel she could deny it. There he stood, hatless, his back to the fire, holding the eggs in front of him like some kind of scraggy limb, fallen from a tree with nest attached.

"Yes, I will," Eliza said, friendly as possible. "Thee's a neighbor of ours, isn't thee?"

Old Lafe's small, leather-colored eyes, no more than pin pricks set high in two of the crosswise creases of his much-creased face, smiled. "I'm your neighbor," he affirmed, "and I've brought you a present." He held out the eggs.

Eliza took, with what enthusiasm she could muster, the eggs and their container, a round and somewhat strawy object, thinking: Nothing missing here but the hen.

"Thee's sure thee's not robbing thyself, friend Millspaugh?" she asked. "Must be a dozen or more eggs here."

"Seventeen," said Old Lafe, proudly. "One's a bantam, though," he admitted. "No," he assured Eliza, "you're not robbing me. I don't eat eggs. Wouldn't touch 'em. It's against my principles."

Eliza'd heard of people who didn't eat meat, and she could understand that and felt, at times, inclined in the same direction; but Lafe was the first person she'd heard of who didn't eat eggs. "Thee's got convictions against them?" she asked gently.

"No, ma'm," said Lafe, "you've got it hindside foremost. You've put the shoe on the wrong foot. I've got convictions for them."

Eliza still had the eggs themselves, and their container which seemed too flabby to hold the eggs if set down. And her convictions were leading her to believe that there was more life in the nest (if that was what it was) than that of fertile eggs, alone. She held the eggs at some distance from her, smiling down on them in what she didn't misdoubt was a two-faced way, since she had forty Barred Rocks of her own all laying like a mill-race, till Jess had said he'd cackle if he had to face another floating island or custard pie.

Her smiling pleased Old Lafe, though. "No, ma'm," he told her. "Convictions for, not against. To my mind an egg's a perfect thing, one of nature's masterpieces and far too pretty to eat. How'd you set about to improve on an egg, Mrs. Birdwell?"

Eliza shook her head.

"Think it over," said Old Lafe. "Take your time."

Eliza hadn't any idea how to improve on an egg. She tried to think as bade, but she really didn't know; they were handy sized, tasted good, and a hen's way of producing them seemed as sensible as any. "Eggs," she agreed with him, "are mighty satisfactory."

"Satisfactory." Old Lafe snorted. He hoisted his coat-tails and stood so near the fire he made it draw better, Eliza was glad to note; but the heat made him kind of steam, too, in an unpleasant way.

"You might say the moon was pretty as an egg," he suggested, "but can the moon hatch? Can it?" he repeated.

"No," said Eliza feebly, "far as I know, it can't."

"You might say a rose was an egg's equal in the choice way it's made. But can a rose last a century, hold its shape till doomsday, if not broke, the way an egg can?"

"No," said Eliza, looking down at the seventeen she held, "I don't suppose it can."

"You might say," said Old Lafe, "an emerald's more precious than an egg, but which would you rather find on a desert island, Mrs. Birdwell, an emerald or an egg?"

"An egg," said Eliza, seeing what was expected of her but thinking all the same that if she'd just stepped off her boat for a little walk on a desert island and had had fried eggs for breakfast, she'd rather find an emerald.

"You see?" asked Lafe. "That being the case I never touch them. I ain't got a word to say against those who do, that's their lookout—but for myself I'd sooner think of busting a rainbow than cracking an egg. Whyn't you go set the eggs down some place, Mrs. Birdwell," he asked hospitably, seating himself in a rocker on his now well-warmed trousers, "and come back and we'll have a little chat? Weather's too mean to do anything outdoors."

The idea of getting rid of the eggs pleased Eliza anyway and she said, "Thank thee, friend Millspaugh, I'll do that," went into the kitchen and closed the door behind her.

There, sitting at his grafting table, his grafting tools laid aside, head thrown back, laughing till the tears ran down each side his big nose and got caught in the little grooves at the corners of his mouth, was Jess. Eliza regarded her husband coldly.

"Shanghai berries," Jess said, looking at the seventeen eggs. "My precious Shanghai berries. So thee'd rather have an egg than an emerald, Eliza?"

"Thee hush right up," Eliza told him, having listened to all the nonsensical talk about eggs she could stomach for one afternoon. "Thee hush right up and get in there and chat with thy neighbor."

"My neighbor?" said Jess.

"He's a man," Eliza said as if that made Jess responsible for him, "and thee get in there and talk."

Jess was tired of making grafts, so he went, and talked for quite a spell—time enough, anyway, for Eliza to stir up the fire in the cookstove and put another batch of custard pies in the oven. "Shanghai berries, indeed," she said, cracking eggs vigorously and giving no thought to the perfection she was ruining. "If Jess thinks eggs are so funny he can just eat a few more and laugh."

The pies had been in the oven some time when Jess came back into the kitchen. "Friend Millspaugh's a mighty interesting old codger, Eliza. Notionate as all get out, but interesting. He's leaving now and wants his hat. What'd thee do with it?"

"He's bareheaded when he came as far as I remember," Eliza said. "If he had a hat he must've dropped it some place in the sitting room. Anyway I didn't see it."

Jess was back in no time. "His hat, Eliza," he said, "was what the eggs was in. What did thee do with it?"

Eliza regarded Jess solemnly. "Jess," she said, "I burned it. How's I to know it was a hat? Looked more like a hen nest to me. Lice and all. Anyway it's gone," she said. "I'm baking custard pies with it. What's to be done?"

"Fine how-to-do," Jess fumed. "First time a neighbor calls, burn up his hat. Well," he said glumly, "nothing for it, I guess, but to go in and say, 'Friend, my wife says she's baking custard pies with thy hat.' Thee sure thee burned it, Eliza?" he asked.

"Oh, Jess," said Eliza impatiently. "Thee think I'm blind? I shoved it in with the poker and I saw it blaze. Thee go on in. Thee tell him I burned it by mistake."

"Don't sound much like a mistake to me," Jess said doubtfully. "Pushing it in with a poker."

"It was a mistake to burn it," Eliza explained, "turning out as it does to be his hat."

"Well," said Jess, pausing at the sitting room door, "I reckon this'll put an end to any neighboring between us and friend Millspaugh."

Jess was mistaken about that though. Old Lafe was not a man to hold a grudge and Eliza hadn't burned his only hat. He was soon back, wearing, so far as Eliza could see, the egg-container's twin, ready to further instruct and edify.

"Won't thee stay for supper?" Eliza asked him one evening, seeing that he was staying anyway, and feeling that an invitation would dignify the occasion. "Jess's not back from town yet, but we won't wait. Thee knows how Jess is, once he gets talking."

"Thank you," said Old Lafe, "I will. The smell of that cobbler

decided me to say yes—if I's asked—some time back. I'm a fair
hand at cooking for myself, but baking's beyond me. A cobbler'll
be a treat."

Eliza would've asked him for a meal before only Old Lafe was
a kind of strong object to set down amidst the aroma of well-
cooked victuals; but now, seeing his pleasure, her conscience smote
her. Thee's getting too fine-haired, Eliza, she chided herself. Letting thy nose instead of thy heart direct thee. Poor lone old fellow,
so high-minded he won't even crack an egg, and honing for company. Nothing amiss with him that soap and water won't remedy
—and that's more than can be said of most.

Soap and water she set forth in plentitude on the wash bench
outside the house and said in an offhand way, "Here's where we
wash before eating, friend Millspaugh. The boys," she told him,
intending to show washing was a custom of the family and nothing devised simply to fit his need, "have finished and the girls and
I do ours inside. Thee just take thy time," she said encouragingly,
"and when thee's finished supper'll be ready."

Old Lafe seemed to somehow shrink inside his vestments at the
sight of that big basin of steaming water (cold'll never do the
trick, Eliza had decided) like a sinner brought to holy fount.

"Here's the towel," Eliza told him cheerfully, "and soap of my
own making." She put the bar in Lafe's reluctant hand.

He set it down at once and brushed his hand against his pants
as if he'd got hold of a nettle. "Ma'm," he said, "I wouldn't dare."

"Thee wouldn't what?" Eliza asked, thinking she'd misheard.

"I wouldn't dare," Old Lafe repeated. "If I wet so much as a
finger, Mrs. Birdwell, my whole body pants and thirsts after water.
One splash of water and my whole body twitches for a taste of
water like a desert under a noonday sun. If I touched that," he
said, backing away from the wash basin, "I'd have to go jump in
the rain barrel. I'd have to run waller in the horse-trough to satisfy my craving. And that'd never do. Man my age, company for
supper to boot, roistering around in the horse-trough. "No," he

said, and picked up the basin with great care and poured its contents gently on the gravelly spot at the foot of the windmill, "it'd never do to chance it.

"And now," he said, replacing the basin, "I don't know've any reason for keeping that good cobbler of yours waiting longer. They ain't any eggs in it, is they?"

"No," said Eliza feebly, "no eggs." She stood, somewhat dazed, watching the last of the water drain away through the gravel.

"No point loitering, is they?" asked Old Lafe.

"No," said Eliza again, "no point I know of. Thee go right on in, friend Millspaugh," she said, taking, herself, a long last breath of summer air, "and seat thyself."

When Jess heard her report, he scoffed. "Women," he said, as if that explained all.

"Women," repeated Eliza. "How's I responsible for Lafe Millspaugh's craving water all over?"

"Thee should have called his bluff, Eliza."

Eliza lay over onto her side of the bed. "If thee thinks, Jess Birdwell, that I'm going to provide baths for thy cronies before they eat, thee's mistaken. Have my kitchen splashed and naked men sashaying around."

"Wait till next time," Jess said comfortably. "Wait till Old Lafe says that to me."

Eliza waited—and when the time came stayed clear of kitchen and porch, leaving Jess to handle the washing matter in whatever way he saw best; but when Lafe sat down to table he was as plainly undiluted by water as ever in his life, and Jess, in spite of all Eliza's questionings, was mighty close-mouthed about what had taken place.

"His whole body thirsting, indeed," Eliza said. "Whyn't thee call his bluff, Jess?"

"I'm a-going to, Eliza. Thee just bide thy time. I'm a-going to give friend Millspaugh such a drink as will set his cravings at rest.

Going to provide him a draught to suit his thirst—all at once and all over. The way he says it has to be."

Then and there, as Eliza afterwards supposed, that outlandish idea was hatched in Jess' head. Or maybe not. Maybe it was a notion he'd long held and Old Lafe had only roused it up again; but if Old Lafe had any connection with it save as carpenter for its building, Jess never admitted it. To hear him talk, all was planned for her comfort, only; though that planning was pretty far advanced before Eliza got any wind of it.

She was stepping through the house, fluting and flying Jess would have said, glorying in the summer weather. "What would thee change?" she asked herself.

Have the warm wind which was lifting the curtains die down? Have the peaches which were ripening, ripe? Have Lafe and Jess, who were on the back porch talking, silent? Have it another hour, another house, another season?

No, no! This hour, this house, this season. All was as it should be. It was one of those contented peaks a woman reaches and clings to. Not a thing clamoring to be done, not so much as a piece of lint beneath the hired man's bed to keep the mind from resting.

The parlor eased the eye; furniture ranged as neat as checkermen before playing disturbs them. The sitting room was like a welcoming hand: chairs saying, Sit and rock; flowers saying, Sniff and smell. Eliza sat and rocked. She rose and sniffed and savored. She did not see that anything could be bettered. The satin rose on one end of the mantelpiece (clear red with thin petals like silk) balanced the velvet rose (deep red, heavy as plush) upon the other. But not quite, perhaps. Eliza moved the velvet rose a fraction to the right. Now, all was perfect. She stepped along the yellow line of the rag carpet toward the kitchen door, moving inside the picture she had made, the way a painter, differences between air and canvas being ignored, might saunter down a lane his own brush had traced.

She paused on the kitchen threshold, hearing with pleasure Jess' deep-chested tones and Old Lafe's thin ones blending together on the summer air, like bumble bee and wasp.

Then she heard, with no pleasure at all, a word said and quickly repeated.

"Nekid," said Old Lafe Millspaugh. "Mother-nekid. Stretched out in that room, not so much as a pair of drawers between you and your Maker. Not so much as a G-string to signify you're man or fish. A carnal room, Jess Birdwell, a fester on the township, a downright invitation to . . ."

Eliza shut the door firmly behind her and heard no more. She sat again in the sitting room, she rocked and sniffed but she got no pleasure from it. Perfection was a hollow thing after all. A petal from the velvet rose fell to the floor. Eliza let it lie. What was Jess up to now?

Whatever it was it rested easy on his conscience. After Old Lafe left he tiptoed (Eliza could hear) across her freshly scrubbed kitchen, came into the sitting room and stood smiling down upon her. "I declare, Eliza," he said, "thee has things so redd up I'm afraid to set my feet down flat."

Eliza wasn't a whit taken in by all that show of docility and bidability. Jess was what he'd always been, a mighty slippery man to handle once he had an enterprise on foot. Then, for all his mild talk, he could set his feet down mighty flat as Eliza well knew.

She watched him stoop down now, mild as Moses, pick up the fallen petal and rub it gently back and forth across his ruddy cheek. "Thee ever remember a better year for roses, Eliza?" he asked.

Eliza rocked.

"Well," said Jess, "day's closing in. I'd best get back to work."

Eliza stopped rocking. "Jess," she asked, "didn't I hear thee and Old Lafe talking?"

"Why, Eliza," Jess said, "I wouldn't know. I just wouldn't have any way of knowing short of thy telling me. Did thee?"

"Yes," said Eliza, "I did."

Jess seemed perfectly agreeable to talk on the subject. "Lafe's a notionate old fellow, ain't he?" he asked. "But pious and workbrickel as all get out," he assured her. "Don't know a better carpenter anywheres."

"Jess," said Eliza, seeing he'd have to be pinned down, "who's this person Old Lafe spoke of, stretched out"—and Eliza paused hunting suitable words—"undressed?"

"Me," said Jess blandly.

"Thee," said Eliza aghast. "Where?"

"In my own bathroom, Eliza, soaking the dirt off, taking my ease."

It was all planned and ordered, designed solely for Eliza's comfort; and it would be not only a means of lessening labor and increasing cleanliness, but reason for civic pride: the first room of its kind west of the Ohio, surely—who knows but west of the whole range of the Alleghenies; Jess couldn't've been more stirred had politics been his subject or religion. It would be no trick at all for a carpenter of Old Lafe's skill: a part of the back porch next the kitchen would be enclosed; the tub itself would be made of metal, water flowing in from the windmill tank and drained away by pipes toward the kitchen garden where it wouldn't be wasted.

Eliza grabbed at a straw in the passing flood. "I don't know's I'd care for vegetables watered by bath leavings," she said.

Jess stared at her. "Thee taking a stand against fertilizing, too?" he asked.

Eliza saw she'd made a mistake. Jess swept on. The water could also by a very simple piece of work be warmed by winding water pipes about in the stove, a thing he'd often thought of. It would be a good-sized room. "Paint it a pretty color," Jess said. "Put a nice rag rug on the floor to catch the drippings. No reason why there shouldn't be a stove in there in winter to warm it. It'd be a pace-maker, Eliza, a thing we'd be noted for."

Eliza didn't doubt it for a minute. "We'd be noted for it," she agreed. "We'd be a by-word," she lamented, "known throughout the countryside for lolling about with our clothes off."

"No need to loll," Jess said. "Jump in and jump out."

"It'd be a temptation," Eliza warned. "The room so warm and the tub so sizeable."

"See," Jess pressed his advantage. "Thee admits it would be comfortable."

"Comfort," Eliza said with dignity, "is not the whole thing in life, nor what a bath's for, Jess Birdwell. Cleanliness, let me remind thee, is the object there."

"It'd be cleaner," Jess said. "More water and a chance to rinse. Thee'd be cleaner."

"Jess," Eliza said, her black eyes getting blacker, "is thee suggesting I'm not clean?"

"No," shouted Jess, heated both by enthusiasm and irritation. "By sugar, I didn't say that. Thee's the cleanest person I know."

"Then thee needn't build a bathroom for me," said Eliza reasonably. "It'd just be carrying coals to Newcastle."

"Eliza," Jess said, "thee's got less interest in new and better ways of doing things than anybody I know. Except that a series of enterprising, forward-looking men's married into thy family from time to time, thee and thy women kinfolk'd still be living in caves and cooking over holes in the ground. Why, if the world was left to people like thee, we'd still be wearing skins."

"If the world was left to people like me," Eliza said with conviction, "we'd be all nearer the Garden of Eden."

Jess fairly hopped. "Eliza," he said, "thee had just as much to do with what happened in the Garden of Eden as I did. More, from all accounts I ever read. It wasn't my sex started talking to the snakes."

Then bethinking himself that Biblical disputation with Eliza was a thing he was always second best at, he changed his tack. "It's ordered, Eliza," he said firmly, "and for thy convenience. Old Lafe starts work tomorrow."

"Friend Millspaugh's against it," Eliza said. "I heard him plainly say"—Eliza paused before using Lafe's strong language, but, feeling there'd be no virtue in being mealy mouthed about so serious a matter, used his words—"I heard him plainly say it'd be a carnal room. Friend Millspaugh and I don't see eye to eye in many ways—but there we do. It'd be neighborhood talk, Jess, a room like that."

Jess set his feet down flat. "Lafe's starting work tomorrow morning. Thee'll live to thank me for this day's planning, Eliza."

"Friend Millspaugh's against it, Jess. He'll never do it."

"Friend Millspaugh's with bathrooms as with eggs," Jess said. "Eggs are not for him but he don't go around cracking his neighbor's eggs in despite. He's got the plans and he goes to work in the morning."

About one thing, anyway, Jess was right. Next morning Old Lafe went to work; but toward the end of the building Eliza came to feel, in spite of Jess' convictions, that to Old Lafe eggs were one thing and bathrooms another. At first the work went at a slapping pace, everything merry as a wedding bell and noisy as a foundry. All was finished but the partition on the morning Jess left for Madison to attend his yearly meeting of nurserymen: tub fashioned and set up, pipes laid and fitted, and water flowing through them sprightly as a side-hill spring.

Jess stood for a minute admiring the shape his dream had taken before going down to hitch up. "Nothing like this since Roman days," he said to Old Lafe.

"Recollect what happened to the Romans?" Old Lafe asked. Sourly, Eliza thought, though Jess didn't seem to note it.

"Ruled the earth," Jess said, then without giving Lafe time to dispute it, "Reckon this ought to be finished time I get home tonight."

"I reckon," Old Lafe said.

"Come home and wash the stains of travel away. It'll be something to look forward to," Jess said. He kissed Eliza and the children. "Might stir up something a little special for supper tonight," he suggested. "We'll kick up our heels a little. You eat with us, Lafe," he said. "Join in the celebration."

Eliza stirred up something special, Lafe stayed and heels were kicked up, though not, as Eliza could tell by midafternoon, in any way Jess had anticipated. Bathroom building, by then, had taken, even to Eliza's uninstructed eye, a strange turn.

She was of two minds about speaking to friend Millspaugh. In the first place, the matter being between Jess and him, she didn't know that her mixing in it would be suitable. In the second place, she sympathized with Lafe. Building that room must've gone against his grain, for more reasons than one, as it did against hers. Not truly un-Christian, she supposed, but moving toward an ease and a laxness which was far removed from the early churches' admonitions.

At day's close she ventured a question. "Is that," she asked, indicating the boards Old Lafe was securely pounding in place, "part of Jess' plan?"

Old Lafe took the nails out of his mouth. "Ma'm, your husband said, 'Build a partition here.' No more. I'm doing that. If he'd meant more he'd ought to've said it. I don't set myself up to be any mind reader. Don't peep into tea cups nor peer in crystal balls. The whole room's a mistake if you ask me. But nobody asked me. I'm doing what I's told." He put the nails back into his mouth and took up pounding where he'd left off.

He'd finished his work and was sitting outside on the wash bench, peacefully smoking, when Jess turned in the driveway that evening. Eliza hearing him seated Jane and Stephen at the long table in the cool dining room. "It'll be a little space," she told them, "before supper's dished up, but you're to sit where you are and be quiet."

She herself returned to the back porch to await Jess. Jess was a good man, she knew, but he wasn't red-haired for nothing, and there was no point having the children within ear shot if words were to be said. She didn't have long to wait. Jess hastened with the unhitching and in no time at all was coming up the path between the currant bushes.

"Wash up for supper, friend," he called to Old Lafe in passing, asking for trouble as Eliza could plainly see; then bounded up the porch steps to have a look at the finished room.

His look turned to a stare. The room was finished all right; it was finished to a fare-ye-well, sealed tighter than a tomb and neater than a beehive; boarded from top to bottom, not so much as a crack left of a size for an underfed gnat to squeeze through, let alone a good-sized and well-fed Quaker.

"Why, the old vinegar cruet," Jess said low and unbelieving.

He said it low, but Old Lafe heard him, mounted the steps two at a time, protesting as he came. "Never said a word about it," he shouted. "Not a word. I listened for it. I kept my ears pricked. Heared you talk about a tub, talk about pipes, talk about drainage, talk about a partition. Heared you talk about the Romans. But never a word about a door. I thought it was peculiar—I'd have a door myself, I told myself, but every man to his fancy. Jess Birdwell's a man who knows his own mind, and if he don't want a door, that's his business. I ain't no mind reader. I don't pretend . . ."

Jess interrupted him. "Thee old vinegar cruet," he repeated, as much with admiration as anything, it sounded to Eliza; still he had laid aside his hat and was taking off his First Day coat.

Eliza waited to see no more. She hastened to the dining room, and there with the children hovering about her listened anxiously to the sounds from the back porch: words only, at first, an equal number high-pitched and deep-chested, but neither kind, Eliza feared, with any hint that what was to come would be a love-feast.

"Will pa get hurt?" asked Jane tremulously.

"Certainly not," said Eliza. "Thy pa's a strong man."

It wasn't Jess' getting hurt Eliza feared, it was what he might do. Once when riled by a traveling huckster he had belabored the fellow with one of his own saucepans, and though he had grieved about it afterwards, worried and prayed over it, still he'd done it.

The voices gave way presently to other sounds: boards cracking, saws ripping, the squeal of nails being pulled out. I reckon Lafe has heard by now, Eliza thought, the word he listened for and didn't hear. I reckon Jess has told it to him in no uncertain terms. Then the ripping and cracking ceased and all was quiet except for the gurgling sound of running water.

"Is pa going to take a bath before supper?" Stephen asked.

Eliza certainly hoped so but she doubted it; far more likely she feared that Jess was going to give a bath before supper, thuds and snorts and grunts now coming from the bathroom. Eliza tightly clasped her hands. This, then, was what Jess called the march of civilization . . . the whole house shivering with the force of someone's fall or sliding . . . civilization, as far as she was concerned, was rapidly going down hill.

I hope and pray, she thought . . . Then Jess began to speak and she and the children held their breaths to better make out his words.

"Swim, friend," they heard him say. "Satisfy thy cravings. Quench thy thirst and break the drought," these admonitions being terminated by a mighty splash.

The splashings were still continuing when Jess walked into the dining room, sleeves rolled up, breathing hard and considerably dampened by water.

"You young uns take your places," he said shortly, seating himself at the end of the table opposite Eliza.

"Do him a world of good," he said heartily, as if expecting to be contradicted; but no one said a word, and Eliza could tell by the look he gave her before he bowed his head for grace that he wasn't easy in his mind.

Jess didn't keep his head bowed long though. No sooner had he shut his eyes than out from the carnal room, high pitched but strong, came Old Lafe's voice singing. Loud and happy, if not tunefully, he was declaring,

> Yes, we'll gather at the river,
> The beautiful, the beautiful river.

"Sounds as if he'd caught sight of Jordan's flood," Jess said, nodding down the table to Eliza as much as to say I told thee so. Then he did a thing Eliza could never remember his having done before. He let grace pass by with that short shutting of his eyes—no more'n a wink, really—and said, "Cleanliness, being, as it is, next to godliness, and seeing how much has been accomplished in that line tonight, let us eat."

Eliza was taken aback, but Jess said, "First time, not counting rains and heavy dews, friend Millspaugh's been wet in thirty years. But I's satisfied he'd take to it once the shock'd worn off."

Jess nodded his head in time to the strong beat of Old Lafe's song. "Ain't that pretty?" he asked. "Ain't that downright sweet?"

Eliza didn't feel she could go that far, considering Old Lafe's voice, but the words he sang, she supposed, were a kind of blessing in themselves.

> Gather with the saints at the river
> That flows by the throne of God.

"Well, well," said Jess with the air of a man who has earned his food, "will thee kindly pass the gravy, Eliza?"

Eliza, seeing the turn events had taken, passed it.

THE MEETING HOUSE

ONE of Jess' bad times came upon him the night before he was to start south delivering nursery stock. Spring had been late that year and the April nights had the frostiness of a season working toward greater coldness, not greater heat. The stars still held to their winter's outlines, sharp and frigid with none of spring's spreading luminosity; the breath on the night air was long and white, and the body was only truly warm in bed, or close to a fire.

Jess stepped in from the porch where he had gone for a look at the sky and went to the fire. There with fingers opening and closing he seemed to be trying to roll warmth into a ball to take to bed with him.

"Eliza," he said, "it comes over me that this trip I ought to have a last look at the meeting house where my parents worshiped."

"A last look, a last look." That told Eliza all she needed to know. She dropped the carpet rags she'd been sewing into her work basket and went to Jess' side. "Jess, Jess," she said.

Jess was a man who ordinarily looked outward and whose health permitted him to do so; from inside himself came none of those quaverings or raspings which cause others to question how they do, set them to examining liver and lights to discover how these organs are holding up in the long see-saw to fend off mortality. And for this reason he was more vulnerable than most. Some small defection, a grain or two too much quinine, or a rising on a sensi-

145

tive spot, and a remembrance of man's thin hold upon life swept in upon him.

Or in perfect health, standing on a small lift of ground in spring, giving his team a breather after plowing an uphill furrow, or in his own bed in the fall, the house creaking in a rising wind, he would think of young men, dead before their time: David's son, bright Absalom; John Keats, the poet. His own little Sarah. And without willing or anticipation, conviction of mortality would settle down upon him and he would walk back to the house with his team, or down the stairs in the morning, as the case might be, a man from whom life was ebbing. And once this pall had settled there was nothing in all logic to lift it from him. Why should it not be so? Why should he, Jess Birdwell, nurseryman, past middle age, the father of children, be spared when young men were taken? Young men whose feet had not touched a fraction of earth's arc and whose tongues were still burdened with saying how even that small segment blossomed? It was unreasonable to expect it. In all reason and with much sorrow Jess would look about him with eyes that said farewell.

"Jess," asked Eliza, "what is it?"

It was a hard thing to put into words, outwardly so trifling, so picayunish, even, Eliza might miss its meaning, fail to see what its course would likely be, and how fatal . . . since it was only that the wen, which, walnut-size, curved the skin at the base of his skull, was now growing. "Preparing to strike inward toward the brain," Jess said, touching it with solemn fingers.

"Has thee seen a doctor?" Eliza asked.

"No," Jess said. "Seems like I couldn't bear to hear it put into words."

For Eliza, who had borne seven children and been near death, not once, but often, though always too busy at the time to ruminate upon it, these seizures of her husband were very strange. Resigned and even cheerful as Jess often was, the days, for the time his conviction held, were bleak. He had said farewell to the finite—to her, and Maple Grove Nursery—and it was sorrowful and upsetting for Eliza to eat breakfast with a man who already looked at her as from the other side of a headstone.

Eliza yearned toward Jess but there was little she could say. His disease was like measles: lacking gentle treatment it struck inward, festered in silence. Nor did any reminder of bygone attacks, surmounted and lived through, help. Those deliverances had been providential—and a Providence which let young men die, must in time loosen its hold upon even the undeserving middle aged. It was in the nature of things sad, to be sure, but not unreasonable nor unexpected.

"Jess," said Eliza, looking up into his big-nosed, well-fleshed face, "I don't recall thee ever looking in fuller health."

Jess shook his head. "Its being so deceptive," he said, "is what makes it so dangerous. Far gone," he told her, "before thee gives it a thought."

"In my heart," said Eliza, who felt that organ to be the seat of Jess' troubles, and her own as capable as his of discernment, "nothing speaks to me of it."

Jess was gentle with her. He would spare her, in so far as this was possible, the pain of his going. "As for man," he reminded her, "his days are as grass . . . as a flower of the field he flourisheth . . . but the wind passeth over it and the place thereof shall know it no more."

He set out before sunup. He headed downpike into darkness and cold, leaving Maple Grove Nursery, the windows yellow with lamplight, behind him. He drove east and south. His fingers often left the lines to see how his wen did. There was no pain about it, but his heart would harden like a dornicker as he felt its unnaturalness beneath the skin. He, a live man, to die. He extended his hand, recalling its cunning, marveling at the way stiff, unpliable bones could be so cushioned and strung together as to be capable of music, of grafting a tree, of lifting a foal from its mother's torn flesh—and that hand to be dust. And the enemy present, carried with him as a passenger, the live hand feeling its outlines, recognizing the source of its dissolution.

The way of his going was laid out for him. He was delivering nursery stock ordered the fall before and he could not now ask himself which lane he'd fancy to turn up, which pass by. It was all settled, a foregone matter, the names in his order-book and the trees themselves well balled and covered with burlap behind him in the spring wagon. Already the ground which would nourish their thread-like roots was prepared and waiting and even now farmers were saying to their wives, "Call me up to the house if Birdwell, the nurseryman, comes. He's due any day now."

The names of his customers and the numbers and kind of stock they'd ordered were all there, written down six months before when he'd had no inkling of what delivery time would bring. For Jonas Rice, twenty-five Rambo, twenty-five Ben Davis. For Dade Devlin, six Early Beatrice, six Stump the World. For Eli Morningstar, two May Duke, six Flemish Beauty. For Abel Rivers, Jr., twelve Early Harvest.

Jess journeyed deep into spring, the meaning of his wen traveling with him, spreading out web-like to encompass landscape and people. He saw objects two ways, now, both as more beautiful and more pitiable: those which would stay, endure beyond men, stones, trees, the moving air, had new beauty, that of their own endurance and of his leaving; but men and women were more pitiable, his trouble added to their own until their cups were filled with sorrow, pressed down and running over.

Jess sat on the seat of his spring wagon. The wagon itself often seemed not moving: it standing still while scalloped hills and sun-yellowed winter wheat moved past him bringing him without effort of his own to the houses, the voices, the footsteps crossing the creaking floor-boards before the doors swung open and greetings were said. So deep was he settled inside himself and his own affliction, that he was hard put to separate the remembered from the imagined, his mind so busy running forward to the anticipated sorrow that he lost track of boundaries, saw no difference between yesterday and tomorrow.

At Jonas Rice's, surely, the gate had been off a hinge, hung si-gogglin' so that beneath the broken arc of its swing a brown furrow had been plowed in spring's green. A shingle blown from the roof in some past high wind still lay in the yard, tip-tilted now by the blunt, pushing leaves of a Chinese lily. On the porch a plank had rotted through and the trash from bygone sweepings was heaped almost to floor level in a faded cone. This, where in the fall there had been high plans, spruceness and the big order.

Jonas Rice himself led him in. "It's our young un," he told Jess. "It's Jasper. Taken with the little-growth, the doctor says, and no hope held out for getting shut of it."

Jasper lay in the parlor-bedroom in a dark bed which, with roof-tree and siding, would have made a house of rooms for him. He lay like the tiny little goody inside an out-size nutshell. The bed had head- and footboard curving like a sleigh and Jess thought driving along afterwards, "A poor peaked little grain of Rice for such a big conveyance."

"Seven years old," said Jonas Rice, "and dwindling backward toward the cradle. The little-disease, the doctor names it, shrinking backward to where he started from and not a thing to be done to stop it."

Mrs. Jonas Rice stood by the bed and smoothed the coverlid above her son; all the neatness and care which the rest of the house lacked, centered here.

"Jasper's body," she said, "is wasting toward nothingness, but it don't touch his mind. The little-growth, the doctor names it, but Jasper's got the big disease, I say, if you reckon mind and heart. Nothing he can't read or remember, and a heart set on goodness. Say the psalm for Mr. Birdwell, Jasper."

Out of the nut-sized face, the small voice: "The Lord is my shepherd. I shall not want."

✦

Wheels beneath him once again, Jess repeated the words Jasper had said, "The Lord is my shepherd, I shall not want," and remembered the way he had heard it said when he was a boy, "The shepherd I shall not want." A good and holy One, the Lord, no doubt, but not a Man you'd choose for a shepherd. His mind on other things and coming home at night, half the flock missing and no notion where He'd lost them. But why people were so fond of saying the Lord was a shepherd they didn't want, he had had no idea as a young un. Nor Jasper, either, like as not, lying in his big bed, dwindling back toward his beginning.

A pullet touched by spring and in love with dying beneath a horse's hooves, it seemed, flew up and down in front of the spring wagon. The little-disease, Jess meditated, is what we're all bit by. His fingers traced the outline of his wen . . . recoiling. Man's a sizeable hulk reared-up on his wagon seat and pulled about the earth by horses; dead, no more'n a spoonful of dust, not enough, spread thin, to take a small-sized horse track.

Old Eli Morningstar took delivery of his two May Dukes and six Flemish Beauties in a V of his land, leaning at the fence post of the angle. They were good trees, flourishing, the May Duke in season bearing a firm well-fleshed cherry; the Flemish Beauty, a pear whose taste was summer in the mouth. Jess forgot for a minute his trouble in pride of the trees he had grafted and raised but they were nothing to old Eli Morningstar. He set them aside as if they had been canes or switches, or a dried cat-tail, cut down and brought to him by a child.

"Mr. Birdwell," he asked, "how're you grounded in regards of religion? I have no mind to shake any belief of yours."

"Grounded deep enough," Jess said, "so's nothing thee can say will matter."

"When I's a child," Eli said, "I believed as a child, but now I've come to maturer thinking."

Jess looked into old Eli's eyes. They were like the screens a man sets across his windows, reflecting nothing, but hiding whatever lies beyond from sight.

"God's only begotten son," said old Eli, leaning across the fence rail in his earnestness. "Why only one, Jess Birdwell? Why only one? And why a son? Whyn't a daughter? Something fishy there, Jess Birdwell, and the more you think on it, the plainer it becomes. Something mighty fishy."

"Something mighty fishy" . . . Jess sat on his wagon seat and the weather warmed about him. A wind dropped down from the high sky like a shallow-winged bird, able to beat the air only a few times before tiring. The yellow spokes of the spring wagon flashed in the sun, its steel rims ran quietly through sand, or noisily across gravel. Trees were leafed out, sallow, now in their beginnings as they would be again in the time of fall. Small flowers, bed straw, buttercup and dog-tooth violet, were opening, and the dogwood, not small, lifted a spangle of white stars high in the spring woods.

"Me, only, decaying," Jess said in sorrow, hoping to find some change in his wen, feeling it always the same.

Dade Devlin's big house lay open to the midday sun, light shining on the fancy carpets and lace curtains.

"Dade Devlin," said his widow, "passed on six months ago. Short time after you're here. But we want the trees, my present husband and myself. My present husband is a master hand for fruit trees."

Jess, like any other man, had had his thoughts about women, but they never made up for him, out of whole cloth, women like Mrs. Devlin.

"Mrs. John Henry Little," she reminded him.

Judging by outward appearances was a sin Jess had tried to wean himself from, and Mrs. Little, for all she looked like an over-ripe peach, likely to spatter if shook loose from the limb, might be a spiritual woman beneath the billowings of flesh. Though crab or quince, Jess thought, while puckerish, were more to his taste and had better keeping qualities once summer was past.

"Meet John Henry," said Mrs. Little, as her husband, sleepy-eyed and in his sock feet, came to the door.

Jess had met John Henry before; last year he had been the Devlin's hired man. "He's younger'n me," said Mrs. Little gustily, "but a thousand years are as one in the sight of the Lord." She did not let her plumpness hamper her a whit in twining herself over and about John Henry's slab-sided frame. "A master hand with fruit," she said, "and at sweetheartin'."

Jess watched the rich farmlands roll past the spring wagon. Flesh, he thought, is the Lord's invention, and there's no call for me to fault it. God knows my own flesh is dear enough to me: that of my own body and that got by marriage and begot out of marriage. Dear enough. Nothing in me so fine-haired as not to be able to stomach Victoria Cinderella Devlin and her John Henry.

The sky was a deepening blue, and the sun each day seemed to hang nearer earth. Jess took off his coat, hunched his shoulders sunward, eager to meet it half-way, put its heat so deep into his bones that some of it, at least, would go to his grave with him, live beneath the sod and warm, in another spring, some needy root. He had come to the end of his list, three more deliveries and he could turn toward Fairhope Meeting House, and there reconcile himself as best he could to the promise his flesh bore: Scully's peach trees, Mrs. Mayhew's two gooseberry bushes, the Rivers' Early Harvests.

He came to the Rivers' where he planned to stay the night, the dusk of a clearing evening after a day of showers, an unsettled day fairing off just at nightfall as it often will. He had lodged here on his fall trip, found the house commodious and the Rivers, young people without children, clever to company. Nightjars were calling as he drove up the lane and the wheels of the spring wagon turned now and then through water. Apple trees bloomed in the dusk, the last of daylight seemingly sucked up into their white petals. He mounted the doorstep with a feeling remembered from forty years before: that a house was a strange place to come to after a day in the sun. There was no reply to his knocking, though he could see a flicker of light through the windows on each side of the door, and presently he made out a woman's voice bidding him enter.

The room he stepped into was not strange at all, nothing amiss, things set two by two, every chair in line with its brother, even the fire smoldering in an orderly way, no coal out of place. Beyond the center table with its unlit parlor lamp and albums, a little glass lamp lighted and turned low was burning on the wide sill above a cot-bed.

"Mrs. Rivers," Jess asked, "is thee sick?"

"I've been poorly for a time," Mrs. Rivers said, "and I had a kind of sinking spell this afternoon—but not sick. Just poorly."

Jess stood looking down onto the neat bed and onto Mrs. Rivers so neatly disposed beneath a kind of knitted throw that she scarcely curved its surface, feet and hipbones alone lifting the covering to show that the head with its great pile of black hair was not bereft of a body.

"Thee's wasted," Jess said, then bit his tongue; but he was shocked at the young face fined down to nothing but eyes, cheek bones, and mouth.

"The fever eats off the fat," Mrs. Rivers said, "but I don't reckon it takes anything you really need. Trims you down, takes what there's no need lugging around and makes you spryer. The fever burns fat, I reckon, the vay a wick does coal-oil." Mrs. Rivers lifted a hand fever had burned down to its essentials, turned the lamp higher and smiled. "Except for my own mother," she said, "I don't know's there's a person I'd be more pleased to see than you, Mr. Birdwell."

Jess, who had a mind now for his tongue, continued to stare: Poor child, he thought, the wick's sucked the lamp so near bone-dry, there's nothing left but the empty bowl—and a final spurt of flame.

"If thee's poorly," he said, "I'd oughtn't spend the night. Trouble thee, maybe. Put thee out."

"Put up your horses, Mr. Birdwell," said Mrs. Rivers. "I was laying here pining to speak with someone."

Jess smiled. "To tell thee the truth," he said, "they're up. Thee and thy husband were so clever to me last fall I been looking forward to staying here again. I brought thee a little present, too," he said. "Four of the Prairie Queen roses thee said thee'd like."

"Prairie Queen," said Mrs. Rivers in her voice which was half breathing, half spoken words. "Have you ever seen the prairies, Mr. Birdwell? I've often thought of them. High and even, they must be, like a hay field, running on without end, and a strong wind always blowing so it would be easy to breathe."

"Yes," Jess said. "I've seen the prairies. Like a dry ocean, the grass moving like waves."

"And a queen, Mr. Birdwell," Mrs. Rivers said, starting to laugh and stopping, because laughing made her cough. "You ever laid eyes on a queen yet, Mr. Birdwell?"

"No," Jess said. "No queen yet. But if I did she'd be black-haired like thee and Eliza."

"How's Eliza?" Mrs. Rivers asked, hiding her pleasure in talk. But before Jess had time to answer, she said, "I've lost my manners, Mr. Birdwell. Ask you questions and keep you standing. Draw up a chair."

Jess brought a chair to the cotside. "Eliza's flourishing," he said. "Full of health and good works. And thy husband? Is Abel about?"

"Abel's away for the minute. Stepped off for a spell." Mrs. Rivers lay quiet for a time, then she said: "You're like as not famished, Mr. Birdwell, delivering trees all day and feeding on chips and whetstones. And I'm in like case. Empty and famished. As soon as a little more of this faintness ebbs off I'll cook us up something tasty."

Mrs. Rivers' cheeks were burning and her black eyes with so little flesh about them blazed with excitement. "We'll have us a real social time, Mr. Birdwell. If you'd let me know you were coming I'd had the house redd up."

"Redd up," Jess said. "Why, things as neat as a bee-hive now.

Any neater and I'd've been afraid to set foot inside. Would've bedded down for the night on the doorstep, scared to cross the threshold."

Mrs. Rivers began to laugh again, then stopped. "Soon's it passes off," she said. "I got plenty of gravy-timber and fruit down cellar. I don't know how it is. In the mornings I'm spry as a two-year-old, but by sundown something gives way and I'm a hundred."

Jess stood up. "How is thee," he asked, "long about noon?"

"Twenty-three," she said, "at midmorning."

"Thy name's Lydia, ain't it?"

"Lydia Ann," Mrs. Rivers said.

"Lydia Ann," Jess said, "thee's young enough for me to be thy pa, and now I give thee an order. Thee's to lay there while I cook us up a bite. I'm a master hand at cooking. All I need to know is where to find matches, lamp and kindling. The rest I'll root out for myself."

"I'll do it," Lydia Ann said. "I'll lay here and it'll be a treat. The kitchen fire's not died out and the woodbox is full."

When Jess brought the food in Lydia Ann said, "You wasn't story-telling, was you? A real master hand." The side meat was hot and crisp, the gravy brown and just thick enough, neither soup nor pudding. There were soda biscuits to put it on and fried potatoes on the side.

"Cake," said Lydia Ann. "You never baked a cake."

"No," said Jess, "I didn't. That was a present to me a ways back from a lady, and I figured it was just the thing to go with thy canned pears."

"I never knowed food could taste so good. Cooking it, my appetite goes with the smelling and stirring."

"It's a pity," Jess said, "thy husband's not back to eat with us."

"He's where he chooses to be," Mrs. Rivers said. "He'll not be back the whole night more'n likely. Abel can't bear sickness, he says. A weak chest turns his stomach . . . the hacking, you know . . . and worse. He's found someone sound in wind. And limb too, I reckon."

They were finished with their eating and Jess carried the empty dishes into the kitchen, thinking: Here's the two of us, brought together under one roof on the same night. Outside, calm as forever, trees blossoming, owls hooting, and inside us two sickening. Trying to learn to loosen our hold on what we've spent half a century getting acquainted with.

The words half a century gave him pause. "Jess Birdwell," he asked himself fiercely, "what call's thee got to lump thyself with that girl? She's had no half century. She's had no children, got no one to do for her. Thee's got Eliza, strong enough to stomach any misfortune that'd come to thee and never flinch. Leprosy or plague'd never daunt Eliza. Thee's got no pain, no fainting spells, no need to lie lonely through the nights. Thee's an old fool, Jess Birdwell, saying 'the two of us.' Leave thyself out of this. Beside that girl, thee's traveling a flower-edged path. Think on her for a spell and ask God to forgive an old codger eat up with his own troubles."

He clattered the dishes for a while, shook down the ashes, blew his nose, and came back, shamefaced, into the sitting-room. He thought Lydia Ann might feel downcast or bashful because of what she'd said, but her words seemed to have passed from her mind. "Recruit the fire, Mr. Birdwell," she said. "Let's have us a big blaze."

Jess laid new logs on the fire. "Oak," he said. "Hard and long burning."

"I hope you're not thinking of turning bedwards, Mr. Birdwell. I hope you're set for visiting. I lay awake so much of nights, it'd be a treat to have someone to talk to for a change."

"Turning bedwards?" asked Jess. "Why, I wouldn't care it I didn't shut an eye this night. What's thee think on, nights thee can't sleep, Lydia Ann?"

"Times when I was a girl, mostly."

"Not so far back," Jess said, smiling.

"Far back seeming. Another person, almost. Happy and well."

"Ah, yes," Jess said. "Those years. Sound flesh and nothing to ever give the heart a jupe. Morning to nightfall, nothing but pleasure."

"I had a white dress, aged eight or ten, with strawberries printed on it as if they'd fallen there. A long dress, to the ground, not suited for work or best. A thing I'd taken a freak for and my mother made it up. Working nights, with little money or time, because I'd taken a freak in that direction."

"Yes," Jess said.

"I'd sit in a swing and it covered me to the toes, and I'd ride like a lady through the air, it blowing out on either side. Me and that mess of strawberries swooping through the air."

"A pretty picture," Jess said. "One to think on."

"My mother made it working night, going without something herself. When you study on it there's much loving-kindness in the world, Mr. Birdwell."

"Much," said Jess. "At this hearthside, too."

"At a pie supper once twelve boys took it into their heads to have my pie or none. They all bid on it, paid the price of a whole pie for a sliver, and the thirteen of us ate together. They made a song about me, those boys did, and sang it. It was midwinter and I remember watching it snow outside the schoolhouse while they sang. And one boy said anything I made was too precious to eat. So he put his sliver in a match box and said he'd keep it forever."

"What kind of pie was it?" Jess asked.

"Sweet potato."

"Likely gone bad by now."

The moon came up, and its light lay across the clean rag carpet. The oak log fell apart and Jess set another on the fire. A cricket reached the hour for playing, first tuned, then bowed its fiddle. Mrs. Rivers turned on her side so that she faced the fire and spoke in her low voice.

"In the Pigeon Roost country," she said, "quite a far step from here . . ." or "Once I had a cat who slept every night under the bedcovers, curled round my feet . . . a gray cat, a tabby with long white whiskers . . ." And after a while . . . "Promised to love and cherish . . . but a bad one from the beginning.

"The doctor," she whispered, "says . . . but I know better. Just a poorly spell, and I'll pick up with summer weather.

"A thing I'd like to know," she said, "is the names of all the rivers—or maybe all the trees. They'd be nice to say over in the night."

A cock on a near-by farm, roused by moonlight into thinking morning had come, crowed and a Rivers cock answered him. "I'm downright unmannerly," said Mrs. Rivers. "Talk all night myself, and you the company. And there's things I'd like to hear you speak of, Mr. Birdwell. Places you've been and how you've fared."

"Where've I been?" Jess asked, "and how've I fared?" He stood up at the bedside. "Well, I'll tell thee, Lydia Ann, I've been a good piece—" and he thought, I'll tell her how I do. Let her see how it stands with me. It'll maybe comfort her to know suffering's ladled out to all, not any one man's burden to bear alone—and he laid his hand to his wen and found it loose and easy beneath the skin, the size it had been for twenty years, not growing, not striking inward, a trifling little lump, less than egg-size, harmless as a summer squash, and not to be thought of twice by any man in his senses.

"You feeling dauncy, Mr. Birdwell? Did you maybe stand up too fast?"

"No," Jess said, "I maybe got to my feet just in time." But he didn't take his hand down from his neck, making sure his deliverance didn't lay in any manner of feeling his wen, but in its real nature . . . a small lump, the same as his father'd had before him, a wen and no more dangerous than a freckle.

"You got something wrong with your neck, Mr. Birdwell? Got a crick in it?"

"I got a crick in my head," Jess said, "but like as not the healthiest neck this side of the Ohio. Other side either, for that matter."

He was walking about the room, testing the new and innocent meaning of his wen, crossing and re-crossing the bar of moonlight that silvered the rag carpet. He put two logs at a time onto the fire and used the poker so that a stream of sparks flowed upward like a column from a fountain.

"You've come to a kind of waking-up spell, haven't you?" asked Mrs. Rivers.

"Yes," Jess said. "I have for a fact. Wide awake. Thee asked me where I'd been and how I'd fared. I've been quite a step, Lydia Ann, and fared mighty well the whole ways. If a man'd fared any better'n me it'd unsettled his mind. I've had two eyes and seen sights so pretty there's no words to duplicate them. I've drunk the wine of astonishment, Lydia Ann, standing still, gazing. I've had two feet and no better land anywhere to walk on. Green plush grass in spring, and leaves like a carpet in fall. I've smelled white clover in daytime and quenched my thirst with live spring-water. I've earned my bread in the sweat of my brow, and still do, hard-scrabble like any other man, but making out. I've had for wife the one woman I'd choose, and been free to lift my voice to God. Though mighty backward, I reckon, in making out what He's had to say to me. I've fared so well," Jess said, moving his hand off his trivial wen and up across his jaw, already in need of morning's shaving, "that a jot more'n I'd be crying."

He was already, if tears make crying, but he was smiling, too, and pacing back and forth.

"It's like a party we're having, isn't it, Mr. Birdwell?"

"Yes," said Jess, "it is. And I'd give thee for a party present, if I could, a share of the ease I've had in my faring. Thee could put it in a matchbox, like the piece of pie, to keep forever."

Mrs. Rivers smiled at Jess as if she knew his wish to make that gift was real. He was standing now before the fire, seemingly finished with speaking, and Mrs. Rivers, not yet ready for sleep, asked him another question. "You've said how you've done," she told him, "but not where you've been. Name the places for me to remember when you're gone."

Jess turned from the fire and named the places: east as far as Philadelphia. North to Chicago. South to Natchez, Baton Rouge, Louisville. West past unnamed clearings and settlements. While he named the places, said what business had called him there and how the cities stood, on the bluffs overlooking the water or spreading across the upper reaches of a valley like a dam, Mrs. Rivers slept. Jess found another cover and laid it across her, thinking, Deserving don't cut much figure in this life. He banked the fire and came back to sit by the cot. As soon as a little grayness seeped into the room he went outside, noiselessly, hitched his horses and turned homeward.

Eliza'd had a strong feeling all day that he was coming and was waiting for him at the bottom of the driveway when he turned in at nightfall. Jess helped her up onto the seat beside him.

"Thee make out all right, Jess?" Eliza asked, anxiously feeling about for the right words.

"Yes," Jess said, "I did."

"How'd thee find thy customers?"

"Different ways," Jess said. "Marrying. Sickening. Meditating on the Lord. Taken with the little-disease."

"Thee," Eliza asked hesitatingly . . . "get to Fair Hope Meeting House?"

"No," Jess said, "I didn't. I turned homeward soon's the last order was delivered."

"I thought thee said . . ." Eliza began.

"I did," Jess answered with some asperity, "but boards don't make the only meeting houses, Eliza. Here's a spot too, for praying and learning," and Jess tapped his solid chest.

Eliza had never doubted it. She scanned Jess' face in the growing dark. "Thee . . . the swelling thee had . . . ?" she asked delicately.

"Thee means my wen," Jess told her, unabashed. "No swelling. A matter of twenty years' standing. A trifle. A thing I never give a thought to."

Eliza leaned back with a little sigh.

"How's things gone here, while I been away?"

"The cold snap held for quite a spell," said Eliza, "but it's moderated recently. Lilies-of-the-valley opened yesterday."

Jess lifted his big nose and sniffed the air of home. "I can smell them from here, seems like," he said.

THE VASE

J ESS, who had planned the day for work, tried to turn it to some use by regarding the rain which had spoiled it. He walked restlessly from the sitting-room window on the left of the front door to the sitting-room window on the right; but there was no difference in the rain. From either place he saw it fall in a great sheet which, the house splitting, set himself, he figured, in the center of a cavern of water, set him like the clapper in the middle of a sounding bell. He silent, the bell itself resounding with the clatter which water, dropped from a great height, makes on a shell of almost empty clapboard (beds, stoves, carpets, a human being or two in no wise filling it).

He sent his hearing out beyond the house, testing his belief that the ear alone can tell winter rain from summer, and had his belief bolstered, for rain falling upon trees in full leaf has a gentle huskiness which the bare and rigid limbs of winter cannot duplicate.

Jess, who was no great hand at hiding the light of his knowledge beneath a bushel of silence, called out to Eliza, and she, her bread set, came in from the kitchen.

"Thee call me, Jess?" she asked, wiping her hands, rosy from the kneading, on her apron.

"Eliza," Jess said, "blindfolded, thee could tell the sound of rain in winter from rain in summer."

"I couldn't," Eliza said flatly.

Jess regarded his wife morosely. Among women Eliza was, he

knew, peerless; but all women he sometimes feared were flawed, whether in their making or by a throwing away of their natural heritage, he couldn't say.

"Ain't thee interested in knowing how?" he asked. "Ain't thy curiosity pricked? Don't natural phenomena mean anything to thee?"

Some did, some didn't. The sound rain made was one that didn't. Bread rising, house shining, fire dozing on the hearth, these were phenomena, and natural, too, Eliza supposed, and for the time being quite enough for her. "Jess," she said, "I don't see any point being blindfolded and trying to tell winter rain from summer. Leave it off," she advised with great practicality, "and save the guesswork."

Jess turned away from the windows and the rain. Women were too much for him. Still, never despairing of lightening their dark, he said, "Rain on leaves makes a different sound from rain on bare limbs."

"In a stand of pine," Eliza objected, "thee'd have to take thy blindfold off."

Jess sighed. He walked to the secretary which filled a great part of the wall on the south side of the door to the kitchen. "I wasn't speaking of evergreens," he said.

There on the middle shelf of the secretary, in a small clearing between books, stood other reminders of woman's strangeness. A queer race, Jess thought, gazing at the set-out, related to us by marriage but mighty odd in spite of it. What were these objects Eliza had saved, set forth like rarities in a museum, preserved, while articles of greater use were lost and broken? A fragment of stone from the chimney of the old log house, a circle of shining wood stamped "Holy Land," but having, to Jess, the look of a piece of local butternut, well polished; a dried orange fetched home from New Orleans, a thimble which Eliza believed had been used in sewing a rent in William Penn's breeches, six feathers small and much faded, plucked long ago from some California bird and lodged now in a squat red cup; a thing of glass, which

Jess in twenty years of seeing had never been able to fathom, and
which he now took from the secretary and turned about in his
hands.

"What's thee call this thing, Eliza?"

"A vase," Eliza said.

"It couldn't very well be a vase," Jess told her reasonably. "It's
open at both ends."

"A vase," Eliza said, "is what I've come to call it."

Jess held it off. He peered through it. He ran his thumb over
the putty swans, set up above the surface of the glass, he traced
the fluting at the top which putty had enlarged. "Looks like it
started life as a lamp chimney," he said.

"It did," said Eliza.

"A broken one at that."

"Yes," said Eliza, "it was broken."

She took the vase from Jess and curved her white, plump fingers
about it, the fingers which at the time of the vase's making had
been neither white nor plump, but pink and thin like bird's legs,
and as quick in their movements as bird's legs, too.

"Thee's made a neat thing of it," Jess admitted. "Ornamental."
But he had, in all truth, to add, "Useless though. Painted over
so's it won't do for a chimney. Open at both ends so's it won't
serve as a vase. When'd thee make it?"

"Thee saw it the morning I started it."

"I took no notice."

"No," Eliza said, remembering, "thee didn't."

"What'd thee aim," Jess asked, "making it?" Knowledge of his
suppleness, turning in two minutes and with good grace from a
scientific contemplation of rain's varying sounds to an examination
of a misnamed dido, filled him with content.

Eliza, who had been facing the fire, which lay on the hearth
like a red eye, angry with the sight of so much water falling, turned
to face her husband. She touched the vase, scalloped top and
swelling sides. What was her aim? There were more aims in it,
maybe, than she knew, and even if she knew them all, could name

and number them for Jess, would he understand? He, who had seen her when the first swan, buoyant upon its painted ripples, was still wet from her brush—and not noted—would he understand now, so many years later? When the colors on the vase were beginning to fade?

There was one purpose clear enough for her to see and say certainly.

"I aimed to make a pretty thing, Jess."

Yes, that was true. That in the beginning had been her whole aim. A spattering of water dashed against the hot lamp chimney had snapped a circle from it, but she had not thrown it away; she had set the chimney on the pantry shelf, remembering a neighbor's saying that such a broken thing could be so painted and decorated as to be an ornament to any parlor. It had stayed there a long time, waiting an hour when, work slackening, she could set a picture onto its glassy bareness. And as the days passed it gave her pleasure, stepping in and out of the pantry to see it waiting. Between all the necessary thoughts of cooking a design to set upon the chimney began to work itself out in her mind, a plan which in the midst of kitchen traffic opened a place of quiet and aloneness for her.

Jess, watching her turn the vase about in her hands, said nothing, so she repeated her words. "I planned it to be an ornament, Jess. A pretty thing for our parlor."

Could Jess understand that? Prettiness outside, Jess understood, she knew. Many a time he'd roused her, just fallen asleep, to look at the stars, had carried many a flower inside to her, had called out to her to look at a cloud, a sky at sundown, a bird, a curious stone, even. But prettiness inside? Did pillow shams thick with satin stitch and French knots give him a smidgin more pleasure than unbleached muslin bare as when it came from the looms? Did it matter to him whether there were peacock feathers over the grate and gilded cat-tails in the corner? She thought not.

But a woman lived in a house, not outdoors. A sunset didn't

come inside, light the wall behind the kitchen range so's she could see it while cooking supper; clouds taking this shape or that didn't settle down on the mantelpiece to keep her company while mending. The prettiness a woman saw, she had to make, she had to build it up from odds and ends. Did Jess ever note her handiwork? The articles embroidered, painted, stenciled, gilded, dyed? The combcases, footstools, doilies, tidies, fire screens, rugs, penwipers, lambrequins? Did he see how the bareness of timber and stone had been hidden and softened, until the room, to her eye, showed itself as prettier than any cloud, and not to be outdone, even, by a rose.

Jess thrust out a finger, touched one of the swans. "An ornament for our sitting room," he said. "Time on end."

Eliza noted he didn't say pretty. Well, that didn't matter. It had come to mean more to her than prettiness, anyway.

"Jess," she said, "I don't know but what in case of fire this'd be the first thing I'd save."

Jess looked anew at the object she held. "Before the family Bible?" he asked. "The letters? The deeds?"

"For those," Eliza said, "I could count on thee."

"But for some things, not?"

Eliza said nothing.

Jess' big nose wrinkled at the bridge. The lines that ran downward from cheekbone to jaw deepened. His large, well-muscled mouth moved a little as if he were savoring beforehand the words he was about to say.

"There are those," he said, "who say I carry thee around on a chip, Eliza. Figger me a poor apron-tied old fellow, married to a female preacher and not able to call his soul his own."

Eliza knew this to be true; still, for all they said, there were things Jess was not to be counted on for. Or maybe, not Jess. Maybe man, any man.

Jess remembered temperatures: ten below or 102° in the shade. He remembered the dimensions of snow-drifts and the number of

inches that had fallen in a single cloudburst. Eliza remembered
how she had felt and from this determined season and weather.

She had started her vase on a summer morning, she knew, for
she could remember how warm she had felt standing in her nightdress by the bed. In the half-light Jess was only a shadowy mound
beneath the covers, stirring a little as he settled toward deeper
sleep. It was before sunup and outside, birds, rousing, sang their
short easy songs, the ones which could be performed while half
awake.

It was earlier than rising time, but she had no sleep left in her
and was too happy to lie still any longer. In a moment's musing,
she then seventeen, there had come to her such bliss in a sudden
picturing of what her life and Jess' might be, that she felt she
must be out of bed, and advancing toward it; moving forward
into the opening years, toward the children, toward the May
mornings and snowy evenings, toward the fine housewifery and
lovingkindness, toward the old age when she and Jess, sleepless
through the long nights as old people are, would say, Remember,
remember, as they lay listening to wind or rain. It all came to
her that summer morning on waking and she had to be up out of
bed and hastening to meet it.

She carried her clothes downstairs, walking silently with bare
feet across floor-boards still warm with yesterday's heat. She
washed in soft cistern-water and dressed in the kitchen. She wished
that Jess might have been hungry for seven breakfasts in one so
that she could have cooked every dish she'd ever heard him say
he fancied: buckwheat cakes, soda biscuits, sausage gravy, tender-
loin, ham with its taste of salt and hickory smoke.

The fire caught and blazed. The fruity, summer air had to take
the column of autumn smelling smoke with what grace it could.
Biscuits cut and dolloped with cream waited the oven. Her nightdress was folded as precisely as if measured. The best cups were
on the table. Psalm 101 had been read and meditated. But it was
not enough. Bliss was not yet served. It was then she remembered
her vase.

She brought chimney, putty and paints from the pantry and

sitting at the kitchen table, the design, known to her mind a long time, became now a separate thing, began now to live outside herself, and there, seemed able in its expression of her happiness to hasten her advance into the life she had imagined.

Her fingers, remembering flowers, enlarged with putty the meager crimping at the chimney's top to petal-sized scallops. Over the break, mended with putty, she molded a plumed swan, a great bird with arched breast and flaunting tail. About the swan she painted blue water and green reeds and the swan itself she made a dazzling white. Overhead was the sky of summer across which long thin clouds like frayed pencils drifted, and the frayings, all raveling out toward the same direction, made it seem as if a wind, light but persistent, blew across the picture.

There were to be two swans, finally, but now Eliza rested. She rose and walked from the table, set the biscuits to baking and moved the skillets to the front of the stove. Still, it was not they, not the laid table nor cooking food, which seemed nearest to what she had seen, or dreamed, lying upstairs by Jess' side: it was the vase, the swan, the reeds, the summer sky.

"Thee looked it over," Eliza told Jess, "the morning I started it. Came downstairs and rocked on thy toes in front of it."

"What'd I say," Jess asked, "rocking there? I reckon I wasn't speechless."

"No, Jess," said Eliza, "thee wasn't speechless."

"What'd I say?" he persisted.

"Thee said," Eliza told him, "and well I remember, 'What's for breakfast? I'm hungry enough to eat a biled owl.'"

Jess rocked a little on his toes now. "Well," he said, "that was something. Better'n saying I could eat a biled swan, I reckon."

That was something and she had not been unhappy, setting the praised breakfast on the table, speaking with Jess of what fruits he would bring in for canning, saying the day would be another scorcher, lifting the pretty cup, which in itself, set their eating apart from ordinary meals. But when breakfast was over the vase had taken on a paltry look and some of her happiness had ebbed away: it was nothing, she saw, but a mended lamp chimney; the great swan, putty and paint. The wind didn't really blow—that was only a trick of her painting, a thing anybody'd see through. She set the vase away in the pantry again. She looked up at it there on the top shelf and wondered how it could have been for a half-hour, not only a place of stillness for her, beautiful and far away, but a setting forth somehow of all the bliss and eagerness she had felt before sunup, listening to the beginning bird songs and seeing the children's faces.

It was a long time before she touched it again. The children's faces she had seen upstairs were real faces, and their voices and needs were real, not only May mornings and winter evenings, but all the hours between. The house, she trimmed and softened as she had planned that morning, so that now she would rise from her chair, open a door, and surprise herself anew with a room which waited her, as far from bareness as a grafted tree in full bearing is from a seedling.

She often thought of the vase, but there had never come another moment like that of the first summer morning—and time, for her, was always short. Still, she planned to finish it, set the second swan in place beside the first. There were days when its incompletion troubled her mind, gave her the feeling that she had turned away from something more than a painted lamp chimney . . . that all the children, Jess, the house, her church even, were not reason enough for having neglected it . . . that it was more to her than she understood.

In spite of this, the vase waited, unfinished, for years. Then in November, after little Sarah's death, she had taken it from its shelf late one afternoon and with chair pushed close to the sitting-room fire had set about painting the second swan, a companion for the first. It was a miserable day; there had been rain in the morning, but after dinner the air had sharpened and snow had begun to fall, not briskly, so that her thoughts were of sleigh rides or the boys fighting snow battles, but listlessly so that her mind turned toward the year's end and little Sarah's grave. She had passed from the first period of grief when her arms had known the loss of her child as sharply as if a portion of her own flesh had been cut away, and she was able to say God's will be done; still she was left with a great heaviness and it was strange, even to her, that this had seemed the hour to finish the vase.

If little Sarah had been alive she would have stood by her side, watching her brush strokes, saying, "Is thee making a bird, mother?", and outlining the curving breast of the second swan she thought, I can never lose her. She remembered the morning she had started her work, all that joy and vision of joy, as if the whole of life would be nothing but delight, nothing but smoothness with never a setback. How different this was, no vision, never misdoubting that there were sorrows ahead, but somehow a tranquil satisfaction in seeing the second swan, the companion for which the first had waited so many years, take shape, and in believing, once again, that it was a real wind which moved the frayed clouds across the summer sky.

The second swan was never finished, though. It remained a shadow, an outline. As she had begun to touch it with whiteness, Jess, bareheaded, hands and hair wet with melting snow, came in.

"Eliza," he cried, "it is more than I can bear."

She had set her brush aside and said, "What is it, Jess?", though she knew.

"Sarah's grave," Jess said. "Under the snow. She loved the snow, so. Thee knows how she loved it, Eliza."

Then he did a thing he had never done—before or since—he dropped on his knees and laying his head, the red hair darkened with melting snow, on to her lap, had cried, not quietly, for Jess was not a quiet man.

"Eliza," he asked, "has thee forgotten that the first words Sarah ever spoke were about the snow?" He lifted his head from her lap and looked toward the windows. "There she stood," he said, "clapping her little hands and crying, 'Pretty flowers, pretty flowers.'"

Eliza had not forgotten. The words had been in her mind all afternoon. "No, Jess," she said. "I haven't forgotten."

"How can thee be playing then?" Jess cried. "Playing with thy paints? And Sarah's grave there under the snow?"

Eliza smoothed the damp hair. "I haven't forgotten God, either, Jess," she said.

After a time Jess had grown calm, had warmed himself at the fire and gone out to finish his evening's feeding. Then Eliza had set the vase, unfinished as it was, one swan but the dream of a swan, gray and shadowy, and without plumage, on the shelf of the secretary. Let it stand there, she thought. It was, perhaps, the best she would ever be able to do, and she was content that it should have its place among the other things she treasured—reminding her of so much, the dream before sunup, and much beside, that, never dreamed of, had come since that morning.

The rain was still pelting down and Jess had forgotten the vase. "Eliza," he said, going back to his old idea, "not only seasons, but places, I'll venture, could be told from the sound of the rain. The jungle," he said, fired with the thought of so much rain and so much geography, "how'd it sound there? Or on a mountain peak, how'd it sound falling on bare rocks? Or on the sea? Water spanking down on water? Well, here we are," he subsided. "Stuck. We'll never know."

Eliza didn't feel stuck. She felt at home.

Jess peered out the window. He reconciled himself to rain in Indiana. "Got to make a run for it," he said. "Cows bawling their heads off."

He clasped Eliza to him before he went out, as warmly as if bound, as in his mind no doubt he was, on a journey, and Eliza felt between his clasping arms and herself, the vase, which she still held, separating them. And yet, she supposed, seen in another way, it was a link. After he left she set it back in the secretary, but she could still feel the pressure of its fluted rim against her breast as she moved about the kitchen busy with her evening work.

THE ILLUMINATION

IT was a May morning, early. The morning of a piece-meal flicker-light day. It was the time of the return of shadows. The time once again when there was sun enough and leaf enough to give some variety to the monotony of a wall or strip of land.

Jess sat on his side of the bed putting his foot into a white wool sock. He gazed at the sunlight coming through the east windows, like water tinged with a little squeezed juice from a red geranium, he decided. He had a head full of quizzical ideas about himself and the world—at the minute his foot was busy feeling its way into the sock, and his eye with watching the sun set the water pitcher on the floor. There it was on the gray rag carpet.

"Appears to be a big-eared animal," he said, figuring it out finally.

Eliza, who had the May morning in her veins but was giving no thought to it, gartered her stockings neatly with the soft pieces of rolled red silk she used. Since she was a Quaker, Eliza didn't hold with distracting the eye of man with violent colors. But under three skirts, knee-high and visible only to God, she didn't reckon it mattered. And she knew it was there.

"Thee's choosing a poor time to be fanciful, Jess," she said. "I can feel all the steps I got to take before night jolting my spine right now. Kitchen to dining room. Dining room to kitchen." She got up from her side of the bed and walked to the middle of the room, where she gave a little bounce.

"Tickled?" Jess asked.

"Gratified," she said without studying about it. "Praising God in his glory. It'll be a convenience. Beautiful at night. Shining through the trees, too. To say nothing of the novelty."

"It was my idea," Jess reminded her.

"Thee was the vessel. The Lord filled thee."

Jess was used to that. Eliza had given God the credit for all he'd ever done.

She had on all but her dress now. It was hard to say what was plumpness and what was starch. There was plenty of both. "Stir thy stumps, Jess," she said, "twenty people for supper—thirty, maybe, and thee shilly-shallying in thy shirttail at six in the morning."

Jess smiled on her fondly. The best training for a woman, he figured, was to put her early in the pulpit. It didn't cut down any on her flow of talk, but it bettered it, and relieved the pressure. A pity neither of his daughters had pulpit leanings. He pulled his nightshirt over his head. There was more warmth under it than outside.

"I got more heat than the sun," he said.

Eliza didn't encourage him to talk. He watched her, her plump fingers flying in and out of her still black hair. Like birds at dusk. That was his own thought of them. The pleasing thoughts God let him have! So long as he had a head and shoulders to lodge it, he would never be bereft. He was jolted from daylight to dark with pleasing ideas. Whether God was the fount of all he could not say, but for their having he was grateful.

Eliza looking in her mirror saw him naked behind her. She took an eye off her plaiting.

"At thy age," she said through her hairpins.

Jess came to life. "I ain't never been this age before," he complained. "Thee seems never hard put for what's becoming to thy years." He meant it. Whatever she did was becoming, waking or sleeping. A child in her arms or tanning its behind, she had a face of love and beauty. What could a man ask further—with that face opposite him for forty years and ideas popping in his mind like firecrackers? He buttoned his shirt meditatively.

Eliza's face got pink. She'd never learned to take a compliment —and she'd had two a day for forty years. They made her feel uneasy—as if she weren't taken for granted like sun and moon. "Don't put on thy good shirt, now," she said sharply. "Save it till evening—there's a mort of work to be done—unless thee plans to sit in the parlor saving thy strength for the Illumination."

Jess slowly pulled off the fresh shirt. "The Illumination," he said. "So that's what thee calls it? Sounds Biblical. The Annunciation. The Transfiguration. The Illumination. Sounds as if the Lord Himself had a hand in it."

Eliza bridled. "Thee'd be a sorry piece—saying He hadn't. But what," she asked reasonably, "would thee call it, Jess Birdwell? Thee's rigged up a gas plant in the cellar—we light the jets tonight and ask in the neighbors. That's the Illumination. Does thee feel marble cake, coconut drops, floating island, and French custard ice cream will be a sufficiency as dessert, Jess?"

"Scanty pickings," he said. "Scanty pickings. No pie."

Eliza's black eyes searched her husband's face anxiously until she saw his Adam's apple fluttering.

"Pie's kind of commonplace," she said.

The bedroom door opened without a knock. In the doorway stood a figure half-way between all known stopping places. A face too sharp-cut for a Negro—too dark for anything else—too much mustache for a woman, too much bosom for a man.

"Preacher," she intoned, "gravy's gobbling up the skillet, morning's gobbling up the day, pretty soon the daylight's going far away." Then she waited.

"That's pretty, Emanuela," said Eliza. "One of thy best. We'll be right down."

Emanuela walked away limber-legged, satisfaction oiling her knee-hinges.

"There's nothing about that woman I like," said Jess. "Calls thee 'preacher.' Always rhyming. No answer unless she can rhyme it."

Eliza was leaving the room, her Bible for breakfast Scripture reading in her hand. "After twenty years, Jess, thee might be reconciled."

"I'm still sane," the old man said. "Though after twenty years it's a wonder."

Eliza was going light-foot down the stairs. "Thee get thy sanity down to the breakfast table," she called back. "Feed it some ham and gravy. Don't get stuck up there preening thyself on it."

Jess stood fully dressed but not descending. It was his morning's pleasure to stand thus at the day's rim as over a pool of water before plunging in. There was no telling what the day might hold —what vexations seize him belowstairs. Or what joys. He stood now, uncommitted to either, his own man, as silent and at peace as the clapper in a ropeless bell. Silent—silent. Here now at six o'clock in the morning with the pink light on the gray carpet, and the bed not yet made up, shutting out the night, he, Jess Birdwell, sixty-two years old, stood committed as yet to nothing but the unraveling of his own soul.

"Taste eternity," he said aloud, "on a May morning in a white clapboard house on the banks of the Muscatatuck. How to taste it—there's so much of it and none you want to waste."

Gratingly his strong finger stroked his long Irish upper lip—his eyes sharply focused on something beyond the chamber's edge. Then he walked slowly to the secretary which stood between the two south windows and took down Janney's "Life of William Penn." With the stub pencil he always carried in his shirt pocket he wrote quickly, "Eternity," the soft blunt pencil set firmly down, "is experienced in life by sampling as many of the elements as is possible."

Around the sentences went quotation marks and under them the words, "From the writings of Dr. Samuel Johnson." Jess's books were filled with sentences of his own with other men's names under them. He was not a wasteful man, he was pious and he was Irish. The good thoughts God gave him he would save. He kept his stub pencil handy to write them down. But say he wrote them himself—he was too bashful for that—it would plague him to death to have it thought he set himself up to be a John Greenleaf or Henry Wadsworth. So his books were filled with wisdom from Charles Lamb and John Milton and John Woolman. When once in a while he had a thought he was convinced was true, but maybe not one a writer'd like to own, he labeled it "Anon."

"Sample as much as possible," he said to himself, put back the book, shut the secretary, and descended to the day that lay below-stairs, waiting.

Jane bent over the hearth in the sitting room, turkey brush in hand, brushing up the night-before's ashes. She was bent, but not brushing.

"Well, daughter," said Jess.

"Good morning, pa,". the girl said soberly, not lifting her eyes to peer beyond the blinkers of her black frizzed bangs.

"Thee's like a witch, with thy broom—bent double and ready to fly."

"A witch," Jane said, standing bolt upright and staring her father sadly in the eye. Then tears rolled out of her own gray eyes and down to the corners of her crooked mouth.

"Hoity-toity!" her father sighed. There was scarcely a word safe to say to fifteen-year-olds. They took exception to Holy Writ itself. Thinking to take her mind off the witch business, if that was what upset her, he said, "Thee have a fever blister on thy lip, Jane?"

Then Jane sobbed, threw down the wing brush, cried, "Oh, pa," and ran to the kitchen.

Now I'm in the day and fairly launched, Jess thought, and walked into the kitchen.

There Jane sat at the breakfast table, her head in her arms, and Eliza faced him, her black eyes crackling. "A pretty way to start a day of celebration with twitting thy daughter about her looks."

"Twitting!" Jess said aghast. He wouldn't twit a shooting enemy about his looks. There was nothing so personal as looks.

"Call her first a witch—then take notice of a blemish that's plaguing her."

A witch—old, bent, ugly. A fever blister—a blemish big as a mountain and visible miles off and akin to leprosy in repulsiveness. I got to retravel so many miles to get back to fifteen, he thought, and even that don't turn the trick for I ain't female.

He sat down to the table. "Ever hear the word bewitching, Jane?" he asked. Jane raised her sorrowing head. "Bewitching. Like a witch. I don't know about now—but when I was a young blade, there was nothing a man could say in way of praise beyond that. Bewitching. Thy mother was bewitching. Don't thee ever read poetry, Jane? Bee-stung lips? A fev—a fullness such as thine is highly regarded."

Jane's sniffs were drying up. Eliza's eyes had given over blazing. The four of them, Jess and Eliza, Jane and Emanuela, sat at the breakfast table. The hired man had eaten earlier.

"Let us return thanks," said Jess, and the four heads bowed in silent prayer.

Jess meditated on God but asked for nothing. Eliza talked with her Father of gifts and wants alike. Emanuela floated wordless before a blazing throne. Jane prayed, "Take away my fever blister, take away my fever blister." Then being of a reasonable and conciliatory nature, "or if Thee'd rather just make it invisible. Thee has the power, O Lord," she reminded Him. "Make it invisible for the Illumination."

The other three heads lifted while Jane's was still bowed. Eliza said, "Help thyself to the gravy, Jane."

Prayer was a solace, but there were twenty—thirty people coming for supper, and solace didn't chew like bread.

Jane raised her head and looked about the table. No one was paying any attention to her fever blister. Perhaps it was already invisible. She helped herself to ham and gravy and soda biscuits, eating with lifted lip.

Eliza planned her day like a general: terrain to be covered, redans thrown up, posts held. She gave out the commissions: "Emanuela, thee's not to set foot outside the kitchen today. Thee's to take care of the cooking. The chickens and ham should go on now. Those hens are all muscle. I'll make the floating island myself, and the corn pudding."

Emanuela drew a long breath to show speech was welling up. "Preacher, while your back is turned none of the vittles will be burned."

Jess swallowed heavily.

> "Emanuela, it's time thee's learned
> Prose is nothing to be spurned."

"Jess, Jess," Eliza chided. This was no day to get a rhyming hoe-down started between those two. It could go on till candlelighting time with Jess the winner, Emanuela sulking in her room, and Eliza with the work to do.

"Jane," she said, "thee's to redd up the bedrooms, get fresh flowers, dust, set tables, and be at all times near at hand. No dallying down by the branch."

"Yes, ma," said Jane.

"Jess, thee set this down on paper."

"Otherwise," Jess said, "it might slip my mind slick as a whistle."

"Bring up from the spring-house dill pickles, the sour cream jar, the apple butter, and all yesterday's milk. Bring up from the ice-house enough ice for the freezing. Go out to the south wood lot and see if there's dogwood blooming there we could use as table flowers. Take a bucket of hot water and see that all signs of thy ducks is off the back steps. Go out—"

"Whoa there!" said Jess. "Whoa there! When that's done I'll come back for further orders."

✦

They darted like needles through the morning—they wove the bright May morning into a fabric strong enough to support a party. Eliza and Emanuela filled in the groundwork sturdy and firm while Jane and Jess feather-stitched around the edges. Jane sang while she dusted, not clearly, because of her sore lip.

I am a stranger here
Within a foreign land.
My home is far away,
Upon a coral strand.

She believes it, Jess thought, listening to her loud and sorrowing voice. She ain't used to Indiana yet. Life's a shock to the young. Shock to have an old man for a father instead of an angel. Shock to eat ham gravy instead of honey dewdrops. And to like ham gravy. That's the worst shock of all. Find yourself fitting into this sorry world.

Jane came down the back steps, walking carefully so's not to disturb the flowers she was carrying. "Look, pa," she cried. "Isn't it beautiful?"

Jess didn't care for it much. The old gravy bowl, mounded high as a lump of raising bread with white bridal wreath in the center, had red geraniums running in a scarlet circle round the outer edge.

"I just got to find something blue," Jane said. "One big blue flower or four little ones would do it. To go right in the center of the white. Then look what I've got, pa. Red, white, and blue."

Jess saw it otherwise. Blue eye with red rim. Bad case of pinkeye's what it'll look like, he thought, but said nothing.

Red, white, and blue. If he'd been of a suitable age how'd his Quaker principles've stood up during the war? Had he been in his prime could he have held out against fighting for what he believed in? Union and the slaves free? The Lord didn't ask me to make that decision. But it goes against the grain now to have to take these things, things I most believe in, from men I never laid eyes on. He watched a cloud shadow pass over the pail of cooling water at his feet.

Eliza came down the steps bouncing. "Cold water'll never do the trick," she said.

"Time was," Jess answered, "when thee'd of been too fine-haired to direct me in dousing duck manure off the back steps."

She nodded her head, remembering that girl.

"Was we better then, Jess?" she asked. "When we's young? When we couldn't bear nought but flowers and sweet words? Couldn't bear to have a mouse die—let alone a bird? Thought hens unladylike for laying eggs? Now I say clean off the duck dung like 'draw up a chair.' And none of this world's beauties break my heart any more—no nor words, any more, Jess, like once I cried for 'As for man, his days are as grass: as a flower of the field so he flourisheth.' Is it gaining or losing, Jess?"

She hoisted her gray chambray skirts so Jess' final swishing would not spatter them.

"Both, both," he said, leaning on his broom. This was a way he seldom saw Eliza. Ordinarily she fit snug and without questioning into one of her two worlds, this world of work, the next of love.

"Both," he repeated. "The thing being to taste each in its turn."

Eliza shook her head. "I don't know."

The shadows of morning had shortened. Fingers of light came through the leafing maple onto her kitchen-warmed face. Enoch's voice came up from the west forty in the kind of guttural horse talk he used in plowing. Jane walked by not seeing them, intent on her red, white, and blue. Emanuela clanged like a forge in the kitchen. Far off, on a farm out of sight, a dog barked as if to someone returning after long absence.

"The mind," said Eliza, puzzled, to her husband, "the live mind can hardly take in the idea of death."

"No need," Jess said. "No need. It ain't in nature."

"We ought to prepare."

"This is preparing," he answered, lifting his face to the sky.

Jane was finished with her work. She went from room to room, leaning in their doorways, seeing their perfection and seeing Jane, stepping under the gaslights tonight, fair as the Illumination itself. She stepped across a threshold to tauten a coverlet or pick up a fallen petal, and stepped back, to watch the room silent in its waiting.

She had not looked in a glass at her fever blister since morning. She trusted the Lord and felt it to be invisible.

Eliza said, "I've got to have a body bath." She hadn't planned on it. Not on getting that hot. She washed in a corner of the kitchen while Emanuela kept her eyes modestly on the cast-iron kettles.

The day's light flowed over the edge of the western hills. Mud daubers left the road puddles with their last loads for home. The Muscatatuck moved like steel under the light-drained sky. The curtains in the parlor lifted a little in the wind off the river.

Eliza was getting panicky—the way she always did before a doings—fearful maybe the knives had been left off the table, or the salt out of the gravy.

Jess went upstairs to get into his First Day shirt.

"Don't thee leave thy dirty shirt on the floor," Eliza called after him.

He put it in the closet, and as he stood in his undershirt and work pants the thought came to him: Better see if the gas plant's working. Sixty years of living had convinced him that something wry and sardonic had a hand in the world's management, something that arranged for invitations to be sent out to Illuminations and then put a stop to the gas supply. It didn't make the old man bitter—it made him alert. When he was bested he listened for that far-off laugh—when things went without a hitch, he laughed himself.

He went downstairs silent as shadow in the shadowy house.

In the parlor he turned the jet, heard the gas whisper like a snake, set his match to it, saw its tongue of flame.

Eliza crackled in, sweet with soap and sunlight. "If Stephen were home from school, could join us here and see the lighting. . . ."

Eliza's muted voice said what perfection that would have been. Steve was the youngest, the child from whose eyes her lost Sarah looked; without him no occasion, however festive, was complete.

"The boy has his studies to think of," Jess said.

Eliza nodded. Then she looked about concerned. This was the hour when she always feared no one would come to the party.

"Jess," she whispered, "what if no one comes? What'll we do with all the food? I've been casting up in my mind what to do with the food."

"Thee never remembers from one time to the next, does thee?" Jess asked patiently. "Surreys'll be turning off the pike in ten minutes."

"Then why's thee standing here in thy underwear? Ten minutes and the house'll be full of people and thee in thy underwear." She pushed him toward the stairs. "It's enough to rile a saint. Hustle into thy clothes."

The old man hustled.

By the time the threads of his silk tie were catching on his rough fingers, he heard, as he had said they would, the wheels of the first surrey become silent as they turned off the pike's gravel on to the soft dust of the Maple Grove drive.

He lingered at the stairhead before descending. The balloon of party preparations which had swollen to vast proportions now burst belowstairs.

People can't be that glad to see each other, he thought. They's taken aback to feel so little joyful and talk loud to hide it. Half the evening passes before it's natural to them.

"Jess, Jess," came Eliza's voice. "It's time for the lighting. We're waiting for thee to set the match to them."

He walked downstairs slowly. A party for him was like a thunderstorm—a fine sight to see, and music to the ears, but nothing to be caught plumb in the heart of.

"Howdy, Jess, howdy."

"Think it's safe, does thee?"

"Cost a mint of money, I reckon."

"The Illumination, eh? Well, light up."

Jess set matches to the jets, and parlor and sitting room, dining room and parlor-bedroom were light-struck as flowers at midday, clear and shining and orderly as petals beneath the yellow lights. The faces turned upward as if to a marvel—and it was a marvel, here in the backwoods a house lit with something flowing up through pipes from the cellar. No lamps to be washed and filied, no coal-oil splashing over the cornmeal and sugar on trips home from town.

"The Illumination," Jane whispered, marveling, yellow lights in her gray eyes as she looked upward.

They were all there: the Griffiths, the Hoopers, the Peases, the Armstrongs: Quakers who dressed plain and Quakers who didn't. The Reverend Godley and his wife from the Rush Branch neighborhood. Lidy Cinnamond, beautiful but somewhat sad; grieving, Jane hoped, for Stephen, her absent brother. The Venters from down the pike. Talking naturally now beneath the artificial lights, and drifting more often past the dining room, where the cold foods were already set out on the table.

In the kitchen was the crisis of dishing up, but it was over in a minute: chicken with dumplings like yellow clouds floating on top, coleslaw in green and white glacier drifts, and mashed potatoes like cloud and snow together were carried in by Emanuela.

Eliza stood in the doorway, untying her apron. "Friends," she said, "supper is ready."

They were twenty-eight at table. Young and old. Oldsters for whom food had a meaning, and young'uns—and in-between, those whose hearts had not yet fed, and who could eat on bread or stone, so little were they centered in swallowing, so much in seeing, searching.

Eliza was the minister at table, but it was a man's place to return grace. Grace was silent, except on occasions like this—with Methodists present who liked to hear what people were saying to God.

Jess shut his eyes. "Father, for food and friends we thank Thee. Amen." It was over before the youngest had started to peek.

After supper there was a little lull. The men talked crops while the women cleared dishes and had some final bites under the excuse of not letting anything waste.

This was a Quaker home and play-party prancing would never shake its floors—but the songs could be sung even if the feet couldn't be lifted.

As Jess walked outside, "Skip to My Lou" was being sung in the parlor and he thought he could hear Jane's eager, asking voice above the others. He walked up to the little rise they called the pasture knoll where he could see the house, have a look at the fireworks from a sheltered spot.

From the pasture knoll the house was a shell of light. The night was mild and from the raised windows light fell out in golden bars across the dark earth. Jess nodded his head, approving—for man whose time on earth is so short it was a brave job, this installing gaslights and eating chicken dumplings like children of eternity. Considering man's lot nobody could berate him, if he chose to molder in some dark corner, thinking on the sorry upshot of it all. Taste all, he thought, taste all.

As he leaned on the fence that separated pasture from orchard, he heard someone come up the orchard side of the knoll, heard the fence creak as it was leaned against.

"Well, Mr. Birdwell," said a thin grasshopper voice, "I see you're pouring it out tonight."

"Pouring it out?" Jess asked. Thinking he meant the lights, but knowing old Eli Whitcomb, not sure.

"The money," Eli said, "the money," and he moved nearer so that his smell, like leaves wet with the first fall rains, was stronger in the May night than anything spring could muster.

"A lot of money going down the drainpipe, there. Food and lights nobody needs. Don't it irk you?"

The old coot ain't ashamed of being a miser, Jess thought. No need my being ashamed for him. For the first time in his life he spoke to the man he knew his forty-year neighbor to be: said farewell to makeshifts and politeness and plunged right into that hard core where Eli lived.

"Money," he said. "Thee prizes it above all else?"

"No," said old Eli Whitcomb, "not money. Anything you can get your hands on. Anything you can count or weigh or measure. There's nothing else to rely on. Looky," he said, and beat out his words on Jess' arm with a finger as light as a withered flower stalk. "What's the main idea behind this world? A wasting away—a wasting away. Trees rotting. Ground carried off by the rivers. The sun getting less hot. Iron rusting. I run counter to that. I put a stop to it. God don't care. Wreckage is His nature. It ain't mine. I save. Piles of everything. Boxes, papers, I get old papers from as far as Kokomo. Nails, money too. I save all. Me alone. Against the drift. The rest of you letting it run down the spout."

Jess turned to the old fellow he couldn't see. "I never figured it in that light."

"Of course you didn't. If you had there'd be none of that."

He pointed to the house. "Devouring, gnawing away. I got to get home," he said abruptly. "A little of a sight like that is as much as I can stomach. Clean against reason. Farewell, Jess Birdwell. You got it in you to've been a credit to the world if things'd taken another drift."

He went away in the May night with the sound of leaf brushing against leaf.

"Eli," Jess called after him, "Eli, is thee happy?"

"Not in sight of that," he said, and Jess knew he was looking at the house. "but against I get home, see what one man's done by way of putting a check to the wasting away of the world, I reckon I will be."

Jess leaned back against the fence, arms stretched along the top rails. "Well, well," he said.

Here where the woods had been so thick a star could be seen only if a leaf was lifted by the wind, here where the Indians had trod silent-foot, here he, Jess Birdwell, the Quaker, stood under the open sky regarding his farm land, his house, his family.

He turned and looked in the direction old Eli had gone. "That's another way if I don't misdoubt."

He walked into the house and up the back stairs to his and Eliza's chamber. He lit a lamp and took down the book he'd written in that morning, and under his morning's writing he set down, "One or many—it don't matter. Eternity's how deep you go."

Not a finished way of saying it, he thought, but for the first time he signed his own name. "Eternity's the depth you go. Jess Birdwell."

He closed the book and replaced it, turned the light low and walked down the front stairs. Oldsters were sitting at ease, talking and listening while the young people were singing,

Oh, when I'm gone, don't you, don't you grieve,
Oh, when I'm gone, don't you, don't you grieve after me.

Jane came to the bottom stair and looked up at him.
"Where's thee been, pa?"
"Outside to see the lights—from outside."
"How's it look from outside, pa?"
"Like an oversize lightning bug."
"I just love Illuminations. Don't thee, pa?"
"Well," said Jess, "they's much to be said for them." Then he joined the young folks in their singing,

Oh, when I'm gone, don't you, don't you grieve after me.

PICTURES FROM A CLAPBOARD HOUSE

ELSPETH, Gard's and Mattie's daughter, was spending Christmas with Jess and Eliza. The Christmas tree was already up. It stood in the parlor bay-window, wild and shining, awaiting the harness of cranberry and popcorn ropes which would semi-domesticate it, quiet its outdoor cavortings and prancings. In the sitting room its harness was still taking shape. Cranberries and popcorn were being strung; gilded nuts attached to cords, red paper bells opened again for such ringing as the eye could apprehend. Grandma's hands were squeezing ropes of sparkling tinsel back to roundness.

The popcorn Elspeth was stringing squeaked a little now and then, and the lonely sound traveled up Elspeth's arm to her ear—which shuddered to hear it. Grandpa, who looked to be sleeping, with feet almost in the fire, heard it, too. When the squeaks were loudest his stockinged toes twitched uneasily. It was a sound, Elspeth thought, like a wind round a house corner, like the wind around the corners of grandma's house, a house white in the windy night, square except for the balcony upstairs which projected like a watch-tower or a sentry-box into the darkness and looked out across the great woods to her own home.

Elspeth thought of her mother. The clock ticked, slow, slow. It said, as Elspeth listened, For-ev-er . . . for-ev-er. The fire rustled and sighed; grandma's tinsel made a scratchy sound. The popcorn squeaked.

"Grandpa," Elspeth asked, "what kind of trees are in the woods between here and home?"

Grandpa bent his toes comfortably back and forth, stared into the fire as if into a forest. "Oak," he said. "And honey locust. Shagbark hickory and button-wood. Dogwood," he added. "And papaw and May-apple. But mostly farms," he said.

In the daytime Elspeth remembered the farms but at night only the long, black woods, dark even at midday. "Corn?" Elspeth asked.

"Yes, lots of corn," her grandpa said, "and timothy and clover."

All was quiet again, only the lonely sounds in the room: the fire, the wind, the clock.

"There's orchards, too."

"Yes," the old man said, rocking. "There's orchards. Summer Sweetings, Northern Spies, Grime's Goldens. Lots of orchards."

The fire curved like a wave; grandma's tinsel crackled; the old house creaked. Elspeth's needle split a piece of popcorn, halved it so it was no longer a flower. The clock said, For-ev-er . . . for-ev-er . . .

"Grandma," Elspeth said suddenly, surprising even herself, "does thee love me?"

Grandma folded her strands of tinsel "Of course, child. Thee knows I do. With all my heart."

Elspeth knew this. "Better than I did my own," grandma often said. "Then I was too young," she'd say, "to know childhood wasn't enduring." She'd sorrowfully shake her head. "Better than thy mother Mattie or thy Uncle Josh or Laban." But she never said, "Better than thy Uncle Stephen," for no one could be better loved than Uncle Stephen.

The clock struck nine. "Time to call a halt," grandma said and opened and shut her short plump hands, weary with the tedious squeezing. Elspeth looked at her grandma. Tidal wave and avalanche were nothing to her so long as grandma was near at hand and well. But when grandma's face grew sad, when, as sometimes happened, she would look far off and say, "Stephen, Stephen. My poor boy," then Elspeth's world was threatened. Tonight, Elspeth thought, grandma's sad.

"Would thee like me to comb thy hair, grandma, before thee goes to bed?"

"No, child, not tonight," grandma said.

Then grandpa asked, "How about a little music before we go upstairs, granddaughter?"

This was, in a way, a kind of joke, and Elspeth knew it—for she couldn't really play—but it was a joke she was glad to be a part of. The organ, which long ago had stood in the attic, was now in the sitting room open and dusted, waiting someone's touch. The music Elspeth's mother, Mattie, had played, "Gala Water," "Evening Star," "Toll the Bell," had gone with her when she married, and grandpa played by ear; but grandma would not have the organ look bereft. On it she kept the red and gold atlas, larger and more beautiful than any songbook it had ever held, and Elspeth who could not play music played the maps.

"Now," she would say, "I will play Africa." Then she played all the pictures she had seen and all the tales she had been told of dark and distant Africa. She played the great winding rivers, the flash of tusks through leafy jungles, the black men with spears taller than their bodies.

Or she would open the atlas to a map of the arctic regions and play the North Pole, her hands hunting for sounds that said bareness and whiteness and icy winds and flashing northern lights.

And she could play China, too, whose sounds for her were all tiny: tiny bells, tiny feet, tiny chopsticks tinkling against the side of tiny bowls. But tonight Elspeth opened the atlas to a map of the United States and said, "Now, I will play California." She chose California because that was where Uncle Stephen had gone and because he wrote home of its great mountains, its sunshine like arrows, its oranges like gold. He wrote about the warm sea and the rivers with strange names: the Sacramento, the Yuba, the San Joaquin, the Feather. Tonight she would play the mountains, deep heavy sounds to show how big they were and thin high notes for the high, snow-covered peaks. And she would play the Feather River which must surely sound like a torrent of downiness.

But before the first mountain had been squeezed from the organ grandma said once again, "No, child, not tonight."

Elspeth turned on the organ stool to look at grandma who ordinarily liked all sounds which said California and reminded her of Uncle Stephen: but, "Not tonight," she repeated. "I can't bear the name tonight." Then she said something that had no meaning for Elspeth: "Oh, Jess, why'd he have to choose her? Marry outside the Meeting? What he need's a settled, sober-minded wife," but grandpa only said,

"How about the North Pole, granddaughter? I like to hear that north wind whistle."

Elspeth played the North Pole, and for awhile she thought that the cold air that swept about her dangling legs was music from the organ; but grandpa had stopped pumping—there was no sound from the organ and still the room grew colder.

"Shut the door," grandpa said quietly. Elspeth turned and there in front of the closed door stood Uncle Stephen and Lidy Cinnamond, both tall, pink from the cold and lightly dusted with snow.

"How did thee get over?" grandpa asked and Elspeth saw he had known Uncle Stephen was home from California.

"Lidy's father brought us."

"He outside?" grandpa asked.

"He went right back," Uncle Stephen told him and carried their luggage which he was still holding and set it by the door which led upstairs. "We plan to stay here until we go to Lidy's Christmas-day." He spoke very clearly and loudly as if arguing with someone, but no one answered him.

Then he walked over to the organ, took Elspeth's hand and slid her from the organ stool. "Lidy," he said, "this is Aunt Jetty."

Lidy Cinnamond spoke for the first time and her voice was the way Elspeth had remembered it, very low and soft with a sort of humming note in it. "Jetty?" she said.

"Because she's so black," said Uncle Stephen.

"Why is she aunt, Steve?"

"Oh, she's serious as an owl," Uncle Stephen explained. "Aunt Jetty, this is your Aunt Lidy. Say hello."

Elspeth put out her hand. "I've seen Lidy before. Aunt Lidy," she corrected herself.

"Have you?" said Uncle Stephen. "Where?"

"At her house. And with Mr. Venters."

Nobody said a word for quite a long time and Elspeth, feeling responsible for the silence, broke it. "They were having a picnic down by Rush Branch."

"Mr. Venters and Lidy?" grandma asked in a strange dry voice.

"Yes," Elspeth answered. "Mel Venters. They . . ."

But before she could say what she had seen, Uncle Stephen reached across and took his wife's hand. "Mel Venters almost beat my time," he said. "And who could blame him for trying?" he asked them all, but particularly his mother.

Elspeth looked at Lidy again. She could not think of her as beautiful, still it was hard not to stare at her; she was so black and gold and red, so tall and curving, so quiet. And so smiling too, as a bride should be, Elspeth knew.

"She's waiting to shake hands with thee, Lidy," Uncle Stephen said, and Lidy, as if recalling herself from some reverie, reached down and took Elspeth's hand.

Elspeth shook it gravely. "It's past thy bedtime," grandma said to her—and to Lidy. "Take off thy coat. I'll heat thee and Stephen some milk as soon as I've put this child to bed."

Grandma held Elspeth's arm as they went up the cold stairs. "When did thee see Lidy and Mel?"

"Last summer," Elspeth said. "Picnicking. They were . . ."

"That will do," grandma said and hustled her out of her clothes and into her cold bed which stood anchored like a little boat at the foot of grandma's great full-sailed four-poster.

✦

On the ceiling next morning was a sea of light, a radiance like milk alive and dancing. It had snowed in the night and sunlight on snow was sweeping the room with waves of loveliness. Elspeth snuggled deeper into her covers. The snowlight so filled her room that it seemed as if, warmly wrapped about, she were bedded in snow itself. Then into the light something dark crowded; something dreamed, or imagined, or . . . remembered . . .

Grandma with a lamp in her hand and Uncle Stephen by her side: shining upward onto their faces the lamplight had made their mouths forbidding, their eyes shadowed. The light ate the flesh from their faces, made bones look down at her.

"While thee was away," grandma was saying, "while thee was distant, sick, trying to get well, she not caring . . . carrying on."

The lamp in grandma's hand trembled and Uncle Stephen took it and held it for her, as if he would patiently hear her out.

"It isn't that she isn't of thy faith . . . but holding herself so light, and her word given. And California so far away."

Uncle Stephen steadily held the lamp. "Tell him," grandma said, "with your own eyes . . . on Sandy Creek."

"There's no need," said Uncle Stephen. "No need. I know it all. Things work out one way and another. Not as thee'd always choose. This works out this way. Nothing to talk in the night about. I was away and Lydia was young. Did thee want her in widow's weeds?"

Uncle Stephen handed the lamp back to his mother and bent to kiss Elspeth. "Go to sleep now, Aunt Jetty," he said. "It's begun to snow."

Then, his arm about his mother's shoulders, he guided her toward the door and Elspeth heard his voice outside, diminishing, failing as they descended the stairs. "Love is more lasting than . . ." then his voice ceased, was swallowed by the narrow, echoing stairway, and then one more word came back . . . "fire." From a long way off, toward the bottom of the stairs, that word came back so emphasized that Elspeth heard it, though all else was lost.

"Love is more lasting than . . ." Elspeth was still thinking about it when she went into the sitting room after breakfast. The room was already tidied for the day. A holiday-sized log burned in the grate; an enormous bell of honeycombed red tissue paper hung from the suspended lamp and swayed with every movement in the room. Snowlight and firelight mingled on the rag carpet, gold and silver. Uncle Stephen sat by the fire, very fine in his good black suit, his light curly hair dampened by water and still showing the marks of a comb.

"Hello, Aunt Jetty," he said. "Want to help?"

From a half dozen paper bags he was taking handfuls of candy, putting them in grandma's best china and cut glass bowls. First a handful of chocolates, then one of gumdrops, then one of peanut brittle. "Have to mix them up," Uncle Stephen said. "Have to give everybody a fair chance."

"Is it for the Christmas tree?" Elspeth asked.

"No, no," said Uncle Stephen. "The shivaree. Thee knows what a shivaree is?"

She did of course: the bride and groom surprised after they had gone to bed by sudden shots and shouts, by cowbells and horse fiddles and lard pails full of stones. And after that the party inside with cake and candy, hot coffee and cigars.

"Will it be tonight? Christmas Eve?"

"Yes," said Uncle Stephen. "Tonight, I figure. With us leaving tomorrow, tonight's about the only time for it."

The big log settled deeper in the fireplace, the red bell gently swayed.

"Love is more lasting than," Elspeth said and her voice asked her question.

"More lasting than the hills," answered Uncle Stephen.

"Fire," asked Elspeth. "What about fire?"

"Ask thy Aunt Lidy about fire," Uncle Stephen said.

Elspeth saw Aunt Lidy then for the first time, in a chair by the far window, all in white. Not white like a bride, stiff and shining, but heavy and soft—like snow warmed and woven. She was looking out into the snow and she didn't look away from it as she answered in her low, humming voice. "Fire warms," she said.

Elspeth stared at her aunt. "Aunt Lidy looks like a snow queen," she said.

"She docs, she does," Uncle Stephen answered her. "White and wintry and beautiful." Aunt Lidy, when he spoke, rose and walked to him and laced her hand, which was darker than his hair, in and out of her husband's curls.

The whole day was magic for Elspeth. Christmas Eve and the shivaree and in the parlor the waiting Christmas tree. Only at Christmas-time did the parlor come truly to life: in summer a snowball bush, white as a cloud but noisier, tapped at the parlor window. In winter the snow was there, white too, but silent. But on ordinary days, now that the children had left home, it was empty of any eye to see or ear to hear. The tappings went unremarked. The snow-crystal pictures melted and in the common runoff of water at midday bore no sign of what they once had been.

Toward evening when the shadows of the pine trees along the driveway were already long and blue on the snow, Elspeth began to think with longing of the tree. There was no one about. Uncle Stephen was helping in the barn with feeding; grandma was busy with supper, and Aunt Lidy had been nowhere to be seen for hours.

The tissue paper bell swayed a little, but was silent as Elspeth crossed the room toward the parlor door. The Christmas tree was secret, not to be really seen until Christmas morning when the presents were unwrapped, but the parlor door was unlocked and quick peeks not forbidden. It was as if grandma knew that there must be a few stolen glances beforehand if the full sight of the tree's Christmas morning glory were to be endured.

But the opened door stayed open, and when it closed Elspeth was inside the parlor, close to the beautiful and shining tree, able to smell, to touch, to stroke. She stood with eyes closed for a minute, then opened them and the little parlor with its red carpet and stiff white curtains was alive. It was as if a flower had fallen into a dead shell, or a bee had crawled into a thimble. Or as if inside a marble clock that no longer ticked, a live butterfly fluttered. The tree had made the room alive. It was so beautiful Elspeth wanted now to be forever. And it was forever, only Aunt Lidy spoke and now came back again.

"Aunt Jetty," she said in her voice that had to Elspeth the sound of bees in it. She was sitting in her white dress by a window, just as she had sat that morning.

"I'm not supposed to be here," Elspeth said. "I oughtn't to be here," she whispered, feeling wicked to be in the parlor, talking the day before Christmas.

Aunt Lidy held out her arms and pulled Elspeth close to her so that she felt the soft warm springiness of the white wool dress. "Neither should I." Then she said, "Will you do something for me?"

"What is it?" Elspeth asked.

"Take a note down the road to Mel Venters? It's just a step really. It's stopped snowing and the wind's died down."

"Grandma'll never let me."

"I know. I'm sorry—but I'd fix it so you could go without grandma's knowing."

It was all planned. She would take Elspeth upstairs after supper and instead of putting her to bed would bundle her in shawls. "Six or seven, even. You'll never feel the cold. I'll take you down the back stairs and start you on the road to Mel's myself."

"It's just a step," she said again. "The wind's gone, the snow's nice and dry, and you can see the lights of both houses all the way. It's—just—I wanted to say good-bye to Mel. The minute he reads the note he'll hitch up the sleigh and bring you home."

"Maybe he won't," Elspeth said.

"Oh, but he will. You just wait and see."

It was as easy as Aunt Lidy said. No one missed her, no one saw her leave. The night was dark, but quiet with a clear sky full of stars. The snow was dry and light, but hard to walk through.

On any other night Elspeth might have been afraid—but what could harm her the night before Christmas?

The Venters opened their Christmas presents on Christmas Eve and they had a houseful of relatives, old folks and young, children and grandchildren. There were so many people and so much excitement Elspeth was scarcely noticed. She gave Lidy's note to Mel, who was sitting apart from his family warming his feet at a big stove. He read and reread the note. He put it deep in his pocket, then dug it out again as if he had forgotten what it said. No one asked Elspeth to take off her many wrappings and she stood burning with warmth. Then the children gave her some candy, and she squatted in a corner, eating the candy and playing with an unclaimed jack-in-the-box. Grandma's sitting room, the organ with the atlas, the parlor and the Christmas tree seemed remote as a dream. She watched Mel read and reread his note and finally wad it into a ball and throw it into the open draft of the stove. She leaned against the wall, eating gumdrops, and drowsily frightening herself with the jack-in-the-box.

She was almost asleep when she heard from down the road the first shots of the shivaree, the banging of milk pans and the clanging of bells. Mel Venters looked away from the fire. "What's going on?" he asked. "Where's all that noise coming from?"

"From the shivaree," Elspeth told him. "They're shivareeing Uncle Stephen and Aunt Lidy."

Mel lifted her off the floor by one arm. "Come on," he said. "I got to get you home."

He took her without time for explanations or good-byes to the barn and clapped her into the front seat of the sleigh to wait while he hitched. He was a fast hitcher—before the cold had fairly awakened Elspeth he was beside her in the front seat, slapping the reins over the back of his horse.

"They'll stand out on the balcony," Elspeth told him, "and bow to the people. Then," she said, clutching her jack-in-the-box, which she had forgotten to put down, "they'll bow to each other and kiss."

"The hell they will," Mel Venters said. "The hell they will."

The sleigh felt as if it didn't even touch the snow—as if it flew. Mel's big black horse was a part of the dark night. Elspeth touched the latch of the box in her excitement and the jack sprang out with a whirr and rapped her under the chin.

"Oh," Elspeth said.

"Be still, be still, can't you," Mel rasped. "Hush your noise."

There was a blaze of light from the torches and lanterns of the people who had come for the shivaree, but the house itself was still dark, the balcony empty. Mel's sleigh cut hissing up the driveway and the crowd, seeing who had arrived, shouted and pounded louder than before.

"Hi, Mel, come to have your last look at the bride?"

Mel said nothing, either to Elspeth or the shivaree-ers, but brought up his sleigh, sharply and deftly, in their midst.

"She ain't here," someone yelled to him. "Neither one's here. They've flown the coop."

"Go on, Mel, you ask the bride to come out," they shouted. "You got a way with women. She'll do it for you, Mel."

They seemed to know what they were talking about; lights showed through the upstairs windows while they were still calling on Mel to ask the bride to come out. They redoubled their shouting then and in a minute or two Elspeth saw Uncle Stephen open the door onto the balcony, then turn back, give his hand to Aunt Lidy who stepped out and took her place beside him. Uncle Stephen had on his black suit, but Aunt Lidy was in a long red dress, a dressing gown, perhaps; something that in the flicker of light from torches and lanterns looked to Elspeth like a dress which might have had a crown above it, or a garland of flowers. Aunt Lidy's dark hair was uncoiled and hung about her face and down her shoulders in rippling tongues of black.

Uncle Stephen called out, "Hello, folks," and waved and said, "I sure did," to somebody who yelled, "You sure picked a looker,

Steve," but Aunt Lidy said nothing. She simply stood there very quietly with the red-gold of the torches and lanterns on her face, looking down at the crowd sometimes, but more often smiling and watching Uncle Stephen as he and the shivaree-ers shouted back and forth to each other.

Elspeth turned to look at Mel. She had supposed Aunt Lidy's note had said, "Farewell, Mel. I love another. We must part forever." That is what she would have written—and she supposed, too, that Mel would bow, throw a kiss and drive away heartbroken through the snow. But Mel was neither bowing nor throwing kisses. He was leaning far back in the sleigh, head lifted, eyes narrowed. Elspeth watched his small, soft mouth lengthen and thin as he returned Aunt Lidy's gaze.

Once again somebody yelled, "Here's Mel, Lidy, come to have a last look at you. Feast your eyes, Mel. It's your last chance. They're headin' back to Californy."

Then Aunt Lidy did what Elspeth had said she would: she made toward the crowd beneath her a slight bowing movement, then laid her arms, very solemnly and slowly, as if thinking what she's doing, about Uncle Stephen's neck and kissed him, just as seriously and just as slowly. No one of all the shivaree-ers yelled or hooted—because the kiss did not seem playful, but almost a part of the wedding ceremony, dignified and holy.

The first movement, the first sound came from Mel. "Take her and welcome," he yelled. Then he pushed Elspeth into the snow like a bundle of rags, laid the whip across his horse's back and cut across the front yard and onto the north driveway with runners hissing. He pulled out onto the pike, slowing up for an instant to yell back, "Merry Christmas," and to add in a voice that was both sharp and bellowing, "and a Happy New Year."

Elspeth turned from where she had been dropped in the snow to gaze after him—but Mel, his sleigh and black horse, were lost in the night. When she looked back at the balcony Aunt Lidy was standing as before and Uncle Stephen had his arm about her shoulders. He leaned over the balcony and spoke in a matter-of-fact way. "There's food in the house, folks, and warm drinks. Come in and welcome."

Elspeth came in with the shivaree-ers, but grandma hustled her upstairs before the eating and drinking started. In bed she lay listening to the night's many sounds. The sounds, at first from below stairs: the shouting and talking and singing, then the pawing and neighing of horses and the sound of sleigh bells growing fine and thin as the bells of China in the frosty air, and finally the sounds of grandpa's and grandma's talking. Talking, talking, their voices murmuring, rising and falling, until at last the bedroom door was flung wide and Uncle Stephen came in. He held the big china lamp in his hands and his black coat was off so that the fine pleated front of his white groom's shirt showed. He put the lamp on the bureau and leaning against the bureau's edge looked down on his father and mother who lay wide-eyed and unsleeping. Uncle Stephen looked buoyant and well, serene and happy.

"Give over fretting," he said to them. He pushed himself up very tall against the tall dark bureau. "It's my marriage and I'm content. I couldn't love except where there's a core of wildness. It's not in me. It'll be a happy marriage."

Uncle Stephen ran his fingers through his light, curly hair, which was no longer neat or combed. His face was calm but his eyes blazed. He leaned over to blow out the light, decided not to and picked it up again. The light fell on his shining face so that Elspeth thought, He looks like an angel of the Lord. He stood on the threshold for a minute, lamp in hand, as if hunting for some word to say. What he finally said reminded Elspeth that Christmas-day had come. "Wise men came bearing gifts of frankincense and myrrh," he said and closed the door softly behind him.

Elspeth went to sleep thinking of those words and they were still in her mind when she awakened next morning. But before she went down to see the tree again, she wanted to stand out on the balcony where Uncle Stephen and Aunt Lidy'd stood and to think if what she'd seen and heard the night before could be true.

She stood on the balcony, looking out into the fresh, sparkling morning across the front yard. New snow had fallen in the night, hiding the footprints, the sleigh tracks, the charred splinters from the blazing torches. No, it could not be true. She lifted her arms as Aunt Lidy had done, slowly and seriously—but it was unreal. What she had seen and heard could not be true.

Then she saw something in the snow, red and silver and blue, partially covered, but still, shining in the sun, brilliant as a flower. It was the jack-in-the-box. It was true, it was true. The black horse had gone down the road in the darkness; Aunt Lidy's face had shone, gold, with the blaze of the torches on it; Uncle Stephen had held the lamp so that he looked like a Christmas angel. Elspeth gazed far away, across the glittering woods toward her home. "Oh, mamma," she said, "it was all true."

HOMER AND THE LILIES

WHEN Jess was eighty years old, somewhat gnarled but still a very sturdy man, he came to know for a short time an asylum-boy, as he was called, by the name of Homer Denham. Homer was an orphan, aged twelve, black-haired, freckled, pale-lipped, very thin. A pulse, when Homer was excited, would rise suddenly in his throat and beat there as if the life in the boy had grown tired of confinement in anything so meager as Homer Denham, longed to be free, say farewell, become a part of the world outside Homer and upon which his black eyes rested so intently.

Jess first saw the boy on a fine afternoon toward the close of September: Jess sitting on a stump by Rush Branch side, Homer stepping quietly along the further bank. Jess had come down to the stream with some idea of fishing; he had his fishing-pole with him, but after an hour or two on a stump watching the silvery dart and slip of minnows and the slower turnings of a big black bass, he had no relish for eating what had given him so much pleasure. Let it be one thing or another, he thought. Don't let eye and stomach feed on the same object. Don't make a fish, in one afternoon, be first thy picture, then thy supper.

Jess felt bemused by the quietly sliding water. Rush Branch was dappled by sunlight which fell through the little chinks left it by the sycamore leaves. The stream flowing onward, disturbed by the fish beneath the surface, carrying the flecks of sunlight like golden seeds, moved beneath Jess' eyes with such likeness to all the streams he had ever watched, that he felt that Rush Branch at its source might be that small trickle at Colerain where he had done his first wading. And that it might be as well, the Muscatatuck, the White, the Wabash, the Ohio, and finally the Mississippi itself, and those great reaches of water into which the Mississippi emptied.

But upon those final waters Jess did not meditate that afternoon. To them in God's good time he would no doubt come. What he was thinking of when suddenly he had the feeling of being watched was the branch behind the barn at Colerain—and the way a spring freshet would send the waters over the meadow grasses there, bending and silvering them in the same way the wind had bent and silvered them the day before. Aged four, Jess used to think: Does the grass care? Does it know the difference?

When he lifted his eyes, focusing them upon the present landscape, he saw Homer quietly stepping along the further bank, but with head turned so that he could regard grandpa asleep upon a stump, Jess supposed.

"Howdy," Jess called across to him. "Come on over. I'm tired looking at fish. Like to rest my eyes on something without fins for a change."

Homer paused for a second, then waded seriously across the stream as a good boy bade by his elder would be obliged to do, Jess plainly saw. He stood beside the stump, unspeaking, smiling a little, his black eyes trying to make out what kind of man had hailed him, the pulse in his throat jumping.

Jess put a hand in his pocket. "I been sitting here," he said, "studying on fish for so long, I declare I'm famished. Backbone rubbing on my ribs. Have to bolster myself up with a little food. Thee care for peppermints?" He pulled out a handful. Homer held out a thin brown hand and Jess poured a half dozen in it.

"Six for thee. Six for me. Two for the fish." He threw two into the stream. "The fish won't eat 'em—at least I've never seen a fish eat a peppermint, but the flavor ought to be a pleasant change after so much branch water."

The pulse in Homer's throat died down a little, and he, like Jess, crunched away.

"Don't seem as if I've seen thee around here before," Jess told the boy.

"I'm Homer Denham," the boy said. "I live with the Perkinses. They took me from a home."

"Oh, yes," Jess said. "I recollect now I did hear something about it. Well," he told Homer, "Amos and Etty Perkins are good people."

"Yes, sir," said Homer.

Amos and Etty Perkins were very good people and they gave Homer a good home. He had a neat little weather-tight room up under the eaves where in summer he could hear the rap and clatter of rain not six inches from his head, and still lie dry and snug beneath his patchwork quilt. In winter he would hold his breath, for the sound of falling snow is like that of breathing, and only in perfect silence could Homer tell whether or not the first flakes had begun to sift downwards. On spring mornings he could hear the birds prancing across the shingles on their toothpick legs and would laugh to think how surprised the birds would be if the roof could suddenly turn to glass and the birds look down out of their little bird eyes and see a human being so close and staring. He would laugh and wriggle with pleasure upon his button-sized behind at the thought of what he knew and birds didn't: that he was lying beneath them listening to their dry twittering sounds.

Then, having laughed, Homer would step into his pants and run downstairs for breakfast. If food would have fattened Homer, Mrs. Perkins' biscuits and hotcakes, her sausage and cream gravy would have turned the trick; but Homer was never very hungry; he filled fast. Homer was looking for something the Perkins' table didn't provide—he wanted someone to talk to. Homer was lonesome.

The Perkinses were childless, and they were very nearly speechless. They had been married for forty years and such conversation as they had once had, had now about died out. Since they were like-minded they had nothing to argue about; and there seemed little point to either of them in remarking upon events about which they were in perfect agreement: in saying, "Eggs look oval today," or "The cow appears to have had a calf."

The Perkinses were used to oval eggs and to cows that calved; they were used, Homer sometimes thought, to everything in the whole world. There was nothing he could say to them to which they didn't reply kindly, looking over their spectacles, "It's more'n likely, Homer," or, "I wouldn't be a mite surprised." And there the talk would end.

Homer was constantly surprised and wanted to speak with someone about what had surprised him. He was filled with wonder at a hundred sights: with the colors a colorless icicle took on when the sun touched it, and the way flames leaped in to attack a hickory burl, then leaped away again as if the burl were fighting for its life; he noted how the smoke on a cool evening curled about the house like a tongue, and the way grass could push a stone over, and how through the buckwheat batter, bubbles like eyes would make their way up to the surface. And the buckwheat eyes, Homer thought, would stare at him, and Homer, filled with wonder, would stare back. But the Perkinses wondered no more about anything, let alone buckwheat bubbles.

Nothing. Day was their right, and night a time of darkness made for their rest. The earth thawed and froze again; corn leafed and came to the full ear; cows who had dried, freshened, and it was all no wonder to the Perkinses.

But it was to Homer and he often wished for the other one hundred and eighty-seven boys from the asylum, who would have wondered with him. There, they had found out things: whether a tadpole was jelly all the way through or not; whether a mouse, if it had to, could run backwards; and if an ant swallowed alive could chew its way out of your stomach.

"Do you think a mouse can run backwards, Mr. Perkins?" Homer had once asked.

"I wouldn't be a mite surprised, Homer," Mr. Perkins said, so there was no use telling him. Homer wanted to surprise someone.

Jess breathed through his open mouth so that he could feel how cold the air was against his peppermint-coated tongue.

"Seems like I ought've caught sight of thee before this, Homer," he said. "Thee's been at Perkinses since last winter, hasn't thee?"

"Yes, sir," Homer said.

"They keep thy nose pretty close to the grindstone over there, Homer?" Jess asked. "Keep thee carrying in wood and hunting eggs?"

"No, sir," Homer said. "It's easy work. Mr. Perkins is good to me."

Mr. Perkins was good, but he was forthright.

"You're to remember, Homer," he said, "you ain't a native here. You've been taken from a home and for all anybody here knows your pappy may've been a train robber. I'm not saying he was, Homer, and I'm satisfied you're a good boy, but other people don't know it yet. So you're not to be pushy. Wait till you're invited before you go anywheres and don't outstay your welcome when you do."

Jess hunted about in his pockets. "Two more," he said. He put one in his mouth, handed the other to Homer. "If I's right certain how fish felt about peppermints," he said, "I wouldn't do this. Sit here chewing right in front of their noses. But they's no telling, Homer. For all I know peppermints may set their teeth on edge."

Homer gazed at Jess. "Do they set yours on edge?" he asked.

"Nope," Jess said, "not the teeth I got."

"Have fish got teeth?"

"Some have, some haven't. A shark'd probably win a tooth race any day."

"What's a tooth race?" Homer asked.

"Race to see who's got the biggest teeth."

Homer moved his tongue about inside his mouth. "I guess I'd lose," he said.

"Oh, I don't know," Jess told him. "Depend on who thee's running against. Thee'd beat a mouse all holler."

Homer leaned against the stump. "Do you think a mouse," he said, "if it had to, could run backwards?"

Jess pulled his hat down over his forehead as if he didn't want the sun in his eyes while he was figuring on such a weighty problem.

"I'd have to study about it, Homer," he said. "There's some things I'd have to know. Was it an old mouse or young un?"

"Medium aged," said Homer. "This one was."

"A middle-aged mouse," said Jess. "Country mouse or city mouse?"

"City mouse."

"Well," said Jess, "my guess is . . . if properly encouraged . . . it could."

"Yes, sir," said Homer, his eyes sparkling. "That's right. It can."

"Why, Homer," Jess said, "thee's told me something I didn't know. I'll go to bed tonight a smarter man for having met thee."

He pushed his hat to the back of his head again, let the last of the sun warm his face, then looked down at the boy and Homer saw he meant what he said.

"It didn't run very fast though," Homer said.

"Fast running backwards," Jess said, "would be too much to expect, first time tried."

Look old as God to him, I venture, Jess thought. Well, I can get back to him after a fashion, but he ain't got no possible way of going forward to eighty. And no way my telling him, I'm him, only considerably weather-beaten.

"When I's about a quarter thy size, Homer, we had a duck pond at our house, just a little scoop of water it was. On a day about like this, warm and dry, I took it into my head to see how it'd feel to be a duck. Well, it felt mighty good, only I'd gone in with all my clothes, and my mother, undertaking to raise me to be a boy, not a duck, said, 'Jess, if thee goes in there again, thee'll come out faster than thee went in.' Thinks I, it can't be done."

"Could it?" asked Homer.

"No, sir," said Jess, "it couldn't. I went in there faster than a cannonball. Ducks thought the sky was falling."

Homer laughed.

"Didn't do me a parcel of good, though," Jess said. "I came out considerably slower than I went in, but I was scutched for it just the same."

"Scutched?" asked Homer.

"Got a taste of apple tree tea," Jess said.

Homer continued to look quizzical.

"Licked," said Jess, "paddled, tanned, had my britches warmed."

Old fool, Jess thought. Why's the old got to ladle out their past to the young? Got to say, I's a frolicsome sprout if ever there was one? If youngness is what we want here it is under our noses, not second-hand, not warmed over. Live in that. The young's got no time to travel back seventy-five years, watch thee sashay in and out of duck ponds, Jess Birdwell.

"Homer," he said, "if thee ain't due home for a spell, how'd thee like to fish a little? Here's a pole and bait itching to be used. Thee could cut across Venters' on the way home and leave the pole at my place, and it'd not be more'n two steps out of thy way."

After Homer had left the pole with his thanks and shown his catch, Jess said to Eliza as they sat in the twilight over their boiled tea and warm sweetcake, "Puts me in mind of Josh."

Eliza nodded, but said, "More like thee."

Jess turned away from the window, where darkness like water was flowing between the buildings, over the currant bushes, leaving shapes so indistinct it was impossible to say what was real, what the outline, merely, memory bade rise up in the accustomed place. He looked at Eliza, soft and gray like the twilight itself. He wondered how it would be if she were to sit across from him now —as she had fifty, sixty years ago, hair black, cheeks red, eyes searching out his meanings. As they still did. Would he know her, even? Would he say to his own wife, "Thee puts me in mind of someone . . . I can't say who . . . at the minute . . . the name's gone, but thy face, I know." Would he?

"Age twelve, Eliza, thee'd never even seen me."

"Aged eighteen, thee was near enough to that."

"Why, Eliza, at eighteen I was a man. Owned a cow and horse and had cleared ten acres."

"Thee and thy cow and horse," Eliza said and laughed.

"Thee didn't laugh then," Jess reminded her. "Thee was thunderstruck to have a man of my substance come courting."

"I was fourteen," Eliza said. "I thunderstruck easy those days. Even then, I saw thee's nearer Homer than a man of substance."

"No, no," Jess said, "I got, as thee well knows, Eliza, an easygoing streak in me. Not Homer though. That boy ought to've been born in another world—a place, say, where there's a dozen stars, a half dozen trees and maybe a couple of dogs. There's too much here for Homer to take in. It wears on him."

"Thee's cut on the same pattern," Eliza persisted. "When I heard him say, 'Did anybody ever count the scales on a fish,' I thought, That's Jess Birdwell over again. Full of wonder. Peering and prying."

"Eliza," Jess said, defending himself, "when I get to heaven and the Lord says, 'How's things on earth?' I want to be able to answer: name the stars, say how the fruits are developing and what fish live in Rush Branch."

"He made them," Eliza said. "He'll have no need to ask."

"He don't see them from this side," Jess said.

"Like that child," Eliza told him again. "Like that big-eyed, wondering child."

✦

Whether or not Eliza was right, and Jess thought she was not, through that fall and winter he often saw Homer Denham. The boy would stop in on his way from school; would tramp across snowy fields after his Saturday work was done to wonder with Jess, what being frozen felt like, say: if it was like falling asleep as some people said; or if it was, instead, an agony of numbness and rigidity, a turning to stone, while the blood in great pain beat against the walls which had risen up about it; to wonder if a healthy man frozen by the cold and so preserved for a thousand years could then be revived, if people only knew how; to ask if cold were really, not a thing in itself, but only less and less heat.

He would come at night even, his lantern swinging with the jolt of his step, its flame veering in the wind, and sit by the hearthside: some nights eating snow ice cream or cracking hickory nuts on an upturned flat iron; others, reading from one of Jess' books or playing a game of checkers with Eliza, who liked to play, and win, too, sometimes, which with Jess she could never do.

Jess from his side of the hearth would watch the play, Homer's brown hand hovering above the board, Eliza's white one firm and sure. He would see the pulse in Homer's throat knot itself for a minute, when the boy feared he'd left an opening which would let Eliza jump a man clear to the king row, then quiet when the danger'd been passed.

No, he thought, Eliza's wrong. I don't take pleasure in the boy because I see myself in him. Myself when young. No, I was a stolid piece compared to that young'un—besides, I give myself credit for wanting to do more than stare in a mirror, see my own reflection.

More like second childhood, he thought, grinning. The old man working his way back to whiptops and gruel. That's more like it, he thought, that's not so bad. Still he didn't believe that, either.

The pleasure comes from two things, he thought. It comes from seeing, once again, what we started with and lost. Honesty, he guessed, would come as near as any one word to saying what it was. Wonder, fear, love, there it all was in Homer, nothing glossed over, nothing hidden from sight. It was meeting a human being at first hand, not as was the case with most grown-ups, second hand, if at all: not meeting a person assembled, put together so's to present to the inspecting eye the very object for which it was searching. Ah, Jess thought, after eighty years thee gets tired of peering through the chinks and knotholes trying to catch sight of something alive inside the makeshift building. Pleasure to see something all of a piece, alive clear to the outside.

And then, though Eliza was wrong in saying he saw himself when young in Homer, still Homer was in a way of speaking a new lens for his eyes, a means of discovering once again the world as it had been when he was young: bright, fresh, abundantly furnished with mysteries.

The clock struck the hour. "They'll be uneasy about thee at the Perkinses, Homer," Jess said. "It's past thy bedtime and thee needs thy rest. Thee'd best call it draw—finish thy game some other time."

"We'll finish now," Homer said.

But Eliza rose, Jess got the boy's lantern, and well bundled they started him homewards. "Don't hustle too fast," Jess told him, "get out of breath. Take thy time and sleep well."

Homer waved the lantern to them, then while Jess and Eliza watched from the window, traveled slowly up the snowy rise toward home, his lantern shining at last on the farthest hilltop, like a setting star.

Jess turned to warm himself before going to bed. "Do the boy a dis-service, I don't misdoubt," he told Eliza, "making over him so much."

Eliza, too, left the window. "Thee carries him about on a chip," she agreed. Then added, "The poor little fellow."

"Spoiling him I don't misdoubt," Jess said once again, remembering Homer's, "We'll finish now."

Jess tried to remember during the rest of the winter not to spoil the boy but for the most part he forgot it. It was a warm winter, short and soon over. While the tongue was still saying the word, the season had passed: snow gone, branches racing along with humped backs, tree twigs swollen with new sap, grass pushing up through the earth into the sunlight. Jess could not have felt nearer the boy if he had been his own son or grandson and the neighbors grew accustomed to seeing the two together, walking down back lanes, riding behind one of Jess' fast trotters, or simply sitting like cronies together, atop a fence-rail in the sun.

One Saturday, the sun hanging in the sky as if pegged there for good and small flurries of wind like warm fingers riffling the hair, Jess took a turn about the house after dinner to inspect the early blooms. He was standing, sniffing and admiring in front of Eliza's bed of lilies-of-the-valley now almost in full flower, when Homer, barefoot and silent, joined him. Jess was musing and felt rather than heard Homer's approach, as he had the first time he saw the boy.

"Well, Homer," he said, "if stars were sweet they'd be lilies-of-the-valley. If these lilies lit up after dark they'd be stars."

Jess smiled down on the boy, waiting to hear what lilies-of-the-valley were to Homer, to be given the glimpse he had come to value, of the world seen through a pair of eyes somewhat less rusty from use than his own. But Homer said nothing, only stood very still, drawing deep breaths, his pale lips unsmiling, as if a bed of lilies were a serious matter, and the pulse in his throat beating as if they were very exciting, too.

Jess noted that the boy had grown peakeder and thought that he had been mistaken, believing, as he had, that spring and sunlight would set whatever ailed him to rights.

"Homer," he asked, "has thee had thy sulphur and molasses yet this spring?"

Homer did not reply, but dropping to his knees began to fill his hands with lilies. He had a half dozen before Jess could stop him.

"Homer," he said sternly, "thee give me those blossoms."

Homer stood up and without a word laid them in Jess' hands.

"Why, Homer," Jess said, "thee surprises me. I wouldn't pick these lilies myself. They belong to Eliza and she picks a few only now and then to scent the rooms. And here thee comes without so much as a by-thy-leave and falls to picking as if thee's the owner. I'm taken aback and ashamed, Homer, to see thee so unmannerly."

Still Homer did not say a word, only reached out one finger to touch the flowers Jess held, as if saying good-bye to them, then ran off toward the barn, hunting, Jess supposed, the new kittens. When he came back to the house he was as cheerful as if nothing had happened. He sat at the kitchen table, ate a thick slice of Eliza's good custard pie, and if he noticed the six lilies-of-the-valley which now stood in a cut glass bowl on the center of the table, he didn't show it.

But Jess noticed them. After Homer had left, the six lilies propped up by cut glass and kept moderately alive by water troubled him. He sat long at the supper table that evening; he lingered after the dishes had been cleared away regarding the flowers, thinking of them, of himself, and the boy. He didn't doubt he'd done the right thing . . . still, doing the right thing shouldn't leave such an ache under the breastbone; those lilies were Eliza's and Homer shouldn't have made free with them, yet saved, restored to their rightful owner, the boy chided, the flowers no longer pleased him. He sat until Eliza called him, and when he rose, finally, to join her in the sitting-room, he was somewhat easier in his mind, he had come to a decision.

The weather next morning had changed, however, and for the better part of a week Jess was housebound, watching alternations of sleet and rain, watching the lilies Homer had picked droop and grow yellow. Watching those in the bed outside become splotched and shattered by the storm. There was, beside the sleet and rain, a heavy wind: telephone wires were down; a limb was torn from the mulberry tree, smashing in its fall a window in the carriage-house.

"Winter dies hard," Jess said to Eliza, walking restlessly from window to window, waiting for the weather to moderate. The change came at last; in the night while they slept the storm let up and on the sixth morning the air was as bland and soft as if all that tempest had been the matter of a single night's dream: only the gashed tree, the broken window, the shattered flowers there to bear witness for reality.

After the midday meal when the sun had somewhat dried the ground underfoot, Jess put on coat and hat, picked the few lilies the storm had spared—not many more than Homer himself had first gathered—and set off with them toward the Perkinses.

He half expected to meet Homer on the way; it was weather which would make staying inside hard and he smiled, thinking what Homer's account of the storm of the past days would be. In his attic room, the wind and rain six inches from his ear-drums, Homer must've heard fine things. Now the day, Jess thought, so balmy and warm it almost seems to lay a hand on the naked heart, to lead one onward. Underfoot the sloshy earth, but overhead the summer sky, grown deep with a blue past all half-promises. Mounting the rise which led to the Perkins house—a desolate place, Jess always felt, exposed as it was on the brow of a small hill, with no other shelter than a clump of dark, ragged pines—Jess saw further damage of the storm: budding trees riddled, new washes started, the road rutted and in many places its gravel covering swept completely away. But that's past, Jess thought, trudging along, that's bygone, the storm over, time now for repairs. The lilies warmed both by the sun and his own clasping hand were as sweetly scented as if they had never felt wind or hail and Jess thinking of the pleasure he would have putting them in Homer's hand was very easy in his heart.

Still, he was neither surprised nor, for the moment, touched by sorrow at the concourse, the gathering of rigs and people he saw beneath the pines and in front of the small, white house, nor did he for a moment doubt the meaning of their gathering. His feet, of themselves it seemed, continued his forward motion, while his mind in quiet lucidity stood apart and saw himself travel toward that meaning: saw, it seemed, this old man start eighty years be-

rore a journey destined to proceed from that branch at Colerain,
through duck ponds, courting, the substance of father and house-
holder, to mount at last this particular small rise on a spring day
carrying lilies which would be heaped with other flowers on a
trestle in a neighbor's front yard and there soften, but not hide
what that trestle had been set up to bear.

His feet carried him onward . . . this is the time, the hour, the
minute thee has walked toward, he told himself—and it seemed
to him then that neither marrying nor praying, worshiping nor be-
getting had held for him such significance, and that he either
now saw or forever missed such meaning as his eighty years on
earth might have. Set on earth . . . believing this or that to be
thy call, thy duty. Hunting thy apportioned way. Thinking in
terms of Jess Birdwell, husband, countryman, churchman . . . all
maybe wrong. Maybe no more than this . . . this maybe the end-
all, and meaning, if any, here in climbing this hill with storm-
damaged flowers for a small boy's funeral . . . and to lay them
there with the others, likewise storm-damaged, concluding for the
time, nothing . . . listening . . . asking.

There was no need for any words of explanation, he could have
said them all himself, turned and told the others: Homer's heart
had finished beating . . . in his small room he had lain as if
asleep, smiling and with a look of listening. Jess wasn't sorrowing
for Homer. Homer, he didn't misdoubt, had seen more of the
world in his twelve years than this whole gathering lumped together, their experiences of seeing, hearing, wondering, bound together in a bundle and counted as that of one. He didn't sorrow
for Homer, having some idea, as he did, of the way this world
would have used him . . . how people like himself, with the best
of intentions . . . trying to do their duty, merely . . . would
have hurt and hampered him at every turn.

He didn't sorrow for himself, even—for the mischance at the
end, yes—but he rejoiced that for a short time when all of his own
young people were gone, a boy who had no father had been a son
to him . . . and now he too was gone. He stood with the others

and heard the familiar words . . . " 'Let not your hearts be troubled . . . in my Father's house are many mansions . . . I go to prepare a place for you.' "

The spring sun was setting when he turned homeward, his feet still taking care of his going while the whole longer journeying of his life busied his mind. Jess didn't sorrow for himself, nor for Homer . . . still he knew there were words he had misused, questions he had never asked, answers he had missed and he felt heavy with searching.

He sat in the kitchen beside the table where the six lilies, now much yellowed, still stood and he spoke to Eliza of the afternoon, his walk and his thoughts. They sat there together until dark had come, and Eliza had lit a lamp and set forth some food. Then while he ate and drank, the meaning he had searched for that afternoon, and maybe his whole life, seemed to shape itself. He took a last bite of bread, a last sup of tea.

"Eliza," he said, "I'm eighty years old. All my life I've been trying one way or another to do people good. Whether that was right or not, I don't know, but it comes over me now that I'm excused from all that. I loved Homer, but I tried to do him good . . . the way I see it now, that was wrong, that was where I's led astray. From now on, Eliza, I don't figure there's a thing asked of me but to love my fellow men."

He got up from the table and went to the window. The earlier resplendence of the sky had faded, leaving only a small fingershaped stretch of yellow light to show where the sun had been and where it had set. But the coming of dark had never dispirited Jess, and he spoke now with cheerfulness. "No, Eliza," he said, "as far as I can see, there's not another thing asked of me, from this day forward."

Books by Jessamyn West
available in Harvest paperback editions
from Harcourt Brace & Company

COLLECTED STORIES OF JESSAMYN WEST

THE FRIENDLY PERSUASION

HIDE AND SEEK

THE MASSACRE AT FALL CREEK

THE WOMAN SAID YES